ALIBIS
CAN BE
MURDER

Connie Shelton

ALIBIS
CAN BE
MURDER

Charlie Parker Mysteries, Book 17

Connie Shelton

Secret Staircase Books

Alibis Can Be Murder
Published by Secret Staircase Books, an imprint of
Columbine Publishing Group
PO Box 416, Angel Fire, NM 87710

Copyright © 2017 Connie Shelton

Book layout and design by Secret Staircase Books
Cover illustration © Ken Cole
Cover silhouette © Ayutaka

First trade paperback edition: June, 2017
First e-book editions: June, 2017

Publisher's Cataloging-in-Publication Data

Shelton, Connie
Alibis Can Be Murder / by Connie Shelton
p. cm.
ISBN 978-1945422294 (paperback)

1. Parker, Charlie (Fictitious character)--Fiction. 2. Women
private investigators--Fiction. 3. New Mexico--Fiction. 4. Teens
and cell phones--Fiction. 5. Social media--Fiction. 6. Infidelity--
Fiction. I. Title

Charlie Parker Mystery Series : Book 17
Shelton, Connie, Charlie Parker mysteries.

BISAC : FICTION / Mystery & Detective
813/.54

As always, this one is for Dan, my husband, best friend and constant inspiration through all the years. Occasionally, a real person inspires one of my fictional characters—thanks to Sue Badar for being my inspiration for Susie Scott in this book. Maybe one day we'll do one called Wine Festivals Can Be Murder.

Special thanks go out to my editors Susan Slater and Shirley Shaw for spotting my errors and helping me to make this book as good as it can be. And to my beta reader team members who helped with this title: Joanne Horak, Jeannie Jackson, Isobel Tamney, Debbie Wilson, Gail Wolf, Marcia Koopman, Susan Gross, Jane Parker, Katherine Munro, Lisa Train, and Carol Blacklock— each of you added something of value to the book. Thank you for your time and attention to detail.

Chapter 1

Springtime in New Mexico is a tricky season. There are beautiful, warm days that fool the trees into blooming, followed by hard freezes that knock your socks off and mean death to those tiny apple blossoms and potential peaches. You never really know it's arrived until, oftentimes, it's gone and summer has sneaked right up on you. But this spring I knew there had been damage when I walked out the back door on April eleventh and heard a curse word from my ninety-something neighbor, the sweet little lady who somehow raised me through my teen years without resorting to sailor language even once.

"Gram?" I called through the hedge that separates our properties. "Everything okay?"

A wide-brimmed cotton hat, topping her fluffy white hair, appeared at the break in the hedge. "My cherry tree is toast. The plums don't look a whole lot better."

It didn't take a glance at the thermometer to know it was freezing out here. I'd come out with only a flannel shirt and jeans and I was already shivering. By noon it would be seventy degrees, but that didn't much matter now.

"I should have put the fans out last night," she lamented. "I knew it."

"So sorry," I said. "You know, Drake and I would have been happy to come over and help."

Elsa Higgins is a sweetie but she has the hardest time being dependent on anyone. Even when it's a simple fifteen-minute chore, she won't ask. Of course, the forlorn look over the lost fruit crop gave me a case of the guilts. If I'd not been at the office until midnight, working on tax returns, I might have thought to bring up the subject of figuring out how to warm her trees.

"Hey, I was about to put some blueberry muffins in the oven …" Providing I still had that mix on the shelf. "Want to come over in about fifteen minutes and have some?"

Freckles, our brown and white mixed breed dog, heard the phrase 'have some' and she raced from the far corner of the yard in response. Elsa and I both laughed.

"I'd say that's a yes. Come on, any time. The coffee's already made." I shivered and opened the door into my kitchen.

"Freezing?" Drake asked, holding a steaming mug out to me.

"Yeah. I had this silly notion because it's sunny this morning I would put the cushions on the chairs under the gazebo and we could have coffee out there. No way—it's barely forty."

He set the mug on the counter and wrapped his arms around me. "Maybe by happy hour this afternoon."

We were both eager to use the new gazebo, his Valentine gift to me, which he'd built during the two weeks of unseasonably warm weather in February when he had no pressing jobs for his helicopter business. I loved the turned balusters and white gingerbread trim. In an effort to rush spring into existence we'd purchased wicker furniture and were ready to spend hours out there. Late February turned cold again, March was way too windy and now April—the unpredictable month.

"Oh, I promised Elsa blueberry muffins. Do we still have that box?" I opened a cupboard door.

He handed me my coffee and steered me toward the kitchen table. "Let me handle it."

How on *earth* did I ever find this fantastic husband? He builds and he cooks, and he's still so good-looking it makes my heart beat faster.

Freckles followed Drake around the kitchen as he found the mix, got eggs from the fridge and stirred it all together, actually remembering to turn the oven on first so it preheated. He amazes me. I'm good with boiling water for pasta, microwaving a frozen dinner for myself when he's working out of town, and not much else unless it comes from packages or jars. I'm an accountant, a partner with my brother in his private investigation firm, and frequent helpmate to Drake, who trained me and turned me into a decent helicopter pilot. As a kid I was always outside, rough and tumbling with my brothers, happy to let my mother—and later Gram—handle everything in the kitchen.

As if thinking her name summoned our neighbor, a tap at the back door meant Elsa had arrived. She carried a small jar of cherry preserves, a legacy of last year's crop which had not frozen. It's another thing I never think to do—show up at someone's house with a little gift. I think of it, really I do. Usually it hits me when I'm standing at the door, having pressed the bell. New resolution: start observing the social graces.

She patted Drake on the shoulder, having come from a not-huggy generation. "It smells so good in here." She was looking at him when she said it. She knows who's the cook around our house.

Plates, forks, the butter dish and a bowl of strawberries had somehow appeared on the table while I wasn't noticing. Okay, at this point I'm going to use the excuse that it's tax season and I've had nothing but numbers on my mind for a couple of weeks. Returns were done for the businesses. Somehow between now and the fifteenth I would put it all together, wrap up our personal tax return and get the whole batch in the mail.

Elsa hung her jacket over the back of a chair and Drake took the muffin pan from the oven. I remembered napkins—see? I can handle a few things.

"… at the Delaney house," Elsa was saying.

I made the mental shift. The Delaneys were neighbors three houses south and across the street from Elsa's. Since I normally come and go from the north end of the street, I had no clue what she was talking about. It didn't matter—with Elsa you just wait a minute and you'll get the rest of the story.

"The twins," she said, "I've only seen one of them around."

I gave a shrug and passed her the basket Drake had set on the table.

"Those girls are always together and now it's been

months and months, and I've only seen one."

"Which one?"

She giggled. "How should I know? They're identical twins."

"Maybe the other girl has left home. They must be out of school by now. Maybe she's moved away."

Elsa gave a tiny shake of her head. "Something tells me that's not it. I'm worried about her."

A flash from the past shot through my mind—two little blond girls that Gram sometimes babysat. During the three years I lived with her I'd spent a fair amount of time with those kids. Maybe it was a case of sometimes you know someone so well you don't see them at all. I've lived in the same neighborhood my whole life. Could it be that I've become blind to what's going on around me?

Chapter 2

Breakfast wound down pretty quickly, as Drake needed to get out to the small westside airport where his helicopter is hangared and I still had those tax returns nagging at me. Freckles saw Elsa out to the break in the hedge then came back to join me. I kissed my husband at the front door, watched him get into his pickup truck in the driveway, and picked up my purse and keys.

My destination was a gray and white Victorian house in an older part of town, one we had converted to the offices of RJP Investigations. My brother, Ron, is actually the investigator. I'm the financial whiz. Our offices are across the hall from each other and somehow, too often, I seem to get pulled into helping out with his cases. He does a lot of corporate background checks on new hires, with a smattering of cheating-spouse cases.

Yeah, even in the age of digital openness, there are still people who use a PI to gather dirt on the person they once vowed to love forever—all for the purpose of dragging them to court and extracting the largest financial settlement possible. I back away from those—it all seems so sleazy—but I've been known to find myself in the midst of a murder or two.

Right now, Freckles and I were riding along in my Jeep with the goal of avoiding any of Ron's dramas and heading straight to: 1) the tin of dog biscuits on my shelf and 2) the partially completed tax forms in my computer. We pulled into the driveway beside the office and followed its length to what used to be a backyard, now our own little parking area.

Ron's Mustang wasn't there yet, but our part-time receptionist, Sally Bertrand, was already on the job, as evidenced by her minivan in its usual spot. Sally was in the kitchen, pouring coffee into a stained mug, looking a little ragged around the edges.

"Long night?" I asked.

"Crazy morning. You know, with Ross staying home mornings with R.B., you'd think it wouldn't be so nuts. But getting Chrissie off to school and myself to work without some disaster along the way … it never happens. Today, it was a whole bowl of oatmeal coating the highchair, the baby and the floor."

I gave a perky smile and thanked my lucky stars my only children had been dogs.

She held out the coffee carafe to me but I declined, making a little chitchat about the muffin breakfast at home before calling Freckles inside and heading upstairs. Sally's domain is the reception area and conference room on the ground floor—originally the parlor and dining room in the Victorian days.

Upstairs, the layout is pretty simple—two identically sized bedrooms became Ron's and my offices, each with a bay window facing the street. There was a smaller bedroom which is now storage and a bathroom you'd hate to think that a family of five or six people once shared. A shower curtain hides the old bathtub and there's a standard white toilet and porcelain pedestal sink—nothing glamorous because it doesn't have to be. I rarely have time for home décor, so I'm pretty content with whatever is handed to me.

I flipped on the lights in my office and turned on my new laptop computer. After years with a crazily outdated desktop clunker, this little thing zooms like a race car. Freckles circled the room and parked herself facing the bookcase where the tin of dog biscuits sits. It's our morning routine. She'll sit patiently for about ten seconds, and if I don't get the hint she'll be leaping into my field of view to get my attention. It's just easier to give her the cookie right away.

I patted her little brown and white head and sat down at the computer. An hour had magically vanished when I became aware of Ron standing in my doorway.

"Ever heard of an alibi company?" he asked.

I came out of my Form 1040 like a mole emerging from the ground, blinking and disoriented. "What? Good morning to you too."

"Yeah. Morning, Charlie." He's recently taken to wearing ball caps and T-shirts instead of the Stetson and plaid western shirts he sported for years. Maybe it's an attempt to impress his new wife of four months, to be cooler with his three sons now they're getting into their teens, or merely to seem younger—I have no idea. Victoria is such a classy lady, I can't imagine the ball caps being her idea.

"So?" he asked again. "Alibi companies. Ever heard of them?"

"Em … no."

He held up a magazine, open to an article whose headline I could barely make out.

"They provide alibis."

"Okay … You mean to get criminals off the hook?"

"Not serious criminals, more like cheating spouses."

"Ooh, right up your alley."

"Ha ha."

I shot him a look.

"I've got this case and everywhere I turn, the guy's got proof of his innocence. I know he's sneaking around, but the wife wants proof and I can't come up with it. According to this article, these places provide their clients with the whole deal—restaurant and travel receipts, answering services where a pretend secretary says the boss is in a meeting, the whole thing."

"Seriously. Does anyone really care about that stuff anymore? I mean, there are no-fault divorces and it's a community property state. Why jump through all the hoops when he knows he'll have to split everything fifty-fifty anyway?"

"When fifty percent is several million dollars, I guess it's worth a bit more trouble. It's Bob Lorrento."

"Bobby The Bomb? The football player?"

"The greatest quarterback in NFL history, the one who could land a pass in anyone's hands. Forced retirement last year after that shoulder injury." He went on to spout football stats I couldn't even begin to follow, the kind of stuff he and Drake talk about on Thanksgiving Day after a huge turkey dinner.

All I remembered about the guy was the headline news about his injury, followed by a local flurry of stories last summer about how he was retiring and moving his family to Albuquerque. Even without the injury, he was hitting an age where you didn't see a whole lot of pro ballplayers still in the game.

"Back on target here," I said. "Bob Lorrento is cheating on his wife?"

"Allegedly. Marcie Lorrento believes he is, and she's furious."

"Well, have fun with it. I've got paperwork here." I pointed toward the stacks of receipts and forms littering my desk.

He grumbled a little, to what purpose I have no idea. He knows those aren't my kind of cases.

We met up again in the kitchen around noon, both Ron and I attracted by the smell of the microwave popcorn Sally had made as a snack. She leaves for the day at one o'clock anyway, but always has a little something to tide her over. I had brought a sandwich from home, but when Ron offered to run out and bring me a Big Mac I couldn't refuse. Despite Victoria's best efforts with both of us, the Parkers seem stuck on fast food.

"Any luck with the alibi guy?" I asked, digging into the bag for my fries immediately after he returned with the meal.

"Just getting started, really. I found two of those alibi companies here in town. I'm not exactly having any luck getting them to admit a famous client's name."

"Gosh, why am I not surprised?"

He tossed a French fry at me and it bounced off my hand as I was opening the little box containing my burger.

"You seriously think I just come right out and ask, expecting an answer?"

I shrugged and took a huge bite. That special sauce always gets to me and I let out a sigh of contentment. The repartee dwindled as we both got serious about our food. A few minutes later, with the initial hunger slaked, I thought of something.

"Do you remember a family in our neighborhood named Delaney?"

He wiped his mouth with a napkin. "Like, from when we were kids?"

Things had changed so much over the years. The homes in our neighborhood were built back when my parents and their generation were young couples starting their families. Elsa and I are now some of the few originals remaining on the block.

"Rick and Jane Delaney have been there a long time. They have twin daughters who were tiny when I was a teenager."

He waved it off. "I would have been out of the house by then."

We were all out of the house, technically. When our parents died in a plane crash, I was the only one still home and Elsa Higgins had—insanely—volunteered to take me in until, at my eighteenth birthday, the law would allow me to be on my own.

"Why do you ask?"

I wondered if he was truly curious or if he was only

filling time as he ate the last of his fries.

"A comment Gram made this morning. She thinks there's something odd going on with the twins. I might look into it."

Ron bunched up the fast food bag and boxes from our meal, stood and took them to the big trash basket by the back door. I took what was left of my Coke upstairs to my desk. The tax papers awaited, but my mind went back to thoughts of the old neighborhood and the way it had been.

Chapter 3

Seventeen years ago ...

Oh. My. God. *Pink* curtains and bedspread. I stood at the bedroom door, staring. Apparently, while I was at school Gram had decided to redecorate my room. In pink. The pattern was Hollie Hobbie or some little-girl design that might have been semi-okay for somebody, like, six years old. There was a new lamp on the old mahogany nightstand, a white china thing with pink roses and a ruffled pink shade. No teen in the world could love this. Especially me, a girl who would rather climb a tree than put on a frilly dress.

"What do you think?" Gram had sneaked up behind me. There was no escape.

Inexplicably, tears welled up. I *hate* when that happens. I blinked them back.

"It's—wow—it's pink."

"I thought it was just the cutest thing," she said, reaching an arm around my shoulders.

"You shouldn't have."

"They had a sale at JC Penney's so it wasn't very expensive."

No, I really meant you shouldn't have. I looked away from her prying gaze and clamped my mouth shut. How was I going to sleep in this cotton candy room? I could *never* invite a friend in here. I walked in and dropped my books on the bed. I needed to talk to Stacy, have someone I could vent my feelings to.

The only phone in the house was on a table in the living room. I swear, living with an old person just sucked. I stomped toward it while Gram went into the kitchen, saying something about having baked chocolate chip cookies and bringing me some. Sheesh—didn't she remember chocolate made my face break out?

I picked up the phone and put my finger in the ancient rotary dial, laboriously finishing Stacy's number in about twenty-five minutes.

"Hey, Stace. Can you get out?"

My best friend lived three blocks away and ever since we were kids we would meet at the little neighborhood park. Nowadays, Stacy sometimes got use of her mother's car—mainly, only when her mom needed something from the store. Of course, *I* never got to use a car. Gram was paranoid as hell about something happening to hers with a teenager behind the wheel, so even though I'd gotten my license last fall, I was only allowed to drive if Gram was with me.

"Sure. The usual?"

"Yeah." I heard a footstep behind the swinging kitchen door and raised my voice. "Yeah, if I could get that history handout Smith gave in class today ... I guess mine fell out of my backpack."

If it pertained to homework, there was no way Gram could refuse to let me go.

The kitchen door swung open and there she stood with a glass of milk and plate of cookies. They smelled heavenly but I was determined not to waver.

"You're going somewhere?" she asked.

"Yeah, I need to run over to Stacy's to get a homework assignment. It won't take long."

"Okay, good," she said, working to hide her disappointment. She liked for us to sit at the dining table together, talk about my school day and have a snack. I knew it was so she could be sure I really was getting started on homework.

"Mrs. Delaney is sending the twins over at four o'clock," Gram said. "I told her you've been wanting to get some babysitting experience."

What? Oh, man, shoot me now.

"I'll be here to help out. They'll only be here a couple of hours. We'll give them their dinner and their mom will pick them up around six-thirty."

"Gram, I don't know anything about—"

"It'll be fine. They're out of diapers already. We'll just play some games and—"

"Stacy's waiting on me. Can we talk about this when I get back?"

I practically ran out the door. Kids ... games ... diapers. Oh, god. Across the street, I spotted Mr. Delaney pulling into their driveway and the two little girls ran out the moment his car stopped. Two identical little blondes with hair down past their shoulders, matching shorts and tops, shrieking with excitement at seeing their daddy.

The tears really did flow then. I would never again greet my dad when he got home from work, never eat cookies baked by my mother rather than a neighbor. I stumbled over a crack in the sidewalk but caught my balance and turned the corner toward the park.

Stacy O'Donnell sat in one of the swings, twirling back and forth by stubbing one sneaker-clad toe into the sand, then the other. She'd gathered her permed blonde curls into a clip at the back of her head and changed from jeans to shorts. She's so pretty she could fit in with the popular kids, but she hangs out with me instead. I wiped my eyes during one of her sways in the opposite direction.

"There was no history handout in Smith's today," she said, "so I brought the one from last week. Guessing you need to walk back in the house with *something* in your hands."

She gave me a firm stare as she handed over the sheet of paper. "What's up?"

I flopped onto the swing beside hers. "She decorated my room in pink—*pink*! And she made chocolate chip cookies."

"Wow—that's abusive, if you ask me."

"I know. She's not doing anything wrong. She's doing everything right. So *right* that it sucks. Ron tells me I'd better be grateful every single day. I could have been put in foster care when Mother and Dad—" I dipped my head so my hair would hide my face.

Stacy put her hand on my arm. "Well, you know, with one brother in college and the other living in a dumpy apartment, you wouldn't exactly be able to live with either of them. You've made it through more than a year with your Gram, Charlie. Only a couple more ..."

I nodded and sniffed loudly, wishing I'd put some tissues in my pockets.

"Hey, have you read the latest Mary Higgins Clark? I read under the covers last night until my little book-light battery went out. It's *so* spooky."

I shook my head.

"I'll give you my copy when I'm done." She pushed off with her toe again. "Maybe you can come sleep over Friday night?"

I nodded with a flicker of enthusiasm. Stacy's mom wasn't as cool as the ones you saw on TV but at least she wasn't a million years old.

"Gram's set me up with a babysitting job this afternoon. Twins. I get these little hints she thinks she's preparing me for life as a wife and mother. All this cookie-baking and everything."

"I think having kids would be fun—someday. Not 'til way after college though."

I pictured the toddler twins across the street. Nuh-uh. That was a *long* way off for me.

Chapter 4

I rechecked the figures I'd entered into my tax preparation program. Something wasn't making sense and it had to be my mistake—after all, these programmers guaranteed the math would be correct. I went through it again but the problem with scrolling up and down the computer screen was that I began to lose track of my place—which line on which form. I took a deep breath.

Babysitting the twin girls hadn't been *so* awful, I thought, in retrospect. They were cute kids and well behaved, as I remembered. Gram had handled most of the actual work and I mostly watched them play with a plastic toy where they were supposed to press buttons and cause plastic animals to make squawking sounds. The problem-causer in the room had been me.

I flushed with embarrassment at how rude I'd been to

Elsa in those years. She's such a sweetheart and was so kind and self-sacrificing for me, and all I could do was find fault. Over the years, I've apologized for my behavior back then, but my conscience still niggles at me whenever a scene from the past comes back. How could I have thrown a fit over a pink bedroom? Elsa and I have laughed over that one.

The stupid tax return still didn't make sense. I decided I needed to get some distance and look at it later. I printed the forms and jammed them into a folder. Freckles popped up out of a dead sleep the moment I switched off my computer, recognizing the signal for going home. Going home meant having dinner and, to a dog, any meal is cause for celebration.

Downstairs, Sally's desk sat neat and empty. I'd not heard her leave, nor had I remembered Ron saying goodbye, but by the hollow sound in the office I knew he'd gone for the day. I switched off the few remaining lights and paused in the kitchen to load the coffee maker for tomorrow morning. Those chores done, I opened the back door and raced Freckles for the Jeep. She won. She always wins.

My once-pristine Cherokee was showing her age, victim of a few mishaps during some of my cases—a small dent here, a long scratch there. Although Drake and I are fairly caring about our vehicles, dogs are less cautious and the interior had definitely seen better days, I thought, as I tossed the file of tax papers onto the front passenger seat after letting Freckles into the back. Still, I love the old girl. I slid into my well-worn seat and started the engine.

The afternoon air held a hint of the chill that would descend when the sun went down, but for now it was lovely out—a deep blue sky, abundant sunshine and barely a breeze. I powered all four windows partway down and let the dog stick her nose out to enjoy whatever array of scents she could pick up.

We covered the few miles home in under ten minutes, while I thought ahead to dinner. Drake had taken steaks out of the freezer this morning, which meant baked potatoes and a salad to go along. He's a master at salads and at the grill, so it left me with only one duty: placing two potatoes in the microwave and pressing the button. I can handle that.

I turned onto our quiet residential street, my Jeep knowing the turns all on its own. Ahead, a flash of red caught my eye, a Corvette in a driveway across the street. One of the Delaney twins was walking toward it and she must have hit her key fob button to unlock the car. She didn't look up, concentrating on something in her hands—a smartphone, no doubt.

Another blast from the past hit me then, memories of my irritation with Elsa's having only one telephone in her house. Even in our own home, there were several extensions; none of us had cell phones in those days. The idea of a teenager with a telephone she could carry absolutely anywhere might have intrigued my father but would have scared my mother to pieces.

I chuckled at the thought as I pulled into my driveway and parked beside Drake's truck. Behind me, the red Corvette roared past. I let Freckles out of the back seat and put a protective hand on her, although the sports car had now turned at the corner. I wondered if I should say something to the girls, warn them about driving so fast on a quiet street where pets and kids could dash out. Sheesh— maybe I *was* becoming my father.

In the kitchen, Drake was already working his magic with salad ingredients at the cutting board.

"Hey you," he said, leaning backward to accept the kiss I delivered. "I thought I'd get an early start on this, so we'll have time to sit out under the gazebo a little while before it turns too chilly."

A bottle of merlot already sat open at the end of the counter and two filets were seasoned and waiting in the fridge.

"Did I ever tell you, you're the best?"

"You could say it again if you want."

Instead, I kissed the back of his neck.

"You brought work home?" he asked, with a nod toward the folder in my hand.

"Ugh, tax stuff. I only have a couple more days to finish this. I'll take a look at it after I'm filled with a fabulous dinner, although I'll feel too wiped out to think about details."

"Makes perfect sense to me," he said with a laugh.

The mention of work reminded me of Ron's newest case.

"Have you ever heard of a company called Innocent Times?" I asked as I took two potatoes from the wire basket in the pantry.

"I haven't, but the name makes it sound like something not quite so innocent."

"Funny you should pick up on that. Ron says it's what is known as an alibi company. They're in business to provide alibis for people who don't want someone to know where they've really been and what they've really been doing."

"Or *who* they've really been doing?" He teased with the lightheartedness of someone with a clear conscience. "I'm only guessing ... your brother seems to catch a lot of those cases."

"That's what it is, and the current one involves somebody with quite a pile of money."

"Do we know this horrible cad?"

This time I laughed. "Well, we don't *know* he's a horrible cad, not *yet*. It's Bob Lorrento's wife who hired us."

"NFL Bobby Lorrento?"

"Yeah, but you cannot say anything, okay? We don't know for sure."

"It won't take long to find out," Drake said. "He's got a reputation as a womanizer. I doubt the news would surprise anyone."

"You do know that I would murder you if you ever did that," I said with a wink.

"And I would deserve it."

He put the salad bowl into the fridge, pressed the microwave button for the potatoes, and turned to take me into his arms. Nuzzling my neck, he murmured, "I will never, ever, ever hurt you, Charlie. You are the most important person in the world to me."

Somehow, we forgot about the wine and the gazebo after that, and it was nearly eight p.m. before the steaks went on the grill and we sat down to a very, *very* satisfying dinner.

Chapter 5

Two days later, I dropped three fat envelopes through the mail slot at the main post office and walked out of there, carefree as a three-year-old. Tax season—done. Yeah, I know, it's a weird kind of euphoria, something only an accountant can appreciate. I felt like celebrating.

Drake had rushed to the airport this morning to meet with some people from National Geographic about a photo shoot. I supposed I would get the details when the meeting was finished. Ron had said he was going to call Innocent Times and pretend to be a potential client to find out how their services worked. I promised to tell Victoria what he was up to and he threw a pad of sticky-notes at me.

Now, I stood beside my Jeep in the post office parking lot trying to decide what to do with my newfound freedom.

The choices were many: I could go to the office and catch up on RJP billing and other tasks I'd not done in weeks; at home the roses still needed pruning and the lawn should be fertilized. Elsa's busyness in her own yard reminded me I'd left several things half-finished in ours. A car waiting for a parking slot tooted at me, bringing me back to the fact I was uselessly taking up space woolgathering. I got in the Jeep, started the engine and backed out.

A block away, before I had to make the choice to turn left or right at Central, my phone chimed. Drake. I swung into a gas station lot and picked it up.

"Hey," he said, "you in the middle of anything?"

"Happily, I'm not."

"If you want to fly along, I'm taking a photographer for a little jaunt over the mountains. He claims there's an old mining camp up there and he's doing a story on such things."

Mining camps in the mountains reminded me of the job we'd taken last summer in Alaska, one that unearthed some tragic old secrets, and I almost declined. But here I sat with a beautiful spring day at my disposal and my husband inviting me to spend it with him.

"We'll pull pitch in about twenty minutes, and you can ride along if you're here," he said.

My decision was made. I told him I'd come, then took the on-ramp to I-40 and raced westward toward Double Eagle airport as fast as my Jeep and the moderate traffic allowed. Precisely nineteen minutes later I whipped into a parking spot and waved at him through the mesh fence. His blue and white helicopter sat on the skirt outside one of the maintenance hangars.

Watching Drake in his khaki green flight suit and leather

bomber jacket, I was struck with a hundred memories of days like this—my handsome pilot doing the thing he did so proficiently. Love welled up in my heart. My favorite times were when it was just the two of us, on our way to or from a job, sometimes he would be at the controls, sometimes I took them. The presence of a man with a large camera bag slung over his shoulder reminded me we had company today.

I walked through the fixed base operator's office, said hi to Jimmy at the counter and joined Drake as he was helping his customer with the seatbelt on the passenger side. A quick introduction—the guy's name was Michael-something. I hopped into the back and settled in. While the rotors spun up, Drake gave the standard safety briefing, the stuff about doors and windows and not touching anything. Within a few minutes we were skirting the northern edge of the city toward the Sandia Mountains.

I hiked these mountains a lot in my teens and early twenties, but there are still a zillion places I've never seen. For our purposes today, Michael wanted a general view of the area. I supposed his photographer eye would know what he wanted when he saw it. Drake and I chatted as we crossed I-25, skirted a couple of the Indian pueblos and followed Highway 14 past the tiny town of Los Cerrillos.

"What's that place?" Michael asked, pointing at something to the south.

From my seat behind him I couldn't yet see it, but Drake circled and a little cabin came into view. Made of rough lumber, it had once sported a coat of white paint but most of that had flaked away. I spotted a woman's touch—red-checked curtains at the two windows, a wooden flower box on the tiny covered porch. An outhouse sat a few yards behind. The one thing I didn't see was a road leading to it.

"Can we land there?" the customer asked.

I was kind of wondering the same thing. For some reason, the place caught my fancy.

Drake brought the aircraft to a hover and looked around. The ground was barren and rocky but for a bunch of cottonwood trees near the little house. As we came in low, it became evident a dry arroyo ran through and there must still be enough underground water to keep those trees alive. There was a fairly level spot about fifty yards behind the cabin and he set us down there.

"I'd like to spend a little time, if that's okay," said Michael. "That bluff on the northern horizon is magnificent but the light isn't quite there yet. If we hang out a half-hour or so, the shadows will catch those tiny crevices …"

His eye was far better than mine—I had no idea how he envisioned the high dirt ridge in that way. Drake shut down and we all got out. Michael immediately began roaming.

"Keep an eye out for snakes," Drake called out to him.

"Really?" I scanned the ground nervously.

"I have no idea. Better safe than sorry. Can't have a big magazine suing me for bringing their guy out to a dangerous place." He took a deep breath and looked around. "Wow. Listen to the quiet."

It's one of those things you don't hear when you live in a city. Even in a secluded neighborhood like ours there's always noise—the distant roar of traffic on the freeway, a car starting up somewhere, someone's TV through an open window.

"My place in Hawaii would be like this sometimes," he said. "I'd get up around dawn and sit outside with my coffee, and the only thing I would hear would be a rooster crowing now and then. Even that didn't last long, once people got up and headed for work."

I stood still and really listened. Michael's footsteps on the rocky ground made an occasional crunch-crunch. When he stopped, out of our sight beyond the dip of the arroyo, it was as if Drake and I were truly the only ones on the planet.

"Someone else loved it out here," I said, pointing to the cabin. I would have felt guilty, intruding on their idyllic location, but the place had clearly been abandoned. From the look of it, decades ago. "There's no road. How do you suppose they came and went?"

"There was a skinny little track down there." He pointed downhill. "It's probably washed out now and I have no idea what it connected to. We must be nearly a mile off the nearest road."

"Look at this place, hon," I said, facing the cabin.

For its age, the small building was in remarkably good condition. No doubt its distance from civilization played a part. No squatters or vandals would make the trek out here. Our high desert climate, with dry air and a cold enough winter to discourage termites, was most certainly another factor.

I could picture an old miner having built the place, catering to his wife's desires for something sturdy where she could cozy up and create a home. But that wasn't quite the whole story, either. The nearest mineshaft we'd seen was miles away, not exactly an arrangement conducive to a guy heading off to work each day and coming home every night. There was more to it. I squinted my eyes and envisioned the little house with its white paint fresh and bright and maybe some red trim around the window frames. I skimmed past the outhouse. I'd managed those fine when I was a kid out camping, but I've come to enjoy the finer points of indoor plumbing in recent years.

Drake had circled the structure. "You know, it's not in bad shape at all. There's a back door with no curtain over the window. The kitchen has a woodstove and I have no idea what they did for refrigeration. Nobody's touched it, though there's a double bed in there with a decent quilt on it."

"If the bedding hasn't been shredded by mice, the house must be incredibly tightly built."

"Are you thinking what I'm thinking?" He raised his eyebrows.

In recent months, we'd had several conversations about buying a weekend place somewhere. With commitments to two businesses, there's seldom time for us to go away on cruises or take typical vacations. We'd discussed a couple of ski areas in the northern part of the state—Taos, where we spent our honeymoon, is incredibly beautiful and less than three hours away. But this place ... it was fifteen minutes by air and absolutely no one was going to come around.

I looked at it with a fresh eye. The outhouse was the first thing to catch my attention. "I don't know ..."

An exclamation from Drake's client caught our attention. When we looked toward the bluff where the photographer had headed, I saw what he'd been talking about. The sun struck the tan earth now, bringing out incredible peachy tones and highlighting every fissure and boulder. My breath caught in my chest and all at once I could see myself spending time out here.

Chapter 6

Drake and I sat on the cabin's wooden porch while the photographer snapped away. He'd brought three cameras, we discovered, so he kept plenty busy while we talked.

"You know," Drake said, "a wraparound porch would make this even better. We would set a couple of chairs facing that bluff."

"We don't know who owns it or if it's even for sale," I countered, not wanting to get attached.

"I think my carpentry skills are up to it."

"Getting confident after building the gazebo, huh?"

"Think how great it would be to come out here anytime we want. With the aircraft, we'd just hop in and go back to town if a job comes up …"

"And the bathroom is an outhouse …"

"You could get new curtains and all that girly stuff …"

Michael was coming up the arroyo, one camera on a strap around his neck, the others stashed in the bag again.

"Lots to talk about later," Drake said to me, extending a hand to pull me to my feet.

"Wow—this view will make a perfect backdrop for the story," Michael said, breathing a little hard in the high, thin air. "Now, what were you saying about a mining town up the way? I'd like to get some shots there, as well."

An hour later, we'd covered a lot of ground and the man had taken a *lot* of pictures, ending with shots of the mine shafts near Madrid (which the locals pronounce *Mad*-rid).

Way, way back in history there were coal mining operations up here. The town was abandoned for a long time until modern-day artists discovered it and revamped the old houses and buildings to create a funky little touristy place to visit on weekends. Dressed up, Madrid had even starred in a movie or two.

Drake set the helicopter down near the ballpark, which in the town's heyday in the 1920s was the first field west of the Mississippi with electric lights and a scoreboard. Babe Ruth even played here—or so the legend goes. The other thing the little burg was known for back in the day was its annual display of Christmas lights with scenes covering the nearby hills and attracting families from Albuquerque who made the two-hour drive to get here by road.

These days, there are dozens of artsy shops and—we hoped—someplace good for lunch. A stroll into the heart of town told us immediately there was some kind of event going on. A food and wine festival, it seemed. I discovered I was up for both.

Michael took off on foot to see what picturesque delights he could capture. He said he'd be back within an hour, but since Drake was on the clock we didn't care if he took all day. The arrangement of booths seemed to run along the lines of: a wine, a food, an art or craft, a wine, a craft, another wine. New Mexico is known for some excellent wineries and this little event was here to showcase them.

First, I wanted food. The smell of barbeque wafted toward me; I took Drake's hand and pulled him along as I followed the scent like a hopeful puppy. Not that he needed much persuading.

"Hey," he said, stopping under a shady elm tree, "isn't that your guy?"

Utter confusion on my part.

"Bobby Lorrento, the one Ron's tracking. Over by that wine booth with the chile ristras hanging on it."

I followed his gaze in time to see a large white guy pull a petite, dark-haired woman into an embrace. They had stepped out of the traffic path and were indulging in a kiss. A *long* kiss.

I had to admit I didn't watch enough football to recognize the players in their uniforms, on the field, much less out in the civilian world, but Drake seemed fairly certain.

"It's him. He hired me once to fly him around a ranch property up near Pecos."

Why hadn't he told me this a week ago? "Did the woman go along too?"

"Not that one. The lady I met was taller and blonde and was introduced as his wife, Marcie."

I glanced back over at the lovebirds. Where was our

photographer when we needed him? I reached for my
phone in my jeans pocket, but even zooming it to its max,
I knew the photo I shot would be an unrecognizable blur.
The subjects were too far away.

"I'm going to see if I can catch up with them," I said.
"Charlie—"

The crowd had multiplied and I lost sight of the pair
as I dashed across the road—bringing a pickup truck to
a sudden stop—and sprinted toward the booth with the
bright red strings of chiles. You'd think a guy who's six-
three and well over two hundred pounds couldn't simply
vanish. The pair had been slightly to the side of the wine
booth when I spotted them, maybe they'd ducked behind
to get away from the expanding crowd.

I followed the route I guessed they most likely had
taken, but all I found was the parking area for the vendors.
The row of booths was backed up by vehicles parked at
crazy angles, an assortment of empty cartons and more
than a few guywires waiting to trip me and toss me on my
face if I wasn't careful.

No sign of a big man and petite woman. I turned back
to the hubbub. Drake had crossed the road and apparently
had just asked the slender woman in the wine booth if she'd
seen me. She gave a winning smile and pointed toward me.
He looked relieved. What a sweetheart he is, but really, I
don't need this much worrying-over.

I turned to the woman, whose business seemed
momentarily at a lull. She had enviable long blonde hair
drawn up into a ponytail with just the perfect number of
wisps escaping the band, and she wore a burgundy apron
over her jeans and white T-shirt. A name tag pinned to the
apron strap identified her as Susie Scott. She picked up a

small plastic cup and poured a half inch of wine into it.

"Here, try this one. It's our red-chile cabernet." She offered Drake a taste as well, but he declined on the grounds that he had to fly later.

Momentarily distracted from my football-player mission, I took the cup. A lot of New Mexico winemakers are getting creative with flavors, but I'd never tried one of these with chile. I took a tentative sip. It was actually very good, with just a hint of chile nip as it settled into my mouth.

I noticed Susie was watching the crowd as we chatted, so I decided to see if she had noticed Lorrento. I described him.

"You mean Bobby Lorrento," she said. "I recognized him right away. He was one of my fantasy football picks last year." She lowered her voice. "The girl with him—that wasn't his wife. I've seen Marcie Lorrento in the stands. You know, they do those crowd shots sometimes on TV. Uh-uh. This was somebody else. I didn't know he and his wife had split."

As readily as she shared information I figured I'd better not tell her about our case. "Did he buy anything from you?"

A credit card receipt could give Ron some additional ammo, I supposed.

Susie shook her head. "No, but I noticed they stopped at the booth over there where the guy sells the Polish sandwiches. Bobby wolfed down two of them. Oh—and the girl? She was carrying a little bag from The Spice Rack. It's the booth about three down from me that sells all kinds of spices and teas."

"You'd make a great detective," I told her.

She beamed. "You think? My mother always told me I was too nosy. My sister just says I'm very observant."

I thanked her for the information and we bought a bottle of the wine. I spent the next forty minutes visiting the two booths Susie had pointed out—no luck finding Lorrento at either one. I turned my attention toward ferreting out the best of the barbeque sandwiches on offer. When we decided, we settled at a picnic table under an awning to eat and watch the crowd.

At one point I thought I saw the dark-haired woman Bobby Lorrento had been kissing, but she was alone and I couldn't be sure. I was becoming impatient with the search—this was Ron's case, after all. I wanted to return to my earlier euphoria, but even Drake's mention of the little cabin we'd found didn't quite bring it back.

Drake's client came ambling up to our table, a happy grin proof he'd gotten everything he wanted out of the day's excursion. We balled up our sandwich papers and tossed them in the trash, and the three of us strolled back to our aircraft. Bobby Lorrento might be rich and famous, but we were the ones in this crowd who knew how to come and go in style.

By the time I got home, leaving Drake and Michael at the airport to finalize their business, it was late afternoon. I was still full from the late barbeque lunch, so I planned nothing more complicated than to take Freckles for a quick walk followed by an evening devoted to nothing much at all.

I'd barely clipped the leash to the dog's collar and stepped out the front door when Elsa woo-hoo'd at me from her front yard. We walked over to say hi. I immediately noticed she seemed concerned about something.

"Everything okay?"

"Oh, I shouldn't be such a worry-wart," she said, "but I still think something's wrong over at the Delaney's. Ever since we talked before, I've been watching those girls. I haven't seen the two of them together in ages."

"Yeah, you mentioned that. Is it unusual? Maybe one girl has been away."

"Hm, maybe. But it's been a long time, and both their cars are there."

I looked up the street and saw that, yes, two Corvettes sat in their driveway—a red one and a blue one.

I did a quick age calculation. The Delaney twins must be eighteen or nineteen now, certainly old enough to be on their own. I remembered my own late-teen years and how girls that age almost always hung out in pairs or groups. Even shopping, I always went with Stacy or Brad.

"You told me the parents travel a lot. Maybe she went with them."

"But that's the thing. I see both girls. Zayne comes out and gets into her red car, and other times Clover comes out and goes in the blue one."

"And the problem is …?"

"I never see them *together*. Those girls have always done everything together."

Freckles was tugging at her leash but I took a moment to give my attention to Elsa.

"So, what are you saying?"

"I don't know, but I have a bad feeling."

Chapter 7

Sixteen years ago …

I ducked into The Gap and tucked myself behind a rack of jeans. Why, oh why had I agreed to come to the mall with Gram? *Only* because it's not Saturday and I know most of my friends wouldn't be here. How lame is it to be out shopping with an old lady?

Okay, to be fair about it, she'd gone her own way and let me go mine. I have my allowance, the monthly amount from my soon-to-be inheritance that I can spend on clothes and necessities, but geez-Louise it's barely enough. Two years ago, I'd hoped to save up enough for a car but my cash only goes about as far as a couple of CDs and maybe one new outfit a month.

The only car on the horizon is my mother's five-year-old Buick which still sits in our garage, to be mightily bestowed upon me for my eighteenth birthday. Six more months and I cannot wait, even though it's a Buick. I'll trade it in on something cooler as soon as I graduate and get a job.

From behind the jeans I looked at my watch. Another ten minutes before I needed to meet up with her at the Orange Julius. I *could* just not show up. But that would never fly. She'd wait around or, worse yet, get mall security to look for me. And then I'd be in for a lecture. God, I hate those. The gentle, "Now, Charlie, it's dangerous for a girl …" Blah, blah, blah.

If Gram knew how often I sneaked out at night, if she had a *clue*. She's got no idea that I go over to my house and get the car key off the hook by the garage door and meet up with my friends. She'd faint dead away if she knew how many times Brad North and I have ended up in the backseat. One time when Ron went over to start the Buick and keep the battery charged, he said something about how the gas gauge seemed lower than he'd remembered. After that, I made sure to put more in each time I drove it.

I looked at the price tag on the jeans I'd pulled off the rack and put them back.

A familiar voice caught my attention. Oh geez, it was Gram. She'd stopped right outside the store and was talking to somebody. Maybe if I slid over to the jackets, I could disappear.

"Oh, there's Charlie now," Gram said.

Oh well, I would've had to go in a few minutes anyway. I waved and she motioned me over.

"You remember Mr. and Mrs. Delaney don't you, Charlie?"

I smiled and nodded. The parents of the twin girls

Gram still insists I help babysit now and then. They'd been over only a few nights ago and we played Candy Land until I felt like I'd get a cavity. Now, the two happy-go-lucky little girls were holding hands and skipping around, singing some irritating little song.

"So, anyway," Rick Delaney said, continuing as if I'd gone invisible, "it's pretty boring work but the people we get to meet are so fascinating. There's this young actor in our current project—just getting started, but he'll be somebody. Name's Orlando Bloom."

I started to pipe up and say Orlando wasn't that new. I'd noticed those dark, smoky eyes of his in a movie about Oscar Wilde, and it was already out in the video store. But Mr. Delaney wasn't pausing for a second.

"Our favorite to work with so far has been Steven Spielberg. Can you imagine? I'm handling the camera rigging, right next to Spielberg."

Jane Delaney piped up. "Yeah, you'll see our names, right there in the credits. Watch for it. His newest film hits the theaters next month."

Yeah, like I want to sit in the theater an extra twenty minutes after the show just to see your name in print. I don't think so. But I smiled when she looked my direction.

"And," said Rick, "we'll be on location in Santa Fe on a new action-adventure shoot for the summer. My sister's coming to stay with the kids this time. We'll be put up in the crew housing."

Which is probably some old motorhome or trailer out in the middle of the desert in the summer heat. Call me unimpressed.

One of the twins tripped on the leg of a wrought iron bench and started screaming, which gave Gram and me the perfect chance to break away.

"Would you like to drive on the way home?" she asked me as we stowed our few shopping bags in the trunk of her solid old Ford sedan.

"Whatever." *Yes!*

"Boy, that couple sure can go on," Gram said as she sank into the passenger seat. "That whole world of movie people seems so superficial to me. Do they honestly think actors and big-name directors are going to be their friends? Neighbors and family—those are your real friends."

I knew it was another of her not-so-subtle life lessons, so I put on the appropriate face and thought about my date tonight with Brad. I hoped she didn't notice I was ten over the speed limit as we headed down Lomas. A song from the background music at The Gap kept running through my head.

"The little girls are cute, though, don't you think?"

I continued to hum as I diverted my attention back to what she was saying. Oh, the little twins. Yeah, sure. They were okay, as kids went.

"Brad asked me out to a movie," I said.

"On a school night? Huh-uh. You know the rule."

"It's not really night. It's an afternoon matinee that starts at five. We'd be home by seven-thirty."

Actually it didn't start until after six-thirty and there was no way I'd come directly home anyway. We were going to grab a Bob's Burger first, and then would probably hang out with some friends after. She wouldn't like it but, shit, I'm seventeen and she can't treat me like I'm ten anymore.

She gave a sigh of resignation, which I recognized as her way of deciding this was one battle not worth fighting.

"If you've got your homework done."

"I do." *Mostly. I'll finish the history essay during English in the morning.*

Of course, the movie went late and the friends bailed, so it was Brad and me making out and drinking rum and Cokes in his car for an hour. Gram surely noticed my lipstick was completely gone and my hair a tousled mess when I walked in at ten. She didn't say a word, just went around and locked the doors and went into her bedroom. On the kitchen table sat a glass of milk and plate of homemade cookies. I felt bad. Not bad enough to go apologize to her, just bad enough to finish off the milk and cookies.

The next morning at school, my head pounded and I swore off ever taking another taste of rum. Topping it with a heavy snack had been a mistake and my stomach was rebellious. When I got a note in homeroom that my guidance counselor wanted to see me, I almost turned the other way in a desperate attempt to flee school. But I didn't. The consequences at home weren't worth it.

"Charlotte, hello," said Mrs. Reynolds. "Come on in and have a seat."

I complied, mainly because I was rather shaky on my feet. All I remembered of this woman was how we'd had a few meetings my sophomore year, after my parents' plane crash. She'd done her best to assure me that life had to go on, the school would make allowances for my trauma, and the best way to handle it was to get on with it and concentrate on my work. I basically blew it all off.

"As you know, we like to meet with each graduating senior and talk a bit about your plans for the future. I see you've applied and been accepted to UNM for the fall term." She was reading from a manila folder on her desk. "Have you thought about what you'd like to major in?"

I went blank. Other than freedom from my surrogate grandmother, I hadn't thought much about my future at all.

"Many students have plans in place. Others have no inkling," Mrs. Reynolds said with an indulgent smile. She'd read me like a book. "For those who haven't already expressed an area of interest, we like to give some ideas. I notice here on your transcript, and from the standardized tests you've taken, that you have very strong math skills."

I do? Right offhand, I couldn't say what grade I'd earned in any class for two years. My general impression was that I was barely holding my own, although I supposed the university wouldn't have accepted me if I was a total failure.

She continued. "Have you considered a career path in accounting?"

Chapter 8

Freckles and I walked to our little neighborhood park, the one where Stacy and I used to meet. I unclipped the dog's leash and tossed a tennis ball across the grassy space.

Elsa's comment about the teenaged twins had put me back in the world of my own high school days. Unlike a lot of friends who remembered high school as a time of dances, football games and singing in the choir, my experience had been completely overshadowed by the loss of my parents, the uprooting of routine during my life with Elsa, and spending too much time in the world of lies and deceit that kids create when they start hanging out with the wrong crowd. The counselor who'd suggested accounting classes had no idea how decisively she had set me on the right path.

Back to the twins. I decided I would start paying more attention, see whether it seemed Elsa's observations had any merit. She may have turned into the neighborhood busybody, but she's far from senile. I thought back to what she'd told me so far. The parents had been away for awhile now, most likely on one of their movie jobs.

The girls were apparently living at home alone, but they were eighteen or nineteen years old—I'd done the same at that age. I realized I knew little else about them. Were they in college, did they have jobs, did they have a lot of friends? I had no idea.

I must have thrown the ball a whole lot more times than I realized. Poor Freckles was beat. She had taken the ball off to the side and now she was lying in the cool sand beneath one of the swings.

"Okay, baby, we can go home."

The suggestion revived her and she trotted over to me. I snapped the leash on once again and stuffed the ball in my pocket. We retraced our route and I caught myself staring at the Delaney house as we passed. One of the girls came out and noticed me. Oops—caught spying.

She said hi, I said hi. She wore a skin-tight black mini dress, impossibly high platform shoes and her blonde hair hung straight as a plank to the middle of her back.

"How are you girls doing?" I asked. "Elsa Higgins says your parents have been away. Everything going all right for you two?"

"Oh, yeah. We're fine." She turned her attention to the phone in her hand and started thumbing a message to someone as she walked toward her driveway.

"Okay, well … good."

So, there you have it. They're fine. I wasn't sure whether

I'd spoken to Zayne or Clover, and wasn't at all sure she remembered how, long ago, I had babysat the two of them. Anyway, I could now report to Elsa next time I saw her, although I had a feeling this was exactly the response she'd already received when speaking with the twins.

The girl paused beside the blue sports car and looked up at me. I realized I'd stopped in front of their house. I gave a little wave and yielded to Freckles's tugging at the leash. The car didn't start moving until I'd reached my own yard, which seemed a little strange. Normally those girls got in, threw their cars in gear and raced out of the neighborhood. I took a moment to get mail from our box, glancing back up the street as I did so. The red car was still in the Delaney driveway.

I supposed I could walk over there and ask the other girl a question or two, but wasn't that putting me in the same busybody mode as Elsa? And, frankly, I had plenty of other things going on in my life right now. It wasn't my place to insert myself into someone else's family situation.

To underscore the point, Drake pulled into our driveway just then and Freckles bounded toward him. As soon as his truck came to a full stop I dropped the leash and let her run to greet him. He got out and bent over to ruffle her ears and speak to her in baby talk.

"So, your customer seemed happy with the photos he got," I said.

"Yeah, he did. Depending on his editor's feedback, he may want to go again in a few days. And we earned several hours of flight revenue even though the job was close to home." He stepped onto the porch and pulled me close. His flight suit smelled of jet fuel.

"We're just back from a walk," I said. "How about I

feed this kid while you shower and then we'll meet at the gazebo with some wine and cheese?"

I puttered around the kitchen as Freckles scarfed down her kibble as if it were a race to finish. In a short time I had a small platter of sliced cheese, salami, some olives and an assortment of crackers. I was rummaging for the wine opener when Drake came in, wafting the scent of his favorite soap, a vast improvement over jet fuel.

"Shall we open the new bottle we bought today?" he suggested, taking over the duty.

I carried the food plate and some napkins outside. "Better bring light jackets," I called out when he opened the back door.

Once the sun goes down in a desert climate the temperature can drop dramatically. And our shady spot chosen for summer appeal had not exactly warmed much during the day. I slipped into the fleece jacket he brought me and took my wineglass from him.

"Here's to a possible new venture," he said, raising his glass to touch mine.

At my puzzled look, he added, "The little cabin? I'm serious about checking it out, finding out who owns it."

"It could be a great little getaway. As quickly as we can get there by air, we'd both be handy to our businesses if need be." I made myself a stack of cracker, cheese and olive.

"And a fun project," he said, sitting back in his cushioned chair and staring up at the gazebo's ceiling. "I really enjoyed making this little retreat for us."

We finished our light dinner and sat bundled in the blankets I retrieved when I went back for the rest of the wine. The day's events kept playing through my head, starting with the discovery of the cabin and going through our sighting of Bobby Lorrento at the wine festival. The woman I'd spoken with at the wine booth had been very certain Lorrento was with someone other than his wife. I could call Ron and report, but the evening was too pleasant to bring his investigation into it. The news could wait for morning.

Chapter 9

I arrived at RJP Investigations around mid-morning, the late start being my little reward to myself for finishing the taxes yesterday. My plan today was to assemble file boxes for the year's accumulation of receipts, bank statements and other yearly crap the IRS makes us keep. The storeroom would now give up the oldest box to the shredder and add this new one to the collection. Another of those dreary, drudgework tasks only a financial person can love.

Freckles had ridden with me today and she parked herself in the square of sunshine on the Oriental rug in my office. By the time I'd pulled a batch of folders from my desk drawer, the dog was stretched out in tummy-up bliss.

All that ended the moment a loud crash sounded downstairs. Sally screamed.

I pictured the front door flying open and banging against the potted rubber plant beside it. Was that a tinkle of broken glass, or did I imagine it?

Freckles ran to the top of the stairs, barking like twenty-five pounds of vicious wild killer.

"Who's been talking to my wife?" demanded a booming male voice. *Fee-fi-fo-fum.*

Between barks from the dog I caught hints that Ron was on the phone in his office and Sally's voice sounded cowed in a way I'd never heard her before. My first instinct was to reach under my desk for my purse and get my hands on my Beretta.

When I looked up, Ron had appeared in his doorway. I tucked my pistol into my waistband when I saw he was already armed.

"*Well?*" demanded the voice.

Sally stammered something, and I caught sight of my dog racing down the final few steps preparing to launch herself at the intruder.

"Freckles!" I shouted. But the dog was deaf to the sound of my voice and clueless about everything but her mission.

Ron pointed his Smith & Wesson toward the ceiling as he took the stairs one at a time. I was only a couple of treads behind him. We reached the bottom and got our first real look at the situation. Sally stood behind her desk, her normally tan complexion so white her freckles stood out like a constellation of brown stars across her nose. A large man faced her. When she glanced around him toward Ron, the man spun.

It was Bobby Lorrento.

Wow—he sure seemed a lot bigger in the confined

space of our office than he had yesterday from a distance in the open air market. I made a grab for my dog's collar but she eluded me.

"You! You been puttin' ideas in my wife's head." Lorrento stared daggers at Ron.

A quick assessment showed the football player didn't seem to be armed—well, with anything other than his two huge fists. Ron lowered his weapon but I noticed he kept both hands on it. His voice was cool and modulated as he went through the motions of getting Lorrento to introduce himself. As if we didn't know.

Still, it was a good move on Ron's part. The man calmed by about three notches on the anger scale.

"My wife, Marcie, she's been talking to you," he stated, his voice rising again.

Ron nodded. "I've spoken with her."

"So, are you the s.o.b. who told her she ought to sell my Super Bowl rings?"

Ron's gun hand fell limply at his side. "What on earth are you talking about?"

"The little bitch took my rings to a pawn shop! All *three* of 'em—I can't *believe* it. *My* rings that I earned at the *Super Bowl*. Three winning games!"

Freckles was circling Lorrento's legs with evil intent in her eye, and I figured the last thing we needed was a dog-bite charge leveled at us along with his other accusations. I edged past Ron, got the dog by her collar and led her upstairs where I sent her to her crate with a cookie for her bravery.

"Look, Mr. Lorrento," Ron was saying when I came back downstairs. "I don't know anything about your Super Bowl rings, other than the fact I enjoyed like hell watching those games and seeing you win."

The belligerent manner dropped another two notches.

"Can we talk in here?" Ron asked, steering Lorrento toward the conference room.

Sally let out a shaky breath, although she didn't take her eyes off the two men. "Should I call 911?" she whispered to me when I got close.

I gave a tiny shake of my head. Things seemed to have calmed down quite a bit. I edged closer to the open door where the men had gone.

"I'll tell you Marcie hired us to find out if you were cheating on her," Ron said.

I noticed his body language showed he was ready to run, if the response proved to be a negative one. Ron isn't cowardly, but he's no fool either, and now in his mid-forties he's not looking to be taken down by a pro ballplayer.

"Marcie hired you?" Lorrento scratched his head. "Well, that's just stupid. She knows I cheat. I've had girlfriends all along. We players travel ... we got needs ... The wives get treated pretty damn good with clothes and jewelry and great big old houses. Now she wants more?"

This guy could not be serious. I felt my jaw clench.

"Are you familiar with a company called Innocent Times?" Ron asked.

Lorrento shuffled a little, giving away the answer.

"Look, I don't care what kind of arrangement you and your wife have, whether she agrees with your version of this story or not. I was hired to do a job and I started to look into it."

The athlete tensed up again. "My rings ..."

"You're sure she pawned them? Do you know which shop?"

"Yeah, that's how I found out. I found this ticket." He pulled a slip of paper from his pocket.

"So ... you go down there and retrieve them."

Did it really take a rocket scientist to figure this out? I chafed at the conversation.

"Them things are worth, like ..." I could see him trying to figure it out.

"Look," Ron said, "just go down to the shop and see what they want for them. They probably gave Marcie a fraction of the real value. As far as your relationship, I can't tell you what to do there. She was my client. She'll have to decide what she wants to do."

I noticed Ron said she *was* the client. Personally, I hoped it meant he intended to resign from the case and this particular dysfunctional couple.

With his ticket in hand, Bobby The Bomb headed toward our front door, which hung a little crookedly on its hinges. At least, thank goodness, the leaded glass insert hadn't shattered.

I watched him walk away and get into a jacked-up truck with huge tires that sat at an angle in our driveway. It started with a rumble and was soon out of sight.

"Well, that went swimmingly," I said with a grimace toward the door. "Do you now have a clue why I don't like us taking these cases?"

Ron ignored me and walked over to examine the door frame. "Some longer screws ought to fix it." He went toward the kitchen and I heard the back door open and close. He would get his toolbox from the shed out back and spend his afternoon fixing a problem that hadn't needed to happen. Sally and I exchanged a look. *Men.*

Back upstairs, I boxed up last year's files and labeled it

with a thick black marker. I'd just stashed it in the storeroom when I heard voices at the front door. These were much more civil, and in a minute I heard light footsteps on the stairs.

Victoria, Ron's wife, met me at the top.

"Hey there," she said. "Looks like you guys had a little excitement this morning."

I rolled my eyes.

"I'm on my way to take fabric swatches to a client in Old Town," she said, "but thought I'd stop by on the way and invite you and Drake to our place Saturday evening. We're grilling steaks and ribs. I'm guessing Ron didn't already mention this?"

"He didn't. He was a little busy."

She laughed. As she left, I watched her stop beside the door and give Ron a kiss. I hope the big dodo appreciates her. With what happened on their wedding day a few months ago, we're lucky we have her.

I spent another hour wrapping up my little organization project and then headed for home. Elsa was working on her front flowerbeds and she waved me over when I pulled into my driveway. I knew she was going to bring up the subject of the twins again—I swear, she's become a dog with a bone on this subject.

"I went over there awhile ago," she said. "I saw Clover leave, but since the red car is still home I figured that means Zayne is there. Well, if she is, she's ignoring me completely. I rang the bell and called out, even walked around to their backyard. Something's not right over there, I tell you."

I opened my mouth to list a selection of logical reasons why a person might leave her car home while she's somewhere else, but I saw the look in Elsa's eyes.

"It's just … young girls and the troubles they can get themselves into," she said. "I cared for those two little ones and now I'm worried. Could you check into it? I mean you and Ron and your company?"

I gave a resigned nod, hoping my lack of enthusiasm didn't show too greatly.

She seemed relieved. "What is it about girls when they hit their teens? They change so much."

I thought back to my own teen years. My experience was clouded by loss and grief, but even before that I remembered the onset of puberty as possibly the worst time of my life. Pressures abounded everywhere—girls made snarky comments about your hair, your clothes, your looks. Although I'd never been one of the cool kids, popularity was paramount to so many of them. Boys— well, the sexual tension was always in the air. I'd dated Brad North nearly all my senior year and by the time we entered college we were talking marriage.

Yeah, and look how that turned out.

Chapter 10

Thirteen years ago …

J anuary, two months after my twentieth birthday. I'd fully expected this morning's meeting with the family lawyer to go the same way every other one went: No, Charlotte is too young to be living on her own; no, she can't have free access to her inheritance yet; if she's really going to marry this North fellow then there should be a pre-nuptial agreement.

All the meetings with this impossibly ancient attorney went the same way. Elsa attended as my guardian, Ron as the senior-most family member, and me, slumped into a chair while they all talked about me as if I weren't in the room. *I'll graduate with an accounting degree in one more year. I think I can handle my own money now.*

"… the house, furnishings and vehicle. For now," the attorney was saying. "Upon her twenty-first birthday, she'll receive access to half the trust fund. At age thirty, the remainder."

I patted the tabletop with my hand. "Could you all at least pretend I'm right here." I tried for a respectful tone.

"Sorry." The lawyer actually looked a bit chastened. "Charlotte, the trust fund provision is not my decision. Your parents wrote it that way. Each of your brothers received his share at the appropriate age, as well."

I know I made a face when he used the word 'appropriate.' I couldn't help myself. He turned his attention back to the long sheets of paper on the desk and I fiddled with the ring on my left hand. The diamond Brad had given me when he proposed at Christmas wasn't a large one but it signified that we had a future together. In one year's time I would have my degree and a husband and we would be living in a nice neighborhood, a far cry from our contemporaries in their student-housing apartments.

Today's meeting was momentous for me—my own home. No matter what the rest of them said, I felt like a grownup—finally. I signed the papers the lawyer pushed toward me and walked out of his office not quite believing my luck.

Gram suggested a celebratory lunch. She'd put stew in a big pot on the stove before we left for the meeting. Ron begged off, saying he had to meet with a woman about renting space for his business. He'd received his private investigator's license two years ago and the cases started to roll in, thanks to the guy who'd mentored him. But working from home with his shrewish wife Bernadette and three small kids underfoot was proving nearly impossible.

So the celebration ended up being just Gram and me,

which was fine. I gobbled down the stew and cornbread, mentally cataloguing the possessions I'd collected in five years in this house, while she talked about the practicalities of being a homeowner.

"You'll need to be sure to have the furnace serviced each fall. Ron did it last September so it's working fine now. And he'll help you this spring when it's time to switch over to your air conditioning."

I nodded absently. She probably thought the smile on my face was gratitude for her advice, when in reality I was thinking how great it would be to have Stacy over to hang out tonight. I was pretty sure some of my dad's liquor supply must still be in a cabinet somewhere over there. The moment Gram paused, I jumped up and put my dishes in the sink then dashed to my room to start packing.

The shiny black extension phone I'd bought for myself sat on the bedside table. I was fairly certain the phone at my own house—my house!—wasn't connected yet, so I picked up this one and punched Stacy's number to deliver the great news.

"Tonight? *Yeah!* Wow, that's fantastic, Charlie. I'll tell Jennifer and Karin and Lisa. They'll round up the guys, and I'm pretty sure Dominic was getting a keg for the weekend. If he can get it now, he'll bring it."

"I was thinking it'd be just—"

"Oh, man, this'll be great!"

… *you and me* … But she'd hung up. Wow. I was about to host my first party. I started flinging things into a box.

I spent the afternoon putting my clothes into the closet I'd used five years ago. At some point I would have to go through the old stuff I'd left behind. Clothes the fifteen-year-old me had loved were just plain icky now.

Walking through the living room and kitchen sent me back to childhood with waves of memories, both sweet and painful. My mother's china in the dining room hutch, linens she'd inherited from her mother, my dad's pipe on an end table.

I went into their bedroom, half expecting to see Mother's robe hanging from the hook on the bathroom door, but Elsa and Ron and the other responsible adults of the day had cleared my parents' personal things. When Brad and I were married we would move into this room. It would be weird.

Another thing that had been cleared from the house was all trace of food. There was not so much as a stale cracker or ancient bag of popcorn. I would need to buy groceries. I checked my wallet where I had a whole ten dollars to last me the month. *Welcome to the real world, Charlie.* At least, thanks to Elsa's diligence and my own sneakiness, the car out in the garage was gassed up and ready to go. I went out there and got behind the wheel.

The neighborhood had a whole different feel to me, adult Charlie driving my own car from my own house to do my own grocery shopping. Up the block, I saw a woman at the Delaney house, holding the hand of a little blonde girl with each of hers. They must be in kindergarten or first grade by now, just coming home from school. The woman wasn't their mother. A fragment of conversation passed through my memory, Gram saying something about the parents now having a nanny for the girls. They were apparently making an obscene amount of money now (her words) and could afford such things. It meant nothing to me.

At the supermarket I discovered this stuff was

expensive. Bread was more than a dollar a loaf, and my ten bucks wouldn't go far. I settled on items for the party, for now. Tomorrow, I would have to figure out something that didn't involve Gram or see-I-told-you-so Ron.

Friends started arriving a little after ten-thirty that night. Obviously, Stacy knew that was the magic hour when Gram finished watching the evening news and would be dead asleep, the time I had always sneaked out. By midnight I was beginning to wish they'd all go home. I kept turning down the music. Even though all the windows and doors were closed on a January night, surely the sound was rocking the neighborhood.

The gang had decimated the food supply but the keg seemed bottomless. By two a.m. I was ready to hide under my bed, except Rick and Lisa seemed to have locked themselves in my room. I wanted to be a good sport but I had an exam on Internal Revenue Service rules in—oh, god—six hours.

Where was Stacy? Maybe she could convince the rest of them to wind things down. I walked through the living room, past overturned cups and paper plates gooey with onion dip. A dribble of red salsa trailed across the white rug in front of the TV. I picked up as much of the trash as I could hold and headed for the kitchen. I should have put the big wastebasket in the living room. As if anyone would actually use it. I pushed through the swinging door.

There stood Stacy and Brad. Kissing.

The cups and plates dropped at my feet. Stacy heard the sound and backed away from him.

"Nope," she said with a laugh and a little slap at his shoulder. "Scott's the better kisser."

She was laughing as she walked toward me. "Silly bet. I

told Scott he was the world's best kisser."

My best friend had always been a joker, much more playful than I, full of pranks. Was this just another of those? I didn't know. I only knew I was tired and grumpy and had a huge mess to clean up and an exam to pass very soon.

"Party's over," I said to her. "Go tell the rest of them it's time to go home."

Chapter 11

The memory of that first night in my own home hit me in a flash, as if it had happened yesterday. *Whoo*.

Brad and I had continued as a couple another few months. With finals and graduation I had no time to dwell on my feelings about what might have been a simple misunderstanding, and certainly no time or energy to talk seriously with him about it. There were little signs all along, I saw in retrospect. I walked off the podium with my new diploma in hand, joined him at the back of the auditorium afterward and handed him the ring.

He and Stacy eloped less than two months later and even had the audacity to send me an invitation to their reception. I didn't go and didn't speak to either of them for more than eight years.

"Charlie? You seem a million miles away," Elsa said

from the seat beside me. She held a huge bowl of potato salad on her lap.

I blinked back the old memories and turned onto Ron and Victoria's street. Drake was doing a midday flight and would meet us. Ron had warned that the steaks were going on the grill at six o'clock sharp, and if I knew my hubby he would definitely be here on time. The thought of Drake made me realize that Brad and Stacy's betrayal had been one of the luckiest events of my life.

"It looks like we've been blessed with this weather," Elsa said. "This is the warmest April I've seen in awhile."

She says it every year, but I didn't remind her.

"I brought my jacket anyway. You young kids never seem to notice the cold but I sure do."

She also says *that* every year.

I parked on the street in front of the house and helped Elsa with her potato salad, taking her elbow as she insisted on carrying the large bowl up the flagstone pathway to the front door. With my minimal cooking skills, my contribution to the party was a jar of salsa from Pedro's and two large bags of chips, all jammed into a canvas tote bag.

Ron answered the door, trailed by his ten-year-old, Joey, the only one of the three boys who hadn't suddenly become six feet tall.

"Hey, c'mon in," Ron said. He took the bowl from Elsa. "Vic's in the kitchen."

The scent of barbequed ribs filled the house, almost making my knees weak. I followed my nose and found Victoria lifting a wide pan with two racks of ribs from the oven. She set it on the stovetop and turned around, her face bright pink from the warmth.

Elsa had followed Ron out to the backyard where he

promised there was beer in the cooler.

"Those ribs smell *so* good," I said, taking a seat on one of the barstools at the granite counter.

"They'll be better after we add more sauce," Victoria said.

I must have whimpered.

"You can have one now as an appetizer," she offered. She started to pull the foil from the pan but I held up a hand.

"I doubt I could eat just one. I'll save it for later." I pulled the chips from my tote bag. "We could open this salsa. I picked it up from Pedro's yesterday. And there are two bags of his chips."

"Which are always fantastic." She tore open the first cellophane bag and, like woodland creatures at the sound of prey, two of the boys loped into the room and eyed the bowl as chips filled it. "Take this out back," she told them, "and leave enough for your dad to have some."

The two were gone already, handfuls of chips headed toward mouths.

Victoria was shaking her head as she opened the second bag and dumped chips into another bowl. "It is truly astounding what those three can put away. They eat constantly."

"So, married life is good? Everyone settling in together?"

"It's great. The boys are only here alternate weeks, so Ron and I actually do have some couple time. My design business has kept me so busy since the first of the year, I've barely taken a breath."

Elsa came in from the backyard, a tall glass of iced tea in hand. I'd gotten an especially hot bite of the salsa and decided the tea was a good idea. As I walked out the back door to get some, I heard Elsa say, "I suppose Charlie told you about the new mystery in our neighborhood."

Still on the subject of the Delaney twins?

In the back yard, Ron was doing something at the grill and I discovered Drake had joined the party. He must have come through the side gate. He gave me a quick kiss and pointed out the tea pitcher on a long table that was set up to hold the food when everything was ready. I poured myself a glass while he reached into the cooler for a beer.

The two younger boys, Joey and Jason, were tossing a ball between them, while Justin slouched in a chair tapping away at his phone. I wandered toward him and took the seat beside him.

" 'sup, Aunt Charlie?" He didn't take his eyes from the lines of text on the screen.

"Not much. How about you?"

A shrug. The dismissive attitude and inattention to an adult would have earned me or my brothers a cuff on the head from my dad. At the very least, a mild reprimand from Mother. These days, it seemed the way of the teen world.

I searched for a topic of interest. "You have a girlfriend?"

"I don't know … Kinda. There's some girls I like." No eye contact but it was the longest communication I'd gotten from him yet.

Could I tease another whole sentence from him? "Girls, huh. So they're *all* interested in Justin Parker?"

It wouldn't be a stretch to think so. He had his dad's height and dark hair, his mother's chocolate-brown eyes, and a sexy little smile I'd like to think was similar to mine.

He finally looked up at me and flashed the smile.

"Yeah—you know. Girls don't much settle with one guy. A lot of them just want to hook up."

Teen code for sex without any emotion attached.

"Justin, really? That's what they're saying to you?" I gave a nod toward his phone.

He clicked the phone off, darkening the screen. "I think I'll go get a Coke."

He made it sound as if the girls were propositioning the boys. At fifteen? *Oh, come on, Charlie. You remember high school. The boys were doing the asking.*

With his phone stashed away, Justin looked like nothing more dangerous than a great big kid. He pulled a canned cola from the cooler and watched the younger boys throw the ball while he popped the top on it. Ron said something to him and he walked over and shook hands with Drake. The kids were growing up so fast.

I meandered back inside to see if I could give Victoria a hand. She was seasoning a platter full of steaks and Elsa sat at the counter with her tea.

"This looks like enough food for an army," I joked.

"I suppose the big surprise of my married life is how much food three growing boys can pack away," Victoria said with a grin. "There are five adults and the three boys—do you think a dozen ears of corn will be enough?"

I'm sure my eyes went wide. I'm used to planning food for two.

She kept stacking corn into a huge kettle. "Hey, Elsa was just saying the twin girls who live up the street from you seem to be on their own a lot these days. Do you suppose they would like to be included in some of our gatherings? Maybe meet the boys?"

I thought of Justin's comments about girls and hooking up.

"Um, let me think about it," I said. "The girls are a bit older and probably have their own set of friends. I don't know them very well, but I can go over and talk to them."

From Gram's little smile, I suddenly knew she'd planted the seed of the idea in Victoria's head with little thought as to how it would actually work out. She may have even plotted it all out to get me over there to see what the twins were up to. I sighed.

Well, maybe it was time I did exactly that.

Chapter 12

I tossed and turned most of the night, the result—I admit—of too much heavy food and the pitcher of margaritas Ron made once the afternoon slipped into evening. The other reason was the promise I'd made to go over and talk with the Delaney girls. I do this—make promises I really shouldn't—then regret it. *Why* do get into this stuff?

Finally, around six in the morning I got up and went into the kitchen, hoping I still had some of that stomach-settling herbal tea on hand. Freckles heard me and began to whimper in her crate so I let her out and sent her to the back yard. A blast of chilly air rushed in when I opened the door for her, a wild caprice of nature reminding me how fickle this month's weather can be.

While the kettle heated I leaned against the cupboards and debated my approach. There was no way I could stall about the visit—Elsa would pin me down for a report the very next time I saw her. My gaze fell to a boxed cake mix I'd set out the day before. In a moment of grand-gesture thinking I'd toyed with the idea of baking and decorating cupcakes for the barbeque. Although a time crunch intervened and I'd grabbed chips and salsa instead, the cupcakes were still a possibility as a door-opener today.

Then I discovered I was out of eggs and the whole two-hour process of baking seemed like way more effort than necessary. I had the perfect little ice-breaker right here in the backyard. I let her inside and gave her a bowl of kibble while I dawdled over the daily news on my tablet and finished two cups of tea.

An hour or so later, Drake wandered into the kitchen, wondering what I was doing up so early, happy to accept a cup of coffee the minute the brewing cycle finished.

"I'm taking that photographer back out today," he said as he spooned sugar into his coffee. "You wanna come along?"

"Hm, I'd better not. I promised Elsa something and if I don't get it done right away, I never will."

He filled a bowl with a grownup cereal while I chose the Frosted Flakes and we split the last of the milk. I jotted a list to remind me that a grocery trip would be in order.

"Okay, then," he said, landing a kiss on my forehead, "I'll touch base when I'm ready to lift off and again when we get back."

I hadn't asked where the photographer wanted him to fly. Odds were good it would be a lot more fun than what I had in mind, but I decided there was no time like the present. I dressed in jeans and a T-shirt with a small triangle of lace trim at the throat. The outdoor thermometer showed sixty degrees, but the breeze belied that. I grabbed a light fleece jacket from the hooks near the door and called Freckles.

Up the street, I saw the red sports car was the only one in the Delaney driveway. This could be a wasted trip unless I caught both girls home at the same time, but it was worth a shot. We started walking that direction. As an excuse for ringing the doorbell, I'd brought along a battered paperback book I would claim to have found lying in their driveway.

The plan was then to have Freckles work her little cutie-pie routine and get the girls to fuss over her so I would have the chance for a low-key interrogation. I know—it wasn't much of a plan.

I played my role to perfection, walking by the house and doing a little double-take at the driveway (in case they were watching from their living room window), turning my back partially and dropping the book out of my jacket. Freckles gave it a sniff, for good measure, and I glanced up at the house. An observer would see me debating whether to disturb the occupants over an insignificant book but, good citizen that I am, I would dutifully carry it to the door to deliver it.

Freckles sat on command and I rang the bell. I got that hollow, empty-house feeling so I rang it again. Still no answer.

Well, drat. Was I going to have to replay my ruse several times a day until someone came home? If we had other snoop-bodies around, like Elsa, it would make for a silly show. Now I was in a quandary—if someone had witnessed my picking up the book and now I stuck in it my jacket, I would appear to be a thief. If I left it at the doorstep, the twins would have no clue why, plus there went my reason for stopping.

Dang, Charlie, get over it. Go on your way and come back when you can actually find someone home.

Elsa would tell me to bust down the door—the fact one car was still here and no one answered surely had some nefarious meaning. But it was likely the two girls had gone somewhere early, in one car. I was debating next moves when I heard an engine sound from my end of the street. Sure enough, the blue Corvette slowed and turned in beside the other.

Okay. Showtime.

I couldn't swear to it, but I thought the young woman who emerged was the same twin I'd seen the other day. With her was a guy of about the same age. A palpable thread of tension stretched between them.

"Hi," I said meeting them halfway between her front porch and the driveway. "You're Zayne, aren't you? Remember me? I used to live with Mrs. Higgins across the street. We babysat you girls when you were small."

"I'm Clover," she said, with a vague smile that indicated she barely remembered me and even if she did, it meant next to nothing.

"Oh, yeah. Sure. I guess you get that a lot."

"My whole life."

I looked pointedly at the guy. He had a sort of preppy look—short brown hair with a fringe that came halfway to his dark eyebrows, intense blue eyes, not a zit to be seen. He wore jeans and a T-shirt from some band I'd never heard of.

"This is Ryan."

By this time Freckles had gone into her bit, jumping up to Ryan with the eager trust all dogs have, that sureness everyone will love them. He didn't appear to, but Clover called to her and gave the dog a sweet pat on the head.

"Oh, well, we were just walking by and I saw this lying in your driveway. Figured one of you must have dropped it. I thought Zayne must be home since her car's here."

"Uh … well, if she didn't answer she must still be asleep." She glanced at Ryan as she said it.

"Wow. She must sleep like the dead. I rang the bell twice and knocked pretty hard."

Clover's face flushed a deep pink. The boy seemed tense as a guywire.

"Clover," he said. "It's okay to tell her."

The girl had a hard time catching her breath so he answered.

"Zayne's gone away to school. She's in Las Cruces."

"Really? Hm. I thought I saw her driving the red car a few days ago."

"That—that was me," said Clover. She stood a bit straighter. "Zayne couldn't take the car with her right away, so we're keeping it here. I drive it every few days to keep it running good."

"That's right," Ryan said, reaching for the paperback. "Thanks for returning the book."

It was complete bullshit, but it was a dismissal and I knew enough to leave.

Chapter 13

I tugged the dog's leash and we headed toward the park until the two were inside. Nervous glances and fake smiles aside, there was so much wrong with their story. I didn't believe Zayne would have gone off to college without her car, not to New Mexico State. Las Cruces is a mid-size town without much in the way of public transportation and all the fun places to go are off campus. No kid I ever knew went to that school without a car, if they had one. Secondly, it's April. She wouldn't start school until the fall semester. Plus, it would be too easy to check, which is exactly what I planned to do.

We walked to the end of the block and doubled back, veering to Elsa's front door rather than going on to our own.

"Okay, you've got me ninety percent convinced," I

said, the minute she let us in. "That dark-haired guy—is he the one you've seen around quite a bit?"

"The one you were talking to out in the driveway a minute ago? Yes, he's the one." She bustled to the kitchen and returned with a dog biscuit for Freckles.

Meanwhile, I had my phone out and was already looking up the number for the admissions department at NMSU. A female who sounded about twelve years old answered. I told her what I wanted to know and she put me on hold for a good five minutes.

"I'm sorry," she said when she returned. "I can't find the right records."

"So, Zayne Delaney isn't registered?"

"Well, she could be. I just can't find the record, and Mrs. King isn't here today. If you call back tomorrow, she might be able to tell you."

I tamped down my impatience and said I would try again.

"Well, that was frustrating," I said, declining Elsa's offer of coffee. "You said you know the aunt? That's Rick Delaney's sister?"

"Yes. Donna. Let me see if I can find her number."

I still wanted to look for a logical explanation that didn't involve anything sinister. With luck, Donna Delaney could provide it. I dialed the number Elsa gave me, then put my phone on speaker so we could both follow the conversation. Donna answered, slightly breathless, and apologized that she had been out in the yard when the phone rang.

"No one hardly calls my landline anymore, and I've fallen out of the habit of listening for it," she said.

I introduced myself and told her I was with Elsa. They

gave each other happy little hellos.

"We're a bit concerned about your nieces. Elsa's noticed some odd doings at their house and their parents haven't been around in awhile. Clover told me Zayne has gone away to New Mexico State, but I can't seem to verify it. Would you happen to know?"

We heard a long sigh over the line. "No one keeps me in the loop. I'd like to think the girls are in school, not just hanging around the house, but I really don't know."

"I've noticed the two of them coming and going at all hours," Elsa said, "but never together. They used to do everything together. Now there's this boy hanging around. I suppose he's clean-cut enough …"

But looks could deceive.

"I'll try to reach my brother by phone. I think the crew is on location in some foreign desert, but maybe they'll have cell service or be able to get a message. It's possible Zayne is traveling with them."

Possible, but why wouldn't Clover have simply told me so?

"Elsa, thanks for keeping an eye on the girls," Donna said. "I've worried about them for a long time, but Rick and Jane didn't seem to think it was necessary to send them to live with me. I suppose life in small-town Colorado would have bored them to death anyway, and I would have had my hands full."

I glanced at Elsa as she and Donna said goodbye. This miraculous woman had certainly had her hands full with me. I was lucky she'd given me a strong upbringing and, although not all my choices are great ones, at least we both came through it alive and well. And we've remained friends.

Chapter 14

Six years ago …

So, I'm wondering what to do about my job. Sloan and Mercer is a great accounting firm, but I see my future there going either into a rat-race spiral or turning completely dead-end. If I don't hurry and get on the fast track for promotions I'll be stuck forever preparing the simplest tax returns."

I looked across the table at the guy I'd been dating for three months. He looked totally bored.

"Gary, have you heard a word I said?"

He let out a huge sigh and signaled the waitress to bring him another beer. Didn't bother to ask if I wanted more wine. I tried to see what I'd found attractive about him in the first place. He had nice hair. That was about it.

His career in electronics was 'on hiatus' as he liked to tell people, but it basically meant the company had let go of the dead weight in an overall downsizing maneuver and he hadn't yet found another job. Our so-called dates had degenerated to where it was mostly a case of my suggesting we go out somewhere as long as I was willing to pick up the tab.

He flashed a smile at the waitress as she set the beer down, and he fussed with a lime wedge while I thought back to what I'd been saying. The lagging economy was the main reason I hadn't quit Sloan and Mercer—there was no certainty I'd find anything else very soon. And although my inheritance money would take care of me for awhile, I couldn't imagine myself being like Gary—using up my savings and sitting around the house all day.

"So, how was your day?" I asked, although he'd pretty well covered it in the five minutes it took to say hello in the parking lot and walk into the restaurant.

"Are you asking whether I got myself out and applied for a job? 'Cause that line's getting really old, Charlie."

"Okay. You don't want to talk about my work and you don't *have* any, and we really have nothing else in common." I pulled a twenty out of my wallet and slid to the edge of the booth. "This should cover the drinks. Have a nice life."

I walked out, expecting that shaky feeling when you aren't sure you've done the right thing. But the feeling never came. Gary had been sweet and attentive in the beginning, and we'd both had career hopes that made us seem like an up-and-coming couple. And he wasn't bad in bed. But you can't build a life on such fragile pinnings, and at twenty-seven I was looking to settle in with The One. I just didn't have a clue who it might be.

My mother's Buick sat in the lighted parking lot—

another piece of my life where I'd become stuck. It had seemed a practical matter to keep the car that was paid for, rather than rushing out to buy what I really wanted, but sheesh. The thing was more than ten years old now. I climbed in and listened to the battery strain a little to start it. Another thing I'd better attend to before next winter.

At least my red Lab would be waiting at home for me. A dog is the one thing you can count on in life. I pulled into the McDonald's drive-thru lane and got the pooch a cheeseburger and myself a Big Mac and Coke. The evening was looking up already.

I turned on my street and noticed a bunch of extra cars a few houses up the way. Four teens piled out of one and made their way, laughing and kidding around, toward the Delaney house. Looked like a party—on a Tuesday? A little wave of disapproval coursed through me. The twin girls must be about thirteen now. What were they doing having a party on a school night?

Drop it, Charlie. It's probably their birthday and the parents are throwing a bash for them.

My disapproval turned to faint envy. Even on my birthday there wouldn't have been a big party with lots of friends on a school night. It would have been a sleepover Friday night with a few girls. Gram always baked me a huge chocolate cake and she let us girls have run of the house all night long. Now, I can only imagine how she was handling the noise we made. Locked away in her own room, she probably turned up her radio and fell asleep to some old big-band tunes. The envy turned to gratitude. My birthdays were always fun.

The phone was ringing when I walked into the house. Most likely it would be Gary, calling to apologize and suggest we get together again. Translated to: hey, we didn't eat anything tonight. I ignored the ringing until the answering machine took over.

Standing by the kitchen counter, I let my greeting message play while I handed the dog his cheeseburger. He scarfed it down in two chomps. The voice which spoke to the recorder wasn't Gary, thank goodness.

"Hey, sis. I've been wanting to talk about an idea I had. Just want to run something past you … Call me—"

I picked up the receiver before he hung up.

"Ron? Sorry, I just walked in the door. What's up?"

"Hey. Yeah, I wanted to talk about something. We could meet at Pedro's."

I looked at my Big Mac. "I've got dinner already, but come on over if you want. There's absolutely nothing going on tonight around here."

"Okay. Be there in twenty minutes."

Ron used to live a lot closer, but since the split last year with Bernadette, she and the boys stayed in their house and he moved up to the northeast heights to a dumpy apartment only a bachelor could love. He doesn't love it, but he's there. I think it's his version of a hair shirt.

I finished my yummy fast food dinner and had put coffee on by the time he arrived.

He parked himself at my kitchen table with his coffee and the new bag of peanut butter cookies I'd bought yesterday.

"Dinner," he grunted.

"Sorry there's nothing better. I ate the one and only Big Mac, and well, you know what kind of cook I am."

"The Nutter Butters are good."

"So?" It's rare that my brother says we should talk, and

I admit to being a little apprehensive.

"I hear you're not thrilled with your job at Sloan."

No big secret.

"So, how about you and me become partners?"

"Me, in the private investigation business? I don't have the credentials for a license."

He chased three cookies with a big swig of his coffee. "Not what I had in mind. I'm thinking you'd be the financial brains—keep the books, send bills out, answer the phones sometimes."

I ran it all through my head. "A partner, not an employee? So how much money do you need from this *partner*?"

He glanced down at the table for a second. "Enough to cover the current bills. I guess I've been better at spending than keeping on track of what people owe me."

I pictured the dim little windowless office on the second floor of a has-been building up on Wyoming. It would mean driving halfway across the city for me to spend the day without seeing the sun. My job at Sloan and Mercer wasn't the greatest but the downtown offices were nice and they were close to home.

"My terms would include a new office, someplace in a decent part of town. I'll front the money for the upgrade, if that's what it takes. I'll need to see your financial statements as they stand now."

He gave me a blank look.

"You don't have financial statements?" Yikes. "How do you figure out what to declare on your taxes?"

"I got a little receipt book that makes a carbon copy. At the end of the year I add them up."

Fine until you get audited. I paced the kitchen floor.

"Okay … Here's the deal. I'll set us up with a real accounting system, computerize everything. I can come up with the money to get started, but I can't financially support the business if it isn't making a profit."

"Oh, it is. I mean, there's money every month."

"Yeah, but now you're in trouble with unpaid bills."

"Bernadette—"

"Okay, I'm not placing blame. Let me take a look at your last couple of tax returns so I get a basic picture."

His mood brightened by a dozen notches. "We can do this, Charlie. You and I have always gotten along real well."

True. Our other brother, Paul, is from a whole different planet, but Ron and I have always been close.

"One other provision," I said. "I don't want to get into the investigation end of things. You bring in the cases and work them. I do finances only."

We hashed out the details for several more hours, until I realized I really should get to bed if I was going to be worth diddly at work tomorrow. The idea in my head was that I would give two weeks' notice and use evenings and weekends during that time to locate new digs for RJP Investigations.

He stood up and gave me a hug. "It'll be a great partnership."

A big unknown, as far as I was concerned. But the thought of walking into Sloan and Mercer and handing in my notice raised my spirits way up the scale.

"I'll go home and gather the information you need," he said, suddenly motivated. "Let's get together again tomorrow night and go over it again. When can you get away so we can look at offices?"

I laughed. "A step at a time, Ron."

We walked to the front door together, the dog trailing at our heels. Out on the porch, the music from the Delaney house was roaring louder than ever and at least a dozen kids had spilled out into the front yard.

"Gram would have sent them all packing a long time ago, if I'd tried that," I said.

"She'd have tanned your hide. I can't believe the parents are letting them do this. It's almost midnight on a school night."

"I doubt they're *letting* them. They travel a lot and I have a feeling they aren't home."

"Thirteen-year-old girls home alone?"

"Hey, boys do this stuff too. I hope Bernadette is keeping a better eye on your kids than this."

His mouth went into a firm line. "Yeah. She'd better be."

Chapter 15

Drake and I decided to have a rare late-morning breakfast at a restaurant where we love the eggs Benedict. It's out on the west side, so we each took our own cars. He'd lined up another flight with Michael the photographer. This time they would fly to the western part of the state to get shots of the dramatic red rocks in the Gallup area.

I pored over the menu at CeeCee's, deciding which version of the eggs I wanted. I'm partial to the traditional Benedict, but the Florentine version was also very good. Across the table from me, I sensed Drake's movement and I looked up to see his customer standing near the door.

"Okay if we invite him to join us?" Drake asked.

"Sure."

He waved Michael over and he greeted us with a tired

smile. "Sorry—late night," he said after he'd attracted the waitress's attention and signaled for coffee. "My wife called from Virginia. It was after two a.m. when our daughter got home and Joanne was fit to be tied. I guess Dru met up with some kids she talks with on Instagram all the time."

I can't say I'm so out of it I don't know what that is—social media is everywhere these days—but I so rarely check my Facebook page the few friends on there just assume I must have died or something. My real, actual friends still email or phone me when they want to chat.

"I tell you, teenage girls are something else. They literally live with that phone in their hands every moment the darn thing isn't on the charger."

I thought of the girls across the street and the few times I'd seen them recently, and yes, he was right about the constant presence of the cell phones.

"So you guys are off to Gallup this morning?" I was tired of the teen subject.

"Yeah, my editor thinks the whole Southwest consists of that type of stunning rock formations, so even though I've got a lot of other footage around the state he wants red rocks included in the spread."

Drake spoke up. "Getting tribal permission from the Navajos is why this part of the job has taken awhile longer to arrange."

I remembered a few other jobs that took us over Indian nation lands. Their sacred sites are normally completely off limits, so the flight plan has to be pretty specific.

We ordered our eggs and chatted about helicopter work in general, Drake telling Michael about some of our adventures, particularly the one in Scotland where I had an incident over the North Sea. He made it sound as if I'd been more heroic than I actually was—at the time I'd been terrified.

"What about that little cabin we landed by, the first day we went out over the Sandias?" Michael asked.

"I'm still checking the land records," Drake said. "There doesn't seem to be a clear legal description for the plot. We'll see. It may not work out."

I'd made the first cut into my egg dish when my phone beeped with a text message. Ron's name showed on the screen, with the words "Bobby Lorrento is back in the news …" in the visible portion of the message. Unless this was an emergency, I wasn't going to miss my favorite breakfast for an update on the client and his dysfunctional marriage.

I read the message, replied to Ron that I would be in the office within an hour, and dropped the phone into the depths of my purse. I shouldn't have left it out on the table in the first place. We finished our breakfast in peace, and I kissed Drake before getting into my car.

At the office, I helped myself to a second cup of coffee and went upstairs to find Ron on the phone in a conversation that sounded like routine questions. Employment background checks have become the bread-and-butter of our business. I waved at him through the open doorway and proceeded to my own office to take a look at my email. He appeared in front of me about five minutes later.

"So, what's the latest news our football player friend has got himself into now?" I asked, distracted by a notice saying Macy's had a big sale on jeans.

"Apparently, he went down to the pawn shop yesterday evening and discovered Marcie had not pawned the rings—

she sold them. On that basis, the owner had put them in his display case and one ring already sold. So Lorrento goes completely ballistic, leaps over the counter and punches the guy out before the shop security guard could pull out his truncheon. He gave Bobby a quick jab to the gut, called the police, and the cops hauled Bobby The Bomb to jail."

"How's the shop owner?"

"Broken jaw, but it will mend okay. He's pissed as hell."

"And this affects us, how?" The link showed a super-good price on those jeans.

"Marcie Lorrento called this morning and wants me to go down and post bond for Bobby. I wasn't here and she left the message on the machine. I haven't returned the call yet."

"Don't they have an attorney for such things?"

"I plan to suggest she call one. I could go down there and put up the bond money, but I sure can't give Lorrento advice on this legal mess."

"I wasn't aware the Lorrentos were even speaking. Wouldn't she rather just leave him in jail, teach him a lesson?"

"I don't know what the situation—"

His sentence got cut short by a ruckus downstairs.

"Ron!" It was Sally's voice and she sounded panicky.

We both hit the stairs running. Marcie Lorrento stood in front of Sally's desk, wearing a designer dress, six-inch heels, and a furious expression. Her hair hung in luxurious curls past her shoulders and her makeup was freshly applied, so I guessed she was hardly distraught over her husband's situation.

"There you are!" Marcie shouted at Ron. "Didn't you get my message?"

She shot a poison look toward Sally, who took a step back. Next, our employee would be demanding hazard pay for the receptionist job.

"Marcie, tone it down. I got your message. Can we talk in the conference room?"

"We'll talk right here. Why haven't you got Bobby back yet?" Her teeth showed as she snarled the words.

Ron stood taller and squared his shoulders. "The retainer you paid us has been used up, and until we talk about this calmly I'm not doing anything more on your case."

"Fine." She reached into her little clutch purse and took out a Gucci wallet, from which she drew five one-hundred-dollar bills. "Here's more money. How much will you need for his bail?"

"Wouldn't you rather your attorney handle this?"

"My attorney won't speak to Bobby. She got an earful from him the other day when he received the divorce papers, and she says she'll only talk to me now." Marcie paced to the front door and back, the high heels clicking on the hardwood floor like angry typewriter keys.

"So, who's Bobby's attorney?"

"Tom Hawkins, back in Texas. He says he's not licensed in New Mexico and, besides, he's had it with Bobby's temper getting him into trouble."

"Your husband needs legal advice I can't give."

"Yeah, I'll find somebody. Meanwhile, I need you to bail him out. How much do you need?" Her fingers were inside the wallet again.

"I have no idea until I call the station. I don't know what the charges are, or whether he's even eligible for bond, so can you settle down?"

She continued to pace and I'd finally had it with the staccato sound. I went upstairs to Ron's Rolodex and prowled through the A's until I came to an attorney we don't especially like. It would be such great fun to know he was having to deal with Bobby and Marcie Lorrento. I copied the man's name and phone number onto an index card and took it downstairs. Marcie seemed so grateful for the information I almost felt guilty for giving her the name of such a jerk. Almost—not quite.

Ron, the big sell-out, took Marcie's money, made a couple of calls and headed downtown to get Bobby. I couldn't, in my wildest dreams, imagine the weird dynamic between that couple. He cheated, she wanted a divorce, she stole from him, he lost his temper, she bailed him out using money from selling his own jewelry. Somehow, apparently, it worked for them.

I got home a little after five, to be met at the driveway by Elsa. Belatedly, I remembered I had planned to call NMSU again, but business hours had gotten away from me.

"I talked to Donna Delaney," Elsa said, a little breathless after dashing across our yard. "She finally reached her brother somewhere in Egypt. Zayne isn't with them and they don't know where she is. I told Donna about that boy who's hanging around."

"And?"

"Rick told her he knows Ryan Subro. The families have been friends for a long time."

"Did they ask us to do something to help?"

"Well, not really. According to Donna, Rick and Jane aren't worried. They say they've talked with both girls on the phone in recent days and everything's fine."

"So, then … everything's fine. We should butt out."

"It isn't fine, Charlie. I just know it isn't."

I really, really tried not to look as impatient as I felt.

Chapter 16

Five years ago ...

So, what do you think of the colors?" I asked my brother. Ron and I were standing at the curb, staring at the half-painted Victorian house we'd decided to buy for our offices. The old house, in a neighborhood of similarly sized places, had good bones but was in severe need of TLC when we found it. We'd done a lot of the interior cleanup, wallpaper removal and refinishing the floors ourselves. When it came to the exterior, with two stories of trimmed wood, plenty of shutters and gingerbread, we'd hired a crew. My contribution to this part of the project had been to choose paint colors. The house would be light gray, shutters dark gray, and white for the fancy bits.

So far, three weeks had been spent sanding away the

old, peeling parts and priming the poor old dear until she looked like an ancient woman with a bad case of age spots. Now, the west face of the house, the side where a long driveway led to the back, was done in our color scheme, our first chance to see how it all came together. The painters had gone for the day and the midday heat had abated a little as the afternoon grew later.

To my question, Ron gave a nod. "Looks good to me."

What did I expect from him anyway, a rousing cheer? This was the guy who'd not even bought a houseplant to brighten his previous dingy office. I needed a woman's point of view. I was having lunch tomorrow with my friend, Linda Casper, who, after finishing medical school and her residency, was in the process of setting up her own practice. She'd be the ideal person to give an opinion about our project.

Right now, my body was bone-tired. I rubbed an aching shoulder muscle and gave the structure a final appraisal.

"Well, I like it. When it's finished I think I'll love it."

I brushed at the layer of drywall dust coating Ron's shirt, but it was hopeless. Each of us arrived home at night to throw our clothing into the wash, take a long shower and fall into bed. If I'd known how exhausting the project would be, I might have steered toward a property without so much labor attached. The good part was, I now felt emotionally invested in the business, and the more I worked alongside Ron each day, the more certain I felt our partnership would be a good thing. I didn't regret leaving Sloan and Mercer, not one little bit.

"I could go for a margarita," he said.

I knew what he was hinting at, and Pedro's is one place we could eat without having to go home and clean up first.

"At least shake the dust off your shirt first," I said. I

looked at my own appearance, but I'd stayed away from the kitchen area where the new wallboard was being installed. I could get by with brushing my hair and washing my hands and face.

We went back inside and performed our little cleanup duties, one by one, at the bathroom sink, then went to our vehicles. Another selling point for the Victorian house was its proximity to our favorite restaurant near Old Town. Four minutes later we pulled up outside the small side-street place.

"*Hola*, Charlie and Ron," Pedro called out from behind the bar. "Your usual?"

I gave a nod and waved to his wife, Concha, who had just delivered two steaming plates to another table. Within two minutes we each had a frothy margarita sitting in front of us, along with a basket of chips and a bowl of Pedro's homemade salsa. Concha didn't even need to take our order. I always get the green chile chicken enchiladas and Ron will have a beef burrito. I can bet money on it.

"So," I said, once we'd wolfed down half the basket of chips, "the painter said one more week to finish the exterior, and the inside is nearly done. I think we could move furniture into the upstairs offices any day now."

We'd already gone shopping, so desks, file cabinets, shelving units, a conference table and chairs, and kitchen appliances were ready to be delivered as soon as we made the calls. While I'd handled a lot of those duties, Ron still had investigations to work so he'd been taking advantage of the quiet at his old office for phone calls and such.

"Just say the word," he said. "I've got two buddies with pickup trucks standing by and we can haul everything out of my old office and have it set up on a day's notice. I tell you, I'm more than ready."

Our dinners arrived and I breathed deeply of the fragrant green chile scent.

"All I really want at this moment is to sleep for a day and a half," I said as I cut into my enchiladas to let the steam out. "Which I won't do. Don't worry, I'll be back at the new office first thing in the morning."

Thirty minutes later, my tummy full and my head pleasantly lulled from the margarita, I pulled into my driveway at home. Up the street, it appeared a gathering of some kind was happening at the Delaney house. Matching hatchback cars sat out front and I could see the shine of the twins' blonde hair from the glow of the nearby street lamp. Several teens milled around. The family Mercedes was backing out of their driveway. It came my direction and slowed in front of my house.

Jane Delaney powered down the passenger side window. "Hey, Charlie," she called out.

"Hey. How are you guys? Haven't seen you in awhile." It was sort of my standard greeting, since, in fact, I probably hadn't had a conversation with any of the Delaneys in more than two years.

"Gosh, I know. We're constantly on the go these days. Redford's looking at a new project to be filmed around Santa Fe and we're on our way to a pre-production meeting now."

Rick grinned from his driver seat. "I'll be assistant director on this one."

"*If* it comes through," Jane reminded with a perky little wink. "Nothing's for sure in this business."

He rolled his eyes in a you-know-how-it-is gesture. I smiled, but it felt like a tired one.

"Looks as if the girls have a few friends over," I said.

"Oh, yeah. It's their fifteenth birthday and we got them the matching Audis for their starter cars. If they take good care of these, I've promised something nicer next year. They're *so* excited."

Again, my smile felt forced. At fifteen, I'd felt lucky to drive Elsa's huge boat now and then. I was still stretching a few more years out of my mother's old car, even now.

"Well, we're running a *little* more than fashionably late," Rick said to his wife.

"Right. So … we'll see you around," Jane said.

I watched them drive away, thinking how sad it was they couldn't stay for their daughters' birthday party. Park a lavish gift outside and leave 'em on their own, I supposed was the philosophy. I was too tired to dwell on it. I went inside, gave my own neglected fur-baby some attention and hit the shower. By nine o'clock I was completely sacked out.

I rolled over at some point and detected the beat of rock music nearby. Really, girls? The party isn't over and the neighbors don't matter at all? A glance at my bedside clock showed 3:14. I pulled the pillow over my head and snuffed out the sound.

When my alarm went off at six I slapped the snooze button and winced at the pain that zinged through my shoulder. All this manual labor was getting to me. If I didn't hold the scraping and sanding to a minimum, I'd be too crippled for my accounting work. Beside my bed, the dog's tail beat against the floor. We were starting our day whether I was ready or not.

I zombied my way through the morning ritual and rubbed some muscle-relaxant cream on my poor shoulder, informed the dog he would be staying home again and grabbed my purse. A brisk wind greeted me as I headed toward the old Buick. Once I knew the bottom line on what the renovations were costing, I might just spring for a new vehicle for myself.

The reminder of new cars made me look up the street. The two new ones were in the driveway at Delaney's now, but what really caught my eye was the scattering of trash on their front lawn. Apparently, no one at the party had thrown a single cup or plate into any trash receptacle and now the litter was blowing through the neighborhood.

Enough already, I decided. I tossed my purse in the car and picked up two red plastic cups from my front lawn. The gutter held three more, and a scattering of paper plates were flying across Elsa's yard. Okay, this is ridiculous. I picked up the items I passed as I marched myself up the street.

I don't care what time you went to bed, little chicks, I'm ringing this doorbell until you're up.

The twin who answered was less bleary-eyed than I would have expected, although she was still in her sleepwear—loose shorts and a tank top—and her long hair hung in tangles over a makeup-free face.

"Are you Clover or Zayne?" I asked.

"Clover."

"Look, Clover," I said, losing some of my ferocity. I held up my two fistfuls of trash. "This is all over the place. Not good."

"Sorry about that."

I stood aside so she could see her own front yard, which was by far in the worst shape.

"Sorry is one thing, but it's windy out this morning and your stuff is ending up all over the neighborhood."

Zayne stepped into view behind her sister, giving me

the blurred-mascara stink eye.

"Didn't your parents come home last night?" I asked, really trying not to sound like a grumpy old witch. Seriously, I'm only twenty-eight but sometimes I feel seventy.

"We're fine," Zayne said, ignoring the trash I showed her.

Clover gave a quick glance over her shoulder. "We'll get it cleaned up this morning, Charlie."

"Thanks. I'm sure the whole neighborhood will appreciate it."

Zayne gave a dismissive *pah* and disappeared from view. I stood there with two handfuls of trash. Clover told me to wait while she got a bag. When she came back she'd put on a sweatshirt and she stepped out to the front porch, pulling the door closed behind her.

"Don't mind Zayne. She just wants to have a good time. She got pretty wacked last night. I went to bed after the police left. We told them my mom was visiting relatives and my dad had just gone to the store and would be back soon."

The police had been here and I'd slept through it?

"I guess I'm surprised your parents don't get more upset about this kind of thing. I mean, this is not the first party, by far." I dropped the trash into the bag she held open.

"They don't care. Really, they're so easy on us."

No kidding.

"They've got these fantastic careers now, and they take great care of us." A fond glance toward her new car in the driveway. "Really, Charlie, it's all good."

Chapter 17

Ron came back from the police station around three-fifteen, looking like a bedraggled stray. I was in the kitchen, snitching a couple of Oreos from the package I'd left on the counter earlier.

"Fun time?" I teased.

"Ugh. I'm beginning to see your point about these cheating-spouse cases." He dropped his cap on the table and picked up the coffee carafe, scowling at the two inches of black liquid in it.

I almost offered to make a fresh pot but he'd already reached for his mug, filled it and set it in the microwave. In my mind, the day-old versions of some things are okay, but coffee is not one of them. I stared as he shoveled several spoonsful of sugar and I changed the subject.

"So, you got Mr. Lorrento out?"

He nodded. "Asked him where he was staying and he said, at home of course. So I drive him all the way out there. The second I see Marcie's car in the driveway I figure there's going to be real trouble so I wait around to be sure I won't need to call the police."

"Yikes. What happened?"

"She meets him at the door, and from what I can see she's wearing nothing but a pair of high heels."

I know my eyes widened. "You noticed her *shoes*?"

He may have actually blushed a little.

"So, what happened then?"

"Bobby has a big grin on his face and he goes in the house. I drive away."

"You think you'll be getting another call? Once he gets past being all happy again, the same old issues will come back. She'll remember the cheating; he'll remember his fancy rings."

"Yeah, I know. All the way from downtown out to the north valley, he couldn't stop talking about getting the rings back. Now, I'm hired to do what it takes to make that happen. He pretty much gave me carte blanche to spend whatever it takes using his American Express Black."

"Is the pawn shop guy going to let Lorrento buy back the two he hasn't already sold?"

"That's why I went over there immediately after I dropped Bobby off at home. The owner doesn't know his clerk sold them to me on Bobby's behalf." He reached into his pocket, pulled out two velveteen boxes and handed them to me.

When I opened them I nearly had to reach for my sunglasses.

"Holy cow—that has to be the most diamonds I've ever seen in one place."

The rings had other information—the Super Bowl logo, team name, the year—but the dazzle from the stones kind of blurred the detail. I snapped the boxes shut and handed them back to Ron.

"So, now you have to go back to Lorrento's house to return them," I said.

"Later. I'm not walking in on whatever's going on at that big house of theirs. He'll contact me, I'm sure, once he's out of bed." He pocketed the boxes. "For now, I'm locking these two away in the safe at home while I go looking for the third."

"How do you plan to do that?"

"I managed to get the buyer's name. When I went in to buy these I got the youngest-looking clerk in the shop, said I was representing an anonymous collector who wanted all three. The girl looked up the record and said the ring they sold went to someone named Segal."

"I'm surprised she told you that."

"Frankly, I am too. The owner most certainly wouldn't have revealed the name. Maybe it was the fact I so readily paid for the other two rings."

"Well, I'd be looking over my shoulder every minute I had those things in my pocket," I told him.

The phone at the reception desk rang, and with Sally gone for the day I ran to catch it.

"Charlie, is that you?" The female voice was only vaguely familiar, and I suppose I hesitated. "Donna Delaney. We spoke yesterday."

With Elsa. The Lorrento drama and Ron's investigation had set the neighborhood doings on the back burner for me. I asked if I could put her on hold long enough to go upstairs. At my desk, I shifted thoughts and picked up the phone again.

"I'm sorry if I interrupted a busy day for you," Donna said.

I assured her it was fine.

"I've been thinking about the twins ever since I spoke with Elsa. I reached my brother in Egypt and it turns out Zayne isn't with them."

"Elsa told me."

"Oh, okay. Well, after that I called the girls and spoke with Clover but I just don't feel I'm getting the whole story and I keep thinking about dear little Zayne. You know, in elementary school the kids called her Zany Delaney and the tag stuck. Instead of being offended, she played up to it. Came up with increasingly wild pranks. By fifteen, both girls were living on the wild side. Rick and Jane kind of vanished as parents. I mean, they're gone all the time and now they make so much money they've made up for a lack of parenting with lavish gifts. Those cars. What fifteen-year-old needs her own brand-new car? And that was the first pair they bought—now they're older, they've gotten something even more expensive. They have unlimited clothing budgets and neither kid has ever held a job. I wish I had more influence with the girls these days."

I could tell she didn't approve, but maybe there was a hint of envy too.

"I get the impression Clover is the quieter one," I said, although my memory of the parties across the street definitely included both girls.

"In general, yes. But even as small children I can't tell you how many times they tricked me into thinking one was the other. They are identical in appearance so the only differences I could spot were in their tone of voice and mannerisms. Jane used to tell me the girls could even fool their dad."

I wasn't sure where she was going with all these stories. "So, what can I do for you?"

"Elsa gave me your office number because you're a private investigator now."

Not exactly true but I didn't want to interrupt her.

"So, I'd like to hire you to look into this, to find out that both girls are safe and sound. I discussed it with Rick and although he's sure everything's fine, he did authorize me to check into it. I can't personally do it—we're in spring planting season here and if we don't get these potatoes out right now we'll not have a fall crop. Our growing season is pretty limited up here. There's no chance I can break away and come to Albuquerque right now."

I asked a few more questions, but Donna had no current information on the twins' habits or friends. I quoted our normal daily rate for investigative work and told her Ron would most likely be the person actually conducting the investigation. She seemed agreeable enough and gave me a credit card number to cover the retainer. I also took down contact information for Donna and for both parents.

I ran the credit card for five hundred dollars, thinking the whole case might end up being as simple as Ron showing up at the door and both twins actually being home at the same time. Donna had agreed that a photo of the two girls together would suffice to alleviate her fears. I quickly typed notes about everything I'd learned from the aunt and carried the printed page, the credit card receipt and contact information to Ron's office.

"It'll be at least a couple days, most likely, before I can get to it," he said. "I want to get this whole convoluted Lorrento mess off my desk as soon as I can. Having both spouses on my back about different subjects is driving me nuts. I pretty much have the evidence Marcie requested, but now it's the search for the ring for Bobby."

"A missing person might be more important than a missing diamond ring," I said.

"Probably is. Have the police been brought into this?"

"Elsa called them a few days ago and they treated her like a nutty old lady. They said the girls are over eighteen and, as adults, are free to come and go as they please."

"Exactly."

"But now the family is concerned—well, some of them are—and we've been paid to look into it."

"And in two more days' time maybe she'll come waltzing back home and the case will be solved."

"Elsa tells me she hasn't seen both girls home together in months."

"So, she's—what—sitting at the front window every minute of every day? C'mon, Charlie. I'll get to it when I get to it. Unless you want to start asking around. You're done with the taxes and not doing a whole lot else that I can see. Go ahead and get started."

The 'not doing much else' part stung. I was hardly lounging around with a paperback romance and a box of bon-bons. But it was true my urgent deadlines had passed and Drake hadn't needed me on a helicopter job recently. I resisted the urge to make some childish gesture at Ron, turned on my heel and went back to my office.

Chapter 18

I stewed over Ron's comment as I drove back to my neighborhood. Not so much his obsession with solving the football player's case as the part about my sitting around doing nothing. Well, I would show him. We would just see who solved which case first.

Taking Elsa's word for the fact both girls had not been home together for awhile, I decided to see who I would catch there today. Both Corvettes were in the driveway. I parked in my own driveway and walked up the street, gave a hard push at the Delaney's doorbell. A twin dressed in low-riding jeans and a cropped tank top answered the door, barely glancing at me before her eyes went back to the smartphone in her hand.

"Clover?"

She looked at me. A flicker of emotion—something I

couldn't read—crossed her face, but then she gave a bright little smile. "Huh-uh. I'm Zayne."

"Great—I've been wanting to catch both of you at home. Mind if I come in?"

The smile faltered. "Clover's not here right now. She and Ryan went to the movies."

I reached for the handle on the screen door and pulled it open. "I'd like to chat a minute, Zayne."

She didn't want me to come in but I used my age advantage to get my way. She stepped aside as I pushed into the living room. It was impossible to tell at a glance whether the home's disarray was caused by one girl or two. A bright pink fluffy hoodie lay draped over the back of a dining chair. At least three pairs of shoes caught my attention, two of them by the couch in front of an enormous-screen TV set. Pillows and a couple of fuzzy blankets were tossed there, a cozy nest for viewing the big screen. A scattering of receipts littered the dining table, along with two shopping bags.

"Clover said you were in Las Cruces," I said.

"Oh, yeah. I am. It's spring break." I tried to gauge the truthfulness of her response, but lost eye contact when Zayne glanced at her phone's screen, distracted.

"Your aunt Donna called me this morning. She's worried about you girls."

"Really? Why?"

The question was a little sticky to answer. I couldn't very well admit the elderly lady across the street spent her days spying and she was the one who alerted the aunt.

"Donna said she'd tried to call and no one answers."

"Seriously, she must be using the landline. Half the time I don't even know where that phone is. Anybody who needs us uses our cell phones."

"That makes sense. If you'll give me those numbers, I'll pass them along to her."

Zayne looked me straight in the eye. "Don't worry about it. I'll call her myself."

"She wants to hear from Clover, too. She needs to know you're both okay, and when she talked to your dad recently he said he hadn't heard from you two in awhile."

"Geez, what is this, the phone police? We're living on our own and we're fine." She took a breath and forced the perky smile again. "Really, Charlie, it's all good."

I knew a dismissal when I heard one. Pushing for more information would not accomplish anything, so I turned toward the door.

"Just give your aunt a call and reassure her, okay?"

She kept the smile in place, but the door closed pretty firmly behind me. I crossed their front lawn, remembering the time I'd confronted Clover about the loud party and trash all over the neighborhood. The incident had happened nearly five years ago. Her words and tone had been nearly identical to what I'd heard just now.

It's all good. Great catch-phrase to gloss over an iffy episode or deliver a blatant lie with wide-eyed innocence. I'd used it plenty of times myself, back in the day. It might not be what Elsa thought, but those girls were lying about *something.*

Zayne might, indeed, turn right around and call her aunt thinking that would get us off her back, but Donna knew the girls played tricks at times. She'd specifically asked for a photo of the two together, and that's what I planned to deliver.

I went inside my house and straight to Drake's office. He had a pricey Pentax camera with a lens that brought objects right up to your face. While he used it for grabbing great shots during his jobs, I had purposes other than scenery in mind. I checked the batteries and ran through the menus quickly to remind myself how everything worked.

Freckles whined from her crate and I let her out. With the camera, my purse and the dog's leash stationed near the front door, I called Elsa and asked her to give me a heads up when she saw either twin leave their house.

"Am I helping on the case?" she asked. I heard the eagerness in her voice.

"Absolutely. I need to track the girls' movements and your eagle eyes will be invaluable."

I'd barely finished making myself a peanut butter sandwich for the road when the kitchen phone rang.

"I'm not sure which one it is, but the girl just went out to the red car."

"Keep an eye out while I'm following this one. I need to know if the other girl comes home. Supposedly, she went to the movies with that guy."

So maybe this one really was Zayne. If I remembered correctly, hers was the red car. I grabbed a bottle of water to go with my sandwich, called to Freckles and we headed for my Jeep. Before I could get my key in the ignition, the Corvette raced past my driveway, made a rolling stop at the corner and turned left. I jammed my gearshift in reverse and squealed out of the driveway. I would need to finesse this a bit better if I hoped not to attract attention.

I managed to get close enough to witness each of her turns as she left the neighborhood and headed east on Lomas Boulevard. If she made two turns in quick succession I would definitely lose track. The good news was she probably had no idea I was following her. At Girard, Zayne made a right, and I did a barely legal right-on-red turn to keep her in sight. She slowed as she approached the UNM campus and turned into a parking lot for a couple of the big dorm buildings. I slowed, wondering what I should do if she went inside.

As it turned out she pulled to the curb in front of Hokona Hall and tooted her horn twice. A girl with flowing, dark brown curls came down the steps a little awkwardly on her high platform shoes. Otherwise, her outfit of jeans and tank and smartphone were nearly identical to Zayne's. She smiled widely and reached for the door handle on the 'Vette.

A group of four college-age boys stood near the bottom of the steps, and they called out to the girls. Zayne turned to respond, although I couldn't tell what any of them were saying. Her friend gave a coquettish sway with her hips but stayed with the car.

Fifty yards behind them, I snatched up the camera and got a few shots. At this point, I didn't know if the group of kids had anything to do with anything, but I figured it was best to gather any and all data I could get. The girl slid into the passenger seat and the red car's top began to retract. As long as I could somewhat match her speed, following a bright red convertible with a blonde at the wheel and a brunette riding shotgun should be fairly easy.

Animated conversation took place for about a minute, the girls waved to the guys, then the car began to move. I dropped the camera on my lap and cruised up slowly to narrow the gap between our vehicles. Zayne turned left from the parking lot and roared up Girard with a fair amount of noise. It must have been for the benefit of the boys—by the time she reached the light at Lomas she'd slowed to normal speed and I caught up, only a couple of cars behind her.

She made the right turn then sped up again. By the time I began to keep pace, we were both doing more than ten over the speed limit, not that it bothers me but some of these lights have the traffic cams that get your picture if you shave a red light a little too close. I really didn't need another ticket on my record when the previous one was about to reach its time limit and drop from sight of my insurance company.

Lomas is a major street with traffic lights at all the big cross streets. I managed to keep within one light of the red Corvette until she reached Louisiana Boulevard. She pulled into the left-turn lane where she made the light and I didn't. I watched the convertible longingly until it went out of sight. By the time I got a green arrow and followed Zayne's direction, there was no sign of her car.

Ahead were the city's major shopping centers and a freeway entrance. Two young women, off for the day and heading this direction … I could guess they might be doing a girl's day of lunch and shopping, but the choices were nearly endless. I came to the ABQ shopping mall and pulled off the busy street. The center offered both storefront and underground parking, but a quick recon of both didn't reveal the car I was seeking.

Next up the road was a bigger challenge. Coronado Center was built in the '70s as the biggest mall of its day, and it hasn't shrunk with time. Multiple parking lots with traffic that's constantly changing—I took one look and decided it was a waste of time. Not to mention there were other shops throughout the area. I should have noted the shopping bags on the Delaney dining table for clues on the girls' taste, but I hadn't and it was too late now.

Chapter 19

The only sensible thing was to go back to square one. Ultimately, Zayne had to come home. I headed that way, vowing not to admit to Ron how badly I'd done this surveillance. On the other hand, he's always telling me what a bore it is to watch someone and how this type of spying is frequently unsuccessful. If his questions got specific, that's the line I would stick to.

Back in the neighborhood, the first thing I noted was the blue sports car still in the driveway. So, if Clover had gone out with Ryan, there was no real way to tell if she'd come back yet. My dog had initially been enthralled with the long car ride but was now quickly becoming fidgety. I clipped her leash to her collar and we did a little brisk walk to the end of our street and back. Letting the Delaney twins out of my sight again was something I wanted to avoid.

The view of their house from mine is fairly restricted. I have no windows facing their direction. The view from my living room requires me to stand at one edge of the front window and peer around the trunk of a sycamore tree in my yard, and I'm still limited by shrubs in other yards.

Elsa's place would work far better. Her living room has comfy chairs and corner windows that practically put the Delaney driveway in your face if you're using a decent pair of opera glasses. She keeps those on a small table beside the sofa.

All I needed was to pack a baggie of dog treats and take along my uneaten sandwich, and we'd be set for the rest of the afternoon—provided I could get Elsa to let me in. Since she's rarely anywhere but home on a weekday afternoon, it came as no surprise when she opened the kitchen door at my knock. A quick explanation of what I planned to do and I was in. I didn't even have to converse. Old people can talk non-stop if you only let them.

In her living room, I raised the opera glasses to my eyes. The ones with a little handle down the side are handiest, by the way, unless you want to build arm muscles of iron by holding up a regular pair of binoculars. These days, I'm into the philosophy of easier is better. Freckles waited diligently at my side until the peanut butter sandwich was down to the smallest sliver of crust. Once she got that, she settled on the floor.

I heard all about the doings at Elsa's church, the various health problems of all her friends, and how the monthly pie supper had gone. Truthfully, I had no idea there were so many varieties of pie. You gotta keep up with church ladies to get this stuff. About the time I thought I would overdose from the tales of all the sweets, a flash of red came into view. Zayne and her friend were home.

The red 'Vette pulled in beside the blue one and the top began its journey to the *up* position. Both doors opened at the same time—Zayne and her brunette friend stepped out. They circled to the trunk and began pulling out shopping bags. This time I read the labels and knew the stores were all out of my league. If shopping was on the agenda again, I would know where to find these ladies but, unfortunately, I would stand out as an intruder in any one of those shops.

Lights came on across the street and Elsa excused herself to start dinner. I sat in the dark, feeling only a little like a creep for staring at the lit windows where the girls moved about behind sheer curtains. I couldn't see details but got the idea they were trying on their new clothes to show each other. Maybe deciding on outfits to match. Very twelve-years-old, in my opinion.

If that was the case, I would bet they were getting ready to go out. I made a mental list of what I would need to do if I had to take off with two seconds' notice and follow again. Since the goal of this whole exercise was to get a photo of Zayne and Clover together, I'd better have the camera, and in case I ended up outdoors a jacket would be smart. I assumed a college party could go on all night. It had been a few years since my days at UNM and I'd never exactly been a party animal.

The sky grew dark and I turned down Elsa's offer of a bowl of Campbell's chicken noodle soup. Good thing I did—the two girls came waltzing out the front door, the brunette laughing. I couldn't see that they were dressed much differently than before. They both wore jeans and very similar cropped tops. Boots. These had to be the new items. I didn't have time to ponder the question, though. They were heading toward the car, the blue one this time.

I scrambled to my feet, grabbing my purse and camera.

"Can Freckles stay with you until I get home?" I asked as I whipped open Elsa's front door.

She nodded but I barely saw. I closed the door and dashed across the two yards, making a mad leap for my vehicle. The blue car roared past my house as my engine caught and I practically screeched out of my driveway. This time, surveillance would be a bit trickier than previously in broad daylight. I memorized the car's taillight pattern and wondered whether I had a prayer of keeping up with her.

Zayne (I assumed it was still Zayne) turned toward Rio Grande Boulevard, the opposite direction from her earlier trip uptown. Once we passed Old Town the traffic thinned appreciably and I had no trouble keeping her lights in sight. She kept heading north. A bunch of possibilities came to mind. If the girls planned to cross the Rio Grande and head out to the west side, we would once again be caught up in a tangle of traffic, shopping centers and a maze of streets I wasn't very familiar with. Then again, they could go almost anywhere. Several major arteries could take us back to the middle of the city, to Interstate 25, and from there to nearly any destination, including the airport or the northern mountains.

As it turned out, I had seriously dramatized the possibilities. A couple miles later, Zayne turned left toward the river. Although there's a developed visitor center and hiking paths out here, it appeared the kids were taking a small side road to an area of their own. The narrow road would make it very apparent a car was behind her, but there wasn't much I could do. Another car had followed me. Suddenly it all made sense. The riverside spot had been a teen hangout for a lot of years. It had simply not occurred to me that my generation wasn't the only one who'd discovered it.

The Corvette continued along the trail, passing a couple of areas designated for parking. Ahead, I could hear thumping music and see the glow from a couple of campfires. I steered to the next parking area I came to, letting the car behind me close the distance to the 'Vette. I knew the area well enough to be ninety percent certain the girls wouldn't be more than a quarter mile from this spot. My trainers weren't the best choice of footwear in an area strewn with vines and branches, but I could do this.

I reached into my glovebox for the flashlight I always keep there, praying the batteries were still in decent condition. Most likely I would only need it to get back. Finding my way toward the party would be no problem at all. The music alone would lead me. I tucked the light into my pocket and stuffed my purse beneath the seat. The camera would definitely look out of place, but I hoped to accomplish my mission without being noticed. The two-hundred millimeter lens should get great shots while I played stealth in the woods.

I was about to get out when it occurred to me that if I got in trouble no one knew where I was. I quickly called Drake and gave the basics, asking him to go over to Elsa's and get the dog when he arrived home. Bless him, he didn't ask for details. He's figured me out pretty well over the years.

Two more cars had driven by since I arrived and no one gave a second glance toward me. Rather than walking along the road, I took a path that cut through the woods and most likely led to other picnic sites. As I recalled, there were a dozen or more, each equipped with a concrete table

and benches and an ugly metal grill you really wouldn't
want to actually put your food on. I stayed to the left of
the gathering of kids until I came to a break in the trees
where I could get a good glimpse without actually stepping
out into their midst. I was at least eighty yards away, and no
one in the group seemed to be aware of anything beyond
their own fire-lit circle.

The purpose of the party was abundantly clear—
guys and girls drinking and flirting, raucous laughter and
throbbing music. Pretty much the normal. I raised the
camera and took a peek through the lens, focusing it to
see if I could spot Zayne or Clover. The first person I
recognized was the girl who'd been with Zayne most of
the day, the brunette with all the hair.

During their prep time inside the house, she'd added a
bunch more curls and some flirt to her style with a couple
of coquettish sparkly clips. She was standing near a beer
keg with a red plastic cup in one hand, her phone in the
other. The screen cast a glow upward to her face and I
could see she was laughing over something she read there.

With the camera lens as my spyglass I slowly scanned
the crowd. There must be about thirty kids, most likely
all college age, although a few of them could be high
schoolers. One group at the northern edge stood close
together, passing a joint among them. Nearly all held red
cups from the stack near the keg. A surprising number
were looking at phone screens in lieu of talking with their
friends. Parties sure had changed since my day.

I spotted the twin who could be either Zayne or Clover.
The guy Clover had supposedly gone to the movies with,
Ryan, was nowhere in sight. After thirty minutes or so, cars
stopped arriving and the crowd seemed to be settling in for

the evening. Laughter grew louder; someone turned up the music. No sign of the second twin. The brunette flashed her brilliant smile at a guy with curly, dark hair down to his shoulders. He walked over and spoke to her, running his finger across her bare forearm. On the screen of his phone, I caught sight of a photo. The same girl, nude.

I gulped. Yeah, dating had changed a *whole lot* since my day.

The two of them walked away from the firelight, into a shadowy area where a group of cars was parked. I scanned the area once again, hoping to see the bright flash of two blondes together. It was getting chilly out and my jacket wasn't doing a lot of good on the back seat of my Jeep. I'd like nothing better than to leave this place for the warmth of home and husband. Obviously, both twins weren't here and I was wasting my time.

I used the flashlight to get back to my Jeep, got in and cranked up the heat. Keg parties among college kids were certainly nothing new, but something about the group bothered me. The edgy glances from girls, the palpable sexual tension … but there was more. I couldn't quite define it.

The Jeep roared to life and I retraced the route back to my own neighborhood. Drake's truck was in our driveway and I pulled in beside it. He'd said he would make himself a sandwich for dinner, so I had no obligation to rush in and settle in front of the TV. The Delaney house sat dark and quiet. I picked up my flashlight again and nonchalantly walked across the street.

Chapter 20

Frankly, I'm no expert at breaking and entering. The few times I've done it, my success has usually come from an unlocked door or open window. So, okay, that's really the only method I know. The trick is to make it look as if you belong. I approached the dark Delaney house with a confident step, walked right up to the front door and grabbed the doorknob. Not even a mere budge.

Around back, a sliding glass door seemed promising. A little shaking and jimmying can sometimes get their flimsy latches to release. I discovered the Delaneys did not do cheap. Their doors were good quality and fairly new, which made sense. Some of that newfound money had gone into upgrades on the old house. I made a quick visual scan of the windows on the back of the house—checking first to be sure the shrubbery was thick enough to block views from neighbors behind—but found nothing that looked like a quick entry.

Until I came to the side door on the garage. Should have thought of this first; it's one area a lot of folks miss in their nightly locking-up process, and it often reveals another entrance to the house. I tried the knob. Luck at last!

My flashlight came in handy as I picked my way through the detritus of my neighbors' earlier life. Twin bicycles with pink handlebar grips, a collapsible backyard pool (which at some point had been replaced by an oval in-ground one), a sofa, two big stuffed recliners, a triple dresser of dark wood, its matching nightstands and a king-size headboard all lined the path from back door to front. Cartons spilling bright fabrics and stacks of books filled the dark recesses. Stalactites of coiled rope hung from the rafters and one corner was filled with leftovers from a film set: heavy metal stands and two klieg lights. It seemed as the couple began to earn more money and upgrade their lifestyle, none of the old stuff had left the premises.

Mainly, I concentrated on not tripping. It would be embarrassing to go home impaled on a rusted garden tool from someone else's garage. Eventually, the meandering path brought me to a door which, predictably, was unlocked. I opened it cautiously and stepped into a laundry room. As far as I could tell, the girls had left no lights on; the whole place lay in darkness now. I did a quick scan with my flashlight and saw the laundry room opened to the kitchen, and beyond it lay the open living and dining rooms, the parts I'd seen before. Presumably, bedrooms and bathrooms lay to the south of those.

Knowing how easy it was to watch movement through the sheer curtains, and remembering I'd left Elsa to look for activity over here, I masked the beam of my light with one hand as I entered the main areas. Not that it mattered. My elderly spy-friend had most likely watched me walk over and approach the house. If so, I hoped she would warn me if either of the twins came home.

I got an eerie view of the living room with pretty much the same clutter I'd observed during my previous visit. The dining table held the same shopping bags plus a few new ones, and the same litter of receipts lay beside them. I could come back to those.

A hallway led off the far side of the living room and I headed there, dodging a pair of sneakers that seemed to have leapt off their owner's feet and landed in a heap where they would be in everyone's way. A series of doors revealed a small bathroom decorated in navy blue and tan, a large bedroom with twin beds, loads of purple and a bathroom with a long vanity and half the contents of the cosmetic counter from Macy's. At the end of the hall, a master bedroom seemed in good order, neatly made up when its occupants had left several weeks ago. Their bathroom wasn't nearly in as much disarray (or as interesting) as that of the daughters.

I veered back to the domain of the girls and began a little recon. Both beds were messy and unmade. Discarded clothing covered a dresser and side chair. A bookcase against the wall held a random collection of children's books and a few old Nancy Drew mysteries; the top of the case had two decorative metal trees for earrings and necklaces. They couldn't hold everything, apparently, because a scattering of spare jewelry littered the surface nearby like fallen leaves in a forest.

None of that interested me, but on the nightstand between the twin beds was something that did—a cell phone. I glanced over my shoulder. After watching these kids awhile I couldn't imagine either of them being more than ten feet from this device. But the house was empty. I'd watched Zayne and her friend leave and go to the riverside party. Could Clover have forgotten her phone when she left with Ryan for the movies? Doubtful.

I picked up the phone and sat on the edge of one bed. It responded when I pressed the button, lighting up immediately. The background showed a photo of the two girls, with identical smiles and arms around each other. The little icon for text messages showed only two. I tapped it and saw they were from Zayne. So this must be Clover's phone. It made sense, as I'd seen Zayne at the party with hers.

The list of recent calls was extensive. I'd just begun to look through them to see who I might recognize when the phone vibrated and pinged in my hand. I jumped and it fell to the carpet. I stared at the screen as if it were a poisonous snake. A banner came up showing the sender as Zaynie: **we r at riv, u coming?**

Maybe this was good news. Not quite a photo, but I could report to their aunt that the girls were in contact.

A beam of light crossed the bedroom window, catching my attention. A car had stopped nearby. Uh-oh. Whether it was Clover and Ryan or someone else, I was in deep doo-doo for being in here. I put her phone back on the nightstand and picked up my flashlight where I'd set it beside me on the bed. No one had got out of the car yet but it wouldn't take them more than thirty seconds to cross the yard and open the front door.

I dashed down the hall and through the living room,

stumbling on the stupid sneakers in my haste. I heard two car doors slam, then male and female voices. The scattering of shop receipts on the dining table caught my eye, pale slips in the muted beam of my light. I'd taken a huge chance coming in here and hated to leave with nothing to show for my heroics. I reached out and snatched a fistful of the paper strips, jammed them into my jacket pocket.

Through the kitchen, into the laundry room I dashed. I slipped out the door into the garage and pulled it oh-so-quietly shut behind me. Letting my bright beam guide me through the maze of garage junk I beat a quick retreat to the back door. I peered into the back yard. No lights shone out here, but I figured it was time to stop taking chances. I ducked to the side yard, out the gate and to the street. A look around showed no vehicle in front of the Delaney house. Either Ryan had dropped Clover off and driven away, or the vehicle I heard was someone else. I arrived a minute later at my own front door panting like an exhausted puppy.

I'm getting too old for this.

At home, Drake was in his office with his pilot logbook in front of him. He's diligent about making entries for every flight, and over the years has filled several books with not only the required hours flown but little notes about where he went and who his passengers were. Although he's not a name-dropper in social situations, more than a few celebrity names appear in those pages. He looked up and flashed me the smile that had won me over when we met.

"You and Elsa cooking up something next door?" he asked.

"In a way. I was over there for awhile." I wasn't sure he'd approve of my spying on the other neighbors, and

I felt fairly certain he wouldn't be wild about the fact I'd sneaked into the Delaney's home and searched the girls' personal things.

"Did you eat anything?" I asked.

"Yep. Me and Freckles shared some of the leftover chicken in the fridge. There's more if you want me to warm it up for you."

I declined, needing a few more minutes for my stomach to settle down. I walked into the kitchen and poured myself a glass of wine. Freckles followed my every step. One thing about dogs: they know when they've exhausted one food supplier and are fickle enough to switch loyalties immediately to the next person who might be a likely candidate.

"Sorry, kid. Nothing for you here," I said as I pulled the stolen sales receipts from my pocket.

I smoothed the wrinkles from the slips and spread them out. I'd managed to nab four transactions from four different stores. A little flush of pride as I considered there might be useful information here.

One was a long list from Walmart, a few household supplies and a lot of snack food and soda. How did the twins stay model-thin eating this kind of stuff? I wanted to know their secret. The other three receipts came from clothing stores and the names matched the shopping bags I'd seen. Ralph Lauren and Barneys were apparently their favorite brands. I was about to discard the whole batch as a waste of time—really, who cared that those jeans had cost three hundred dollars?

Then something caught my eye. The Walmart receipt wasn't from the store where I always went. This one came from Las Cruces. The town where I'd been so certain

Zayne Delaney was *not* attending school. But what if she was?

What if the twins had been telling the truth all along?

Chapter 21

I woke from a restless night filled with questions about the girls across the street. It didn't help when the Corvette zoomed past our house somewhat after midnight, just as I'd been drifting off to sleep, reminding me I still wasn't sure which twin had actually driven it to the river party earlier. I'd thought of phoning Donna Delaney with the skimpy information I had, but it seemed pointless. There really was nothing to report yet. I decided I might as well get an early start at the office, so I left Drake asleep under our nest of warm blankets and tried to be as quiet as possible as I showered and dressed.

The Victorian was dark and quiet when I arrived, with only the glow from a lamp on a timer at the front desk. I pulled into the parking area in back and called Freckles to follow me inside. We set coffee to brew and I opened the bag I'd bought at the drive-thru window at McDonald's.

I know—I'm not supposed to be eating this stuff. A warm bowl of gooey, mushy oatmeal at home would have been the healthier choice. My inner critic finally shut up and I bit into my egg on a muffin. Freckles doesn't care what I have for breakfast—she'll take a tidbit of whatever is left.

Upstairs, with coffee mug in hand, I turned on my computer and noticed Ron had left a note in his scratchy handwriting stuck to my desk phone. I was to invoice the Lorrento account for the hours he'd put in yesterday tracking one J.L. Segal, supposedly the purchaser of the missing Super Bowl ring. Did he want me to set up a second account for Bobby Lorrento, or bill these hours against the retainer Marcie had paid? I set the note aside to ask him—it would be simpler to do it once than to do it wrong and have to backtrack.

It took me an hour to run an accounts receivable report, print clients' month-end statements and stuff them in envelopes for mailing. One of these days I would look for a way to automate this more efficiently and send billing electronically, but for now I needed to review each client's account before dunning them.

I had gathered the batch to set on Sally's desk for the mailman when I heard sounds downstairs. It sounded as if Ron and Sally had arrived at the same time, and I walked downstairs to refill my empty mug and greet them.

"I saw your note about the Lorrento billing," I told Ron. "Shall I wait until you've got the ring back or just accrue the hours every day?"

"Well, I thought this was going to be an easy one—look up the buyer, do a quick drop-in visit and offer cash. Bobby said to give him ten percent more than he'd paid for it. Which, I'll tell you, is a sizeable chunk of change. I figure, what guy wouldn't love to make ten percent on his money in a couple of days, right?"

I wasn't at all sure how this answered my question, but I let him talk.

"I can't find him. There are only a handful of Segals in Albuquerque, none with a name or initial J, but it didn't take me long to call them all and inquire."

"No luck, I'm guessing."

"Right. So, I went statewide, which ate up the rest of the day, and still no luck."

"Somebody who collects Super Bowl rings wouldn't necessarily be local. Maybe the pawnshop guy put the word out—I don't know … Craigslist or something?—and the buyer came to town on a mission."

"Yeah. It'll be impossible to track every Segal in the country, so I'm back at square one."

I wished I could help him, but it sounded daunting and I had other things on my agenda today. I went back upstairs, really wishing I'd swiped that cell phone I found in the twins' bedroom last night. It would contain a wealth of information and the girls would never guess their snoopy neighbor was responsible. Daddy would just buy another phone, and there probably wouldn't even be a lecture about taking better care of their things. I doodled on the note Ron had left, realizing he'd never answered my question about the billing.

Across the hall Ron's voice rose. "So, no address or anything?"

A long pause. He was apparently on hold because he began crushing paper and tossing the balls toward the trash basket. I knew this because I could hear them hit the wall each time he missed. The repetition began to irritate me.

I got up from my desk and walked to his doorway. "Can you just—?" I came to a halt when his attention turned back to his call.

"What's the name on the card?" he asked. "Address? Really? You didn't get an address?"

He was scribbling on a notepad and I could tell this wasn't going the way he wanted it to. I started to turn away but heard his receiver drop back to its cradle.

"Charlie, can you give me a few minutes?"

Not really. "Sure." I sat down in the chair across from his desk.

"With the boss away, the young clerk who sold the ring made some fundamental mistakes. She put a name on the sales slip, no address, and she didn't compare it to the name on the guy's credit card. The name on the card was J. Livingston."

I felt a smile coming on. "Ron, seriously? J. Livingston, J.L. Segal. You've been spoofed."

His eyebrows pulled together.

"Jonathan Livingston Seagull. It was a bestseller book way back in the seventies."

"How would I know that?"

Okay, so he doesn't read much fiction. "The guy gave a fake name for the receipt, but it's doubtful he could do that on a credit card, especially one with a high enough credit line to cover a ring like that. You're not looking for a Segal, you're looking for a Livingston."

My brother surely would have figured this out. He's a good detective, really. I think he was simply flustered by the dollar amount and fame of the lost item. A more experienced pawn clerk would have gotten better information and we'd be on the way to tracking the ring.

"All right," Ron said, looking a little sheepish. "But Livingston isn't exactly an uncommon name either, so it still looks like I'm back to square one."

I felt badly about the roadblocks in his path, but I had my own path right now. After all, it was my brother who'd suggested he work the Super Bowl case and I take the mission of getting a photo of the Delaney twins together. My goal wasn't going to happen with me here in the office, so I decided to head back to the home front and go back to old-fashioned surveillance. Goody.

It was becoming second nature to me, glancing up the street to see which cars were home at the Delaney place. Once I'd snapped that all-important photo, I really had to get a life.

This time, the red car sat in the driveway. I'd decided to quit being shy about showing up at their door. Why be cagey, when the request from their aunt was a legitimate one? I put Freckles in the house and walked over and rang the doorbell. No answer, but I wasn't actually surprised. This had become the new format of my days. I rang a second time, to be certain, then walked around to the backyard.

As hoped, I found the garage side-door unlocked, so I went right on in, immediately wishing for my flashlight. The only light came from the space around the large roll-up door, and it was minimal. I picked my way through the same collection of junk as last night and, again, found the connecting door to the kitchen and opened it.

Not much had changed in the living and dining rooms, other than I noticed a pair of lace-up sandals kicked off near the front door, a little spill of dirt beside them. With no idea when the girls left or how long they would be away I made straight for the pink bedroom and looked on the nightstand. The cell phone was gone.

I patted the rumpled bedcovers and did a quick peek under each bed (horrific—you don't want to know). The jeans and shirt the party twin had worn last night lay at the top of a pile of clothes on a chair. I picked up each item and shook it but no cell phone showed up.

Dammit, I *knew* I should have grabbed that thing last night. In the back of my mind I had the feeling if I could see the calls made from that phone I would somehow be able to figure out the locations of both girls, although the whole concept was a bit fuzzy to me.

I turned in a circle, studying the room. The clutter was so prevalent it was hard to focus on any one item, but I made myself give it a really hard look. Same with the adjoining bathroom where the vanity surface couldn't be seen for the litter of hairbrushes, eye shadows, mascara tubes and lip-glosses. Two hair dryers, two sets of giant hot rollers, two lighted magnifier mirrors and a pair of electric flat-irons. I thought of my own single plastic compact of blusher and one tube of lipstick in the shade I'd always worn. I own a blow dryer, and somewhere in the depths of a drawer is a curling iron I rarely see. I think I'm definitely missing something in the girlie-genetics department.

My boggled mind tried to focus once again, but I still saw no cell phone.

I meandered back to the bedroom, resolved to give it one more go-over, when my own phone vibrated in the pocket of my jeans. My heart rate went into overdrive and I must have jumped a foot. I grabbed it before it could ring a second time and tapped the screen without looking.

"No one's home over there," Elsa said. "I saw Clover drive away about an hour ago."

She was guessing as to which twin she'd seen, but I was busted nevertheless.

"I saw you go around to the backyard, but I don't think anyone will answer the back door either."

"Thanks, yeah, you're right. Hey, I'm just checking out something over here. Can you keep watching a few more minutes and call me again if she comes back?"

She seemed tickled to be part of my detective work, and I felt somewhat reassured no one could walk in on me, as had almost happened last night. I set about giving the house a much more thorough search.

Chapter 22

I took a quick peek into the girls' closet. The floor was covered by a huge pile that made it look as if the shoe department at Dillard's had exploded here. The upper shelf contained a few childhood board games—including the same Candy Land I had played with these kids more than a dozen years ago. Plush animals filled a shelf unit like a little button-eyed zoo. If there was a clue that would help me here, I didn't see it.

With the luxury of a lookout across the street, I decided to spend a little time in the rest of the house. These opportunities wouldn't come often.

The parents' room contained a king-size bed, neatly made with a thick comforter of silk in the same navy and tan scheme I'd noticed in the main bathroom. Their adjoining bath followed those tones as well, with tasteful décor items in just the right numbers and the necessities tucked away in drawers. It seemed the kids respected their parents' space and had left it untouched in their absence.

On to the living and dining areas, where the girls and their messy lifestyle once again reigned. I looked more carefully this time at the receipts and shopping bags on the dining table. All came from Albuquerque businesses. The bags were empty, and I resisted the urge to fold or toss them in the trash.

The huge sectional sofa in the living room faced a monster big-screen TV, the seating area littered with popcorn tidbits and candy wrappers. Six plastic drink cups with dried cola residue sat on the tables. The two elephant-ears houseplants flanking the door to the backyard looked desperate for water. I jammed my hands in my pockets to quell my fierce urge to tidy the place. A bookcase contained few books but held mostly travel mementos—a tiny Eiffel Tower, a set of carved wooden camels, a metal pitcher with a distinct Middle Eastern design. Photos of the family proved they'd been to these places, along with some cute casual shots of the two girls as they grew up. Toddlers gathering Easter eggs in the backyard, a first-day-of-school pose, the two with sleek long gowns and prom dates. I didn't see a single handwritten note or a tell-all diary in the room, so I headed to the kitchen.

The front of the fridge brought a few insights: A shopping list with yogurt, green juice, blueberries, M&Ms and potato chips sent mixed messages. Photos of the twins at different ages in a variety of vacation spots stuck there in little magnetic picture frames—Disneyland featured in several of them. Inside the fridge, the same contradiction of taste and lifestyle showed up in boxed salad greens,

which looked fairly fresh, from Whole Foods alongside
a six-pack of beer. The freezer contained fish sticks and
a frozen pizza. The tall trash can in the laundry room
contained three more pizza boxes and a bunch of empty
Coke cans, which really should be in their recycling bin.

Frustrated, I turned to study the whole scene. Was
there not a single clue to tell me what the girls were up to?
I didn't see one useful thing. I felt myself getting grumpy.
This whole thing was a waste of time.

I made my way out the laundry room door to the garage,
through the mess, out the back door, once again leaving it
unlocked as I'd found it, although I doubted another sneaky
visit to the house would produce any further information.
Short of ripping into pillows and dumping the contents
of drawers, I'd pretty much covered the place. I mentally
kicked myself once again for leaving the unguarded cell
phone last time. It had to be the place a modern girl would
leave a wealth of notes and messages. I had let it slip away.

Elsa saw me coming and called out from her front
door, so I veered toward her.

"It sure took awhile to figure out no one was in the
backyard," she said with a grin.

"Yeah … it did. I have to say, I'm no closer to knowing
anything about those girls, other than they are messy
housekeepers. Oh, one might be a health food nut while
the other binges on pizza and Cokes."

"I still say—" She stopped, figuring out her insistence
wasn't going to solve anything. "How about some lunch? I
can make us a grilled cheese sandwich real quick."

Well, how could I say no to that? Her sandwiches had
got me through a lot of problems much rockier than this.
I trailed her into the kitchen.

"What clues do you have so far?" she asked as she

sliced Velveeta off a huge block.

"Nothing much," I admitted. "I followed one girl yesterday while she picked up a friend at one of the UNM dorms. They went shopping, came back here awhile, then went to a party down at the *bosque*. I stayed long enough to pretty much look over the whole crowd, but the second twin wasn't there."

Those sandwiches were smelling wonderful as the buttery surfaces of the bread toasted on the hot griddle.

"Maybe I need to talk to Donna Delaney again, see if I can get a number for the parents." I was basically thinking out loud, passing time while Elsa scooped the sandwiches onto plates and cut each in half. "Surely, they know where each of their daughters is, and the whole puzzle can be solved."

"Donna said they didn't—remember? They told her Zayne has enrolled at State and Clover's here."

I felt fairly sure Zayne wasn't enrolled in school. Spring break had happened a month ago, so I didn't quite buy her glib answer. However, it didn't mean she hadn't moved to Las Cruces. It could be nothing more complicated than her leaving home a few months early and getting a job prior to the fall semester starting in a few months. I kept thinking if I could speak directly with the parents I might get more information. For the moment, though, that sandwich was calling my name.

We finished our lunch and I called Donna. Building upon my skimpy bits of evidence I told her I suspected one or both of the girls had been in Las Cruces recently.

"I'd really like to talk with Rick and Jane if that's possible," I said. "Maybe they will have remembered something else since you spoke to them, or maybe I'll come up with some new questions. Frankly, I'm hitting a lot of dead ends right now."

"I'm happy to give you the numbers," she said, "but it may be awhile before you get through. Rick told me their location was changing yesterday and they would be completely out of cell range for the next week. He said something about needing a satellite phone ... whatever that is ... but I didn't get the feeling he has one yet."

I jotted down the information she gave. It would probably not net me anything new, but it wouldn't hurt to try. She thanked me for sticking with it, expressing worry again over the way the girls' lives were going. I had the feeling she judged her brother's parenting on a fairly strict scale, but she didn't say so.

I was about to dial one of the numbers, not really counting on reaching Jane or Rick, but my phone rang in my hand before I could enter all the digits. Ron.

"Hey, I need you to get over to the Lorrento house and talk to Marcie," he said. "I'm on my way to the hospital. She whacked Bobby over the head with a skillet and he's getting treated for a concussion."

"*What?*"

"That's all I know. Marcie called me in a panic. The police apparently went to their house and I don't have much more than that."

Great. Just great.

He gave the address in an exclusive area of the North Valley, no more than fifteen minutes away.

"If they arrest her, we'll have to go bail her out too, I suppose."

I could not express how very little I wanted to do that.

Chapter 23

I drove north on Rio Grande Boulevard, passed the turnoff where I'd followed Zayne and her friend to the river party, and continued into a pastoral area where the old-time small properties and shacks had been bought up and merged into estates favored by the state's successful business people. Now, McMansions sat surrounded by ancient cottonwood trees and acres of tended grass. I started watching addresses, fairly certain I knew which was the Lorrento place.

The property had originally been acquired and the ten-thousand-square-foot house built by a real estate developer with a flair for the magnificent and good connections in the media. After he got involved in a condo project in Mexico that went bust, he'd been forced to sell his bucolic retreat and move to the less spacious, but equally prestigious, Tanoan country club neighborhood. There, the houses were big but jammed so close together it was hard to appreciate their grandeur. It would have been hard to give up the quiet and surrounding natural beauty for that, I imagined.

The Lorrentos had come along and bought it for the relatively bargain price of four million, something I knew only because the broker who handled the transaction was a friend of a friend and he couldn't keep quiet about his brushes with the rich and famous.

I spotted a white rail fence that ran alongside the road for about a half-mile before it curved inward and met with an entrance. High, wrought iron gates blocked the way but a keypad and small speaker mounted on a brick pedestal told me what I had to do. I pressed the intercom button.

"Marcie, it's Charlie from RJP Investigations. Ron Parker sent me over."

No words came through the little box but I heard a whirring noise and the gates began to roll back. The paved drive was a good quarter mile long, bordered by thousands of purple and yellow pansies and more of the white rail fencing. Beyond the fence, on my left, stood a trio of thoroughbred horses, their brown coats gleaming in the sunshine. One looked up as my Jeep passed, but the others only continued to nibble at the grass. I briefly wondered if they had any purpose or were merely here to make the rest of the estate look good.

The acres of green and the long driveway served basically as a framework for the house itself, three stories of red brick, white shutters and two-story columns holding up a portico and impressive veranda. Very traditional if you lived in the Midwest—completely dramatic here in the Southwest where everything else was either stucco or adobe.

I spotted Marcie standing at the front door so I followed the circle, which looped to the left, and parked under the portico. Somehow, I was certain my seven-year-old Cherokee was the crummiest vehicle ever to have filled that space.

Marcie waited at the top step until I caught up with her, then she led me into the house. I wondered whether she remembered me from the day she'd come into our office in a tirade. I followed her through the two-story entry hall, a floor expanse covered in black and white marble tile with a round pedestal table in the center that held a bouquet of spring flowers to rival anything found at the White House.

A maid was dusting an elaborately carved console table near the curved staircase. I was trying not to look dazzled by the amount of gold rococo ornamentation and size of the crystal chandelier overhead as Marcie led the way into a sitting room. She strode to a pair of tall windows at the far side of the room, but I held my ground near a white sofa. If she thought her home—impressive to the point of gaudy—or the silent treatment would somehow influence my opinion ... well, I couldn't see the point.

"Ron says Bobby is doing all right," I said. "If you were wondering."

When she turned I saw her eyes were red-rimmed and her nose a brilliant pink.

"Oh, god, I can't believe I did that." She reached for a tissue box on a gold end table and lowered herself to the edge of a chair.

I followed and sat on the sofa. "What happened?"

"Oh, I don't know." She dabbed delicately under each

eye, but the mascara damage was already done. Her hair most likely had been styled this morning but had gone over to the wild side now. She wore bright purple workout attire and matching Nikes.

"You have no memory of the events?"

"Well, not that. I remember. I got up early and did my workout in the gym on the third floor, then went to the kitchen to make a smoothie. Bobby was in there, staring into the fridge like he'll do sometimes for, like, an hour. He said something, got that sweet tone in his voice and I almost hugged him. Then I realize he's on his phone and he says, 'I'll see you soon, Darla.' Darla's my best friend!" Her voice broke and she trailed off into sobs.

Ouch.

"Yeah." She sniffed. "I slammed the fridge door on his hand and asked how long he'd been fooling around with her. 'Awhile,' he says, and I just got so angry. They say sometimes you see red—well, I did. I grabbed the nearest thing, which was a cast-iron skillet our chef had left on the stovetop, and I swung. Oh, god, I really didn't mean to hurt him."

"Really? Because if that was my husband, I would have meant to kill him."

She gave a little smile and a tiny hiccup escaped.

"Ron said the police came?"

"The maid came running in when Bobby fell, and there was blood and everything. She asked what should she do and I didn't know, so I guess she called 911. An ambulance took him away. I mean, he was conscious, moaning and cussing and all, but he said he didn't want to press charges so the police went away."

I wondered if the football player would change his mind once he was thinking more clearly.

"I don't know what's gone so wrong with us, Charlie. Bobby and I used to be the best couple. We've known each other since college in Texas. He was so sweet to me. I mean, he was a football star there, too, and all the girls were interested in him. But he just let that roll off. We were an item and stayed together through graduation. He got drafted by his favorite team and we moved, and married life was wonderful. He started bringing in big money and I had so much fun setting up our first house."

"That was in California?"

"Yeah. He was my first real boyfriend. I'd dated a little in high school but I saved my virginity for the right man. Bobby was the one. We moved a couple of times when he changed teams, then there was the injury and he decided to retire. Actually, we made the decision together and we picked Albuquerque because it's a nice city and we could get out of the pro-ball limelight. It seemed like a good way for us to start over, live in the country, start a family ..."

"But there's still some bad stuff going on, obviously."

Marcie nodded and sniffled again.

"His cheating is bad—I'm not minimizing that," I said. "But why the retaliation? Why sell his prized rings?"

"We seem to be in a vicious circle, Bobby and me." She slumped back into the chair and stared into the space between us. "He wasn't the only one. We got into this social whirl. There were parties, lots of flirting, other guys made moves toward me and I dallied a couple times too. I guess they gave me the kind of flattery Bobby was dishing out to his other women. It didn't seem so wrong. It was a tit-for-tat kind of thing."

"If he was going to hurt you, you'd hurt him right back."

"Yeah, I guess. It's just the other women were strangers to me. It hurt, of course, but not like it did when I heard Darla's name."

"You hired our company to find out if he was cheating, but it sounds like you already knew he was."

A long sigh. "I knew this time was different. He was happier than I'd seen him in a long time. I was worried he'd found someone he would leave me for."

"You knew it was Darla, even before this morning, didn't you?" I shifted on the sofa and faced her directly, forcing her to make eye contact. "Isn't that why you sold his Super Bowl rings? Before—the other affairs—they were little hurts. But this was a big hurt and you wanted to hurt him back in a big way. Retaliation never works to make someone love you."

She looked toward the fireplace and her eyes welled up. "I know."

"So? Where will it go from here?"

She turned back toward me. "No, I meant I know who has the ring."

A wave of frustration washed over me. Couldn't she have said this from the start? I stood up, nearly upending another big flower arrangement, and paced to the fireplace. When I faced her, it was all I could do to put a gentle look on my face.

"Marcie, what do you want out of this whole deal—save your marriage, get out, stick with Bobby no matter what … move on? You're sending such mixed signals here, I don't know what you want from us."

She slumped deeper into the chair, staring at the expensive carpet with a zombie-like fixation.

"Okay then," I said, moving toward the door. "You

figure it out and when you get your act together, I hope it all works out for you."

Seeing that I was ready and willing to walk out brought her back to life. "Wait. Um, I'm not really sure how it's *all* going to work out … but I need to find the ring for Bobby. It's the right thing to do."

Well, that was a refreshing attitude, anyway.

"You said you know who has it. Call him and say you need it back."

"It's not quite that simple." She was twisting the gigantic diamond ring on her finger.

I walked back to the sofa where I'd been and sat down again. "Tell me all about it. And this time it had better be the whole truth."

Chapter 24

I called Ron when I got outside to my Jeep and he informed me he'd left Bobby Lorrento in the care of the ER staff at the hospital, where Bobby was to stay overnight for observation. We had a short discussion about whether Bobby should go home once he was released. I felt Marcie was remorseful about the skillet incident, but there was no telling what Bobby might do when he saw her again.

"Does he have somewhere else he can go until things cool down?" I asked.

Ron said he would check, but he'd told me he was already back at the office and I got a feeling he didn't want to go dashing back to the hospital for another talk with the client.

I drove down the Lorrento's long driveway, waving goodbye to the horses as I passed. By the time I arrived at the RJP offices, the sun was low in the sky and I really only wanted to be home, but this day wasn't over yet. I heard Ron on the phone when I climbed the stairs. I dropped my purse at my desk and tidied a few things I'd left undone earlier before he came across the hall to me.

"Okay, it's set that Bobby Lorrento can come home with me tomorrow," he said.

"Wow. That's a generous offer."

"I just talked to Vic and she's fine with him being there a day or two—no more, she said. We have the boys this week and they'll be thrilled. She says if we put Bobby on the basement pull-out sofa he won't be inclined to stay very long."

"Marcie's feeling badly about what she did. I don't think she'd give him any grief about coming home, but who knows what he might do. Those two are a pair, I'll tell you."

"So what's the big story you promised me?"

"I know who has the missing Super Bowl ring."

His jaw dropped. "And you found this out, how?"

"Marcie told me."

"You're right, it *is* a story." He moved over to the small sofa near the bay window. "Tell me."

"His name is Jay Livingston. Marcie met him at a charity fundraiser in Dallas where football was the theme and memorabilia was big among the auction items. Livingston was admiring Bobby's newly won Super Bowl ring from the previous season, but he was also admiring Marcie. Bobby wasn't willing to donate the ring to charity. Marcie, it turned out, had her head turned a bit more easily. Livingston went on an all-out campaign to get close to her—well, that's how it sounded to me. She told me about the charming little gifts he began sending, and apparently he also started showing up at any event where he heard Lorrento would make an appearance. Eventually, drinks at the bar became clandestine little meetings and she confided her marriage wasn't happy. Well, you know what a guy will do with that information."

"I didn't find any matching Livingstons in this area," he said, apparently oblivious to most of what I'd said.

"Apparently, he travels the country for these events."

"So, where does he live?"

"Marcie actually doesn't know. They would meet up and spend an afternoon in a hotel—New York, St. Louis, Miami ..."

He gave me a look.

"I got a phone number. It's how she contacted Livingston to let him know when she'd be traveling. I was just about to look up the area code and find out where it is." I held up the scrap of paper I'd written it on.

"So, Marcie planned all along to sell the rings and tell Livingston where to go buy them?"

"Essentially, but maybe 'plan' isn't the word. She said it was after one especially bitter fight with Bobby that she took the rings. Later, she was feeling a little guilty about it and when Jay Livingston called she told him what she'd done. He acted like he sympathized but, unbeknownst to her, he went to the shop she'd named and bought the one ring. She wondered why he quizzed her about the store, but didn't think much about it."

"I wonder why he didn't get all three?" Ron said.

I shrugged. "Maybe even a rich guy has his limitations when you're talking in the hundreds of thousands of dollars."

"I did a little research, and there are a lot of factors that go into the values of these things—who the player or team member was, his role in the game, etcetera. Every team member, the coaches and the staff get rings, you know."

I didn't know that, had never actually cared before now.

"The pawnshop owner told me the one he sold was the most desirable of the three because Bobby threw the winning pass in that game."

"So, maybe Livingston had a ready buyer for it, himself—someone ready to give him a tidy profit?"

"It's anyone's guess. Let me track that phone number and we'll see what happens next."

I handed over the information, more than a little eager to close up shop for the day and get home to my hubby and dog. By the time I'd shut down my computer, found my jacket and picked up my purse, Ron informed me the area code for Livingston's phone was in El Paso, Texas.

Chapter 25

El Paso sits on that little jag of Texas land directly beneath New Mexico on the map, the little shelf that gives our state its neatly squared edges. It's the border city to Juarez, Mexico, and as such has always been popular with kids who want to duck across the border for some evening fun and tequila. Especially the students at New Mexico State. El Paso is only a hop down the road from Las Cruces.

All this went through my mind as I drove home. I like things tidy and organized, so the idea of clearing two cases with one relatively short drive south made a lot of sense to me. It was the only reason I toyed with the idea of volunteering to help Ron.

Freckles greeted me at the door as if she hadn't seen me in a month. Days alone, apparently, stretch out infinitely for a dog. I ruffled her fur and scratched her ears and babbled sweetie-sweet words at her, to which she wriggled and danced and led me to the kitchen.

Drake had been home awhile. I'd called him when I left the office, and he offered to start the grilled chicken and salad we'd talked about for dinner. He stood at the sink, washing lettuce.

"Don't let her lie to you," he said with a nod toward the eager pup who was sitting with her nose pointed at her empty food bowl. "I fed her fifteen minutes ago."

I gave him a kiss and ignored Freckles.

He set aside the vegetables and pulled me into his arms. "Hey, I didn't get a chance to tell you ... I found out who owns that property, the little cabin we found."

"Really? Do you think it's available?"

"Haven't got that far with it. All I know so far is the piece of land is twelve acres. The road we spotted below is one boundary, and from the topo map it looks as though it wouldn't be too difficult to lay a driveway from it up to the cabin."

"Would we want that? Driveways invite nosy people and vandals."

"It's an option that would make it easier in case we're weathered-out from flying."

"How does the current owner get up there?" It was something I'd wondered from the beginning.

"That, my dear, is something we'll have to ask once we make contact." He turned to the bowl containing two chicken breasts and spooned more of the spicy-scented marinade over them.

I set plates and flatware on the table and poured a glass of wine for myself. Drake already had a beer in a

frosty mug nearby. I filled him in on the latest drama at the
Lorrento household. He just shook his head.

"Bobby Lorrento used to be one of my favorite
players," he said. "Why do people go all weird once they
have fame and fortune?"

I could only make a guess. "People start treating them
as if they can do no wrong, so they suddenly get away
with bad behavior or buy the solutions to their problems
instead of having to work them out. If their antics make
the news, it's covered in a silly boys-will-be-boys way so
there isn't much outrage over it."

"Boys-will-be-boys? Sounds as if the wife was every bit
as wild this time."

"She was. I'm not pointing fingers at men or making
excuses for women. They're both messed up."

Childish. That's what the Lorrentos' behavior had
become.

"Speaking of kids acting up, I thought I'd volunteer to
drive down to El Paso tomorrow to help Ron find the guy
who has the missing ring."

Drake sent me a puzzled look. "He's another kid?"

"Oh." I could see where my stream of consciousness
had skipped a few steps in the telling. "I'm thinking while
I'm down there it would be easy to prowl around in Las
Cruces and see what I can find out about the Delaney girl
who is *supposedly* enrolled in school there but isn't. Ron's
following a lead we have on the ring collector and is trying
to get an address. If we've got that, it could turn into a
twofold bonus if we can solve both cases at once."

As it turned out, simplicity took extra time to
accomplish. By the next day Ron had made contact with
Jay Livingston and, pretending to be a buyer for the ring,

set up a meeting. During our little heart-to-heart, Marcie Lorrento had agreed to use the money she'd obtained from the pawnshop when she sold the rings in order to get them back. This little transaction would, no doubt, cost her a bit extra from her clothing allowance. Jay might be interested in Marcie in the bedroom, but this was business and he wanted to make a profit.

Ron also had the little matter of taking custody of Bobby Lorrento when he was released from the hospital and taking the man into his own home. While he took off to accomplish those tasks, I drove out to the peaceful, green estate on Rio Grande where the last battle in their marital war had taken place. The horses had been moved to the pasture on the opposite side of the drive; otherwise, everything appeared the same.

Marcie was either busy with a charity luncheon (the story I was given), or she was too embarrassed to see me (the version I believed) because she'd left a thick brown envelope with my name on it. The maid who answered the door handed it to me without even asking to see identification or have me sign a receipt. It either meant the household operated greatly on trust, or Marcie was watching from a window and knew I was the one getting the money.

I counted it in front of the maid. One hundred ten thousand dollars in one-hundred dollar bills. From what Ron had told me, this represented a ten-percent profit for Mr. Livingston on an investment he'd held less than a week. Not bad. I wished my retirement fund was doing anywhere near that well.

I admit to being more than a little nervous with that kind of cash so I drove straight back to the office and locked it away in the safe. The following morning I got an early start, retrieved the money, and headed south. In one way, it was a heady feeling—there was nothing to stop me from disappearing into a new life and never having to get involved in another private investigation case. The irony was not lost on me. Here I was, driving toward Mexico with enough money tucked under my car seat to live quite comfortably there for a long time. The downsides would be my dozen-word Spanish vocabulary and the fact I'd go crazy without my husband and my dog.

Our little family was scattered enough at the moment. Drake had taken a job flying some Fish and Game Department men around the northern part of the state. Since he would be gone overnight, Freckles was spending the day with Elsa. Ron had charge of Bobby Lorrento and I didn't even bother to ask how that would go. I could imagine him trying to keep the big football player from going back home, attempting to prevent the battling couple from having contact until we could be sure there wouldn't be another skillet incident. I could possibly end up staying away overnight, too. The drive to El Paso takes nearly five hours.

I shaved some off that time by blatantly ignoring the speed limit in the wide-open areas south of Socorro and was hitting the El Paso city limits before noon. It had been years since I'd come down this way and, of course, the city looked nothing like it used to. But my cell phone had provided me with a neatly organized set of directions and I followed them. One of these days I would modernize with a GPS for my vehicle, one that would talk me through the trip. It's silly that I haven't done so already, given the number of times I'm trekking off somewhere unfamiliar to me.

I-25 turned into Interstate 10 and my directions led me into a complicated spaghetti bowl of interchanges before sending me eastbound into an upscale subdivision. Various twists and turns put me onto a cul-de-sac where I faced a handsome two-story home stuccoed in shades of moss green. Six stately palm trees flanked the drive.

I took a brief moment to gawk. My home turf has nothing like this, and I'm always a little surprised to find what I think of as tropical plants in a desert environment. Patterned tile led the way to the front door. Through the beveled glass double doors, I caught glimpses of a curved staircase with curly wrought iron embellishments. I pressed the doorbell button and waited while a set of chimes played something melodic.

Jay Livingston answered the door himself. He stood a tad under six feet, with a slim waist and broad shoulders. He wore jeans, a dark turtleneck and lambskin jacket. Dark hair with a slight wave to it curled to touch his earlobes, and his green eyes showed golden highlights beneath the dark brows. A warm smile completed the picture. I could see how Marcie Lorrento had been charmed by him.

"Come in," he said when I introduced myself. He ushered me into a living room so well-ordered and perfect either he was the world's neatest man or the cleaning lady had left only minutes earlier. "You brought the cash for the ring?"

The bulky envelope was jammed into my largest purse, which I'd brought for the occasion. "I'd like to see the ring, please."

He reached into the jacket's inner pocket and pulled out a small velvet box. Although I'd seen the other two rings, when he opened the lid I have to confess to being more than a little dazzled. The ring was huge—designed to be impressive on the chunky size-11 finger of a football player—and every millimeter of it was covered in diamonds and rubies. Livingston watched as I took the box and turned it to see the ring.

"I have to say—wow. I can see why you like to collect these things."

I set it on the coffee table, unzipped my purse and pulled out the pack of money. He accepted it and gave me the ring.

"I counted that," I told him, "but you can certainly double-check."

He opened the metal brad on the envelope, gave a deep look inside, and closed it again.

"It looks right," he said. "Thanks for coming by." He stood and moved subtly toward the door, my obvious cue that the deal was done and he had other things to occupy his day.

I tucked the ring box into my purse and thanked him. It sounded a bit silly to thank a guy for selling something at a markup, but I was just thrilled the whole transaction went so smoothly. Back in my car, I lost no time retracing my path out of his swanky neighborhood and getting back on the highway.

Chapter 26

The entire transaction with Livingston had taken less than thirty minutes and I was back at the outskirts of El Paso with plenty of time to grab some lunch and pursue my other case. Las Cruces is a quick forty-five minute drive, and the first exit sent me toward a selection of fast-food choices. I wheeled into the first Mexican food place I spotted and ordered a burrito.

Managing the floppy foil-wrapped packet, I pulled the Walmart receipt I'd stolen from the Delaney dining room table and found the store's address. I'm not terribly familiar with the town, but figured these big-box stores tend to group together on the major throughways. Surely, I could find it by driving around, but the appeal of finishing this task quickly and being home in my own bed tonight won out. I called out to an older couple who sat at the next table.

"Do you live here in town?" I asked. "Do you know how I would get to the Walmart over on Walton Boulevard?"

I got two versions but the woman's directions seemed more straightforward. I left them to discuss it, wadded up my food wrappers and beat a path back to the Jeep. I pulled into the Walmart lot less than ten minutes later—the beauty of a small town.

"I'd like to speak with the store manager," I told the woman behind the customer service desk.

She eyed the receipt in my hand. "If it's about a return, I can help you."

"Thanks, but it's something else."

She asked to see the receipt anyway, examined it, handed it back.

My hundred-thousand-dollar transaction with Jay Livingston had drawn less scrutiny. Eventually, she paged a Bill Morgan who came from somewhere in the back and greeted me politely. He had the country air of a guy who might have been a dairy farmer before the economy changed and corporations dealt out the better-paying jobs. I introduced myself as a partner in RJP Investigations from Albuquerque and said we were looking into a missing-persons case.

We'd been talking quietly off to the side, but I could sense curiosity from the customer service lady so I suggested we go to his office.

"I wonder if you can show me the store's video footage for the day and time this sale was made," I said, giving him the receipt once he'd led the way to the back.

"The asset protection office is right next to mine. Let's check."

The fancified title belonged to a security manager. It took a few minutes' discussion between the store manager and this guy, but they finally decided the video from two weeks ago should still be available. Security guy performed some moves at his computer keyboard and motioned me to step around the desk and take a look.

"Your receipt says the sale was made at one of the self-check kiosks, number three, to be exact, so here's the view of it."

I'd always been aware that the little bluish-black domes in the ceilings of retail stores were cameras, but I'd never seen how much detail they captured. On the screen before me, I saw an overhead shot of a check stand. As he edged the picture forward a few seconds at a time, a slender blonde with her hair up in a long ponytail wheeled her shopping cart up to it. In a few seconds' time she'd run a bag of cookies, a frozen pizza, a six-pack of Cokes, a tube of toothpaste and a pack of toilet paper through the scanner and bagged them. The items matched what the receipt said, and the food choices matched what I'd seen in evidence at the Delaney house.

The girl pulled a credit card from her purse and inserted it in the machine. While it did its thing, she reached up and scratched the top of her head, fiddled with the purse strap, and generally seemed impatient. The moment the machine released her card she grabbed it and picked up her two bags. As she approached the exit door, a face-on view showed me it was indeed one of the Delaney girls.

"I'll switch to the parking lot camera now," said the security man.

When he did, we saw the blonde walking briskly across the lot. She got into a blue Corvette.

"Is she the one?" Mr. Morgan asked.

"Yes, it's the girl I'm looking for. The story is that she's attending school down here but the college can't verify she's enrolled."

"Well, you'd have to check that with them," Morgan said.

"I thought of that, but this being Sunday the admissions offices are closed."

"Could be she just moved here and got a job," he suggested. That very thing had crossed my mind at one point.

"Do you have facial recognition programs?" I asked. "Something that would scan all the videos and see if she's a regular shopper here?"

Security dude shook his head. "We'd have to go through them all manually. It's a lot of work."

Bill Morgan spoke up: "Yeah, it is. Normally, I can't justify that much of an employee's time unless the law is asking and a court order goes along with it."

"I understand." I thought about what my next moves should be, came up with nothing of much use. "Could you do me a favor? If you happen to see her in the store again, would you mind giving me a call? It would be helpful if I could report to her family that she's alive and well and where she's living. That'd be good enough for them—for now, anyway." I handed him a business card.

I sensed reluctance on his part but he agreed. I walked out, conscious that my moves were appearing on the cameras the whole way out the door and going to my vehicle. The feeling was somewhat reassuring, somewhat creepy. There didn't seem any point in my cruising the streets of town hoping to catch a glimpse of the twin. I already knew both Corvettes were regularly at the house in

Albuquerque, so if one of the girls had moved here she'd switched to a different car.

None of the story I'd been given so far made sense, but I didn't think the answers were to be found here in Las Cruces. Home beckoned. I called Ron to update him with my progress in the Lorrento case. He didn't much want to stay at the office into the evening, so I said I would deliver the ring to his house.

By two o'clock I was on the road for home again, glad business was taken care of—at least to the best of my ability. I now had several hours ahead of me to decide what to do next about Donna Delaney's request.

Chapter 27

B y the time I hit the southern edges of Albuquerque, my body was buzzing from all the hours behind the wheel, and my brain had gone numb. I exited at Lomas and wound my way into Ron and Victoria's neighborhood, parking at the curb in front of their house, handing the ring over to my brother as I pled tiredness for my reason not to come in. It was the point in the day when I wanted nothing more than a bowl of soup and a cuddle from my dog before curling up in bed. For once, it didn't bother me a bit that Drake wouldn't be home tonight.

Freckles came bounding out Elsa's back door when she opened it to my tap. I thanked her profusely for watching my rambunctious little one all day, but declined to come in. I suppose she saw the fatigue in my eyes because she didn't push it.

I followed the soup-cuddle-sleep plan, adding only a quick phone call to Drake and a hot shower. I was in bed before nine o'clock. Then I was wide awake at four-thirty, rested and refreshed.

All the way home yesterday afternoon I'd toyed with various ideas for ways to get the Delaney twins in one place and snap the elusive photo to wrap up the case. I'm kind of funny about projects—I like to tie up loose ends and finish them. The Lorrento case still hung in the air as a trail of random threads. I had no illusion about those two working out what they would do about their marriage, but at least our assigned task—my task anyway—had been completed. Now, I needed a photograph. Just one. It shouldn't be difficult.

I'd sorted through the things I did know about the two girls and their recent activities: a store purchase in Las Cruces, two Corvettes now parked in Albuquerque, the shopping sprees, the river party. When I got to that point, I remembered the girl Zayne (well, I thought it was Zayne) had picked up at the dorm and spent the day with. She might provide a lead.

All of this ran through my head while I made coffee and sat outside, sipping it. The sun peered over the top of Sandia Peak, revealing a gorgeous spring morning and the back yard practically bursting with brilliant green. New leaves and shoots were showing up everywhere. The hanging baskets of petunias I'd placed around the gazebo overhang released their heady sweetness into the air.

A flicker of what-the-hell zipped through me. It was tempting to sit out here and give myself over to an entire day off, but I knew I wouldn't. After an hour I was getting antsy. I needed just one photograph. The sooner I got it, the sooner I'd be free to goof off.

I took my empty cup inside and grabbed a couple of cereal bars from a box. Trading robe and slippers for jeans and a T-shirt, I did a little something with my hair and surveyed the result in the mirror. Could I pass for a college kid? I decided yes. Students came in all ages these days.

With an old textbook under my arm and a swing in my step, I headed for the door. Freckles raced to her crate, eager for the treat she always got, and I went out to the Jeep. At UNM I pulled into the same parking lot where the twin's friend had met her. I flipped back through the photos on the camera, the ones I'd taken at the river party, finding the girl and memorizing her face.

Students began milling about, getting into vehicles, beginning their day with yawns and bleary eyes. I scanned every face but it took close to forty minutes before the one I wanted showed up. Her long, brunette hair was more subdued today, pulled into a side ponytail that trailed over one shoulder, and her makeup was far less dramatic. She had a backpack looped over one shoulder and was staring at a cell phone in one hand. I got out of my Jeep, feigned nonchalance, and started on a path that would bisect hers.

When my shoulder bumped hers, she looked up in irritation. I noticed she didn't drop the phone. I grabbed the first name I could think of.

"Sorry," I said. "Oh, hey. You're Kris, right? Zayne and Clover's friend?"

"Missy. Yeah, I know Zayne and Clover." She quickly surveyed me with wary eyes and a half-smile.

"Yeah, I saw you the other night. You went to the party down at the river with ... oh gosh, I can never tell at a distance. Was it Zayne?" I'd fallen into step beside her.

"Clover." Her eyes were back on the phone screen.

"So weird. I've known them forever and I still can't tell them apart."

"Zayne got a little tattoo on her neck." Missy indicated a spot behind her own ponytail. "It's a tiny dragon, but personally I think it's too little and came out looking like a spider."

"Ah, I guess it was so small I never noticed it." I glanced up at the nearest building—Sciences, if I remembered from the old days. "Well, this is me."

I peeled off, noticed Missy kept walking. Her eyes stayed on her phone and she had near collisions with several others who were doing the same. She would never remember the encounter with me, and she'd never know she had just given me a hugely valuable piece of information. I doubled back to the parking lot and drove home.

Freckles was thrilled to see me again so soon, doubly so when I picked up her leash. I'd decided the direct approach was best. I would walk over and come right out with the request for a picture of the two girls together. It wasn't unreasonable for their aunt to want one, and I was merely the messenger. Both Corvettes were in the driveway over there, so this was as good a time as any. Plus, having my little friendship ambassador along couldn't hurt.

For Donna's purposes, a cell phone camera would be fine. I didn't want to walk through the neighborhood with Drake's big camera swinging from its strap around my neck. I stuck my phone in my pocket, clipped the dog's leash on and headed out the front door. The day had warmed nicely and we were just a girl and her dog out on a walk—with one little side mission.

I rehearsed my lines on the way up the street. One

simple, straightforward request—that's all. Your aunt wants me to send a picture.

As I mounted the step I noticed their front door stood open behind the screen door. From inside, I heard a blare of some rock tune. It paused and started again. A cell ringtone. I stepped to the side and pulled Freckles along with me.

"You've reached Zany Delaney," said a voice. "Ha! Yeah, it was a blast. I just got up."

A pause. Laughter in response to something the caller said. It sounded like Zayne, I supposed. I'd only spoken in recent times with Clover, the twin with the quieter demeanor. Maybe if I could get a look and see that tattoo …

I started to step toward the open doorway but another phone rang, this one with a chiming sound like cathedral bells.

"Hello? Oh hi, yeah this is Clover."

My heart thumped a little as I reached for my phone camera. Both girls were here in the same room. I would whip the screen door open and get my picture before they knew what happened. The dog picked up on my excitement, running around me and entangling my legs in her leash. I stumbled, crashing my shoulder into the metal screen, making a clatter.

"Who's there?"

"Um, hi. It's just Charlie."

Clover came toward me, her phone still at her ear. I knew which twin it was because I could see the side of her neck.

"Sorry, just me and Freckles."

She told the person she would call them back then jammed the phone into her pocket.

"Hey Freckles," she said softly. "You're so cute."

She pushed the screen open and knelt to pet the dog.

"I thought I heard your sister talking to someone when I walked up on the porch. Is she here?"

Her head shook, rattling the dog's tags. "Ah, well … no. That was me. She went to the store and forgot her phone. That was a friend she went to a party with last night."

I glanced toward the two cars in the driveway. She noticed.

"She walked. It's just to the little convenience store over on Central."

It was a lie, I felt sure. For one thing, I'd never seen either of these girls walk anywhere their bright speedy cars would take them. As for forgetting the phone … if not for the previous time I'd been in the house, I wouldn't have bought that story either. But what was I to do—confront her and have her shut down altogether?

I decided on the if-you-can't-beat-them-join-them approach. A memory from years ago surfaced. Clover was the quieter of the two and she was also more outdoorsy.

"Freckles and I were going for a hike a little later. Want to come along? Just an easy one up in the foothills."

Her body tensed.

"Remember the time you girls were maybe ten or so? You were spending the day with Elsa and she thought a picnic would be a great idea. She drove up to that picnic area and I came down the trail, all sweaty and hungry. I was never so happy to see anyone, 'cause, dummy me, I'd left my water bottle behind. She fed us all …"

"I do remember that day," Clover said. "You were kind of my hero back then."

"So, what do you think? I'll grab a little something from the fridge and we can picnic again."

The thing inside her which had been so closed off to me opened the smallest bit. "Okay, yeah. Why not?"

Chapter 28

I had no clue what—aside from pizza, fast food and soda—these girls ate. Sandwiches seemed tricky. I could make four kinds and still get it wrong, so I opted to toss a couple of cheeses, a small salami and some fruit into a little cooler. Sodas and bottled water rounded out the offering, which I hoped covered the choices well. It wouldn't surprise me if she bailed anyhow and I ended up putting it all back in the fridge.

I carried the cooler out to my Jeep, checked the gas tank and was teasing Freckles with the promise of a car trip when I saw Clover come out to her front porch. This was the moment of decision. She caught sight of the dog and came walking toward us. See? Pets really are the world's ambassadors.

Clover climbed into the passenger seat, turning to

reach over the console and pet the dog, who wriggled with excitement at our newfound company as I backed out of the driveway. We hit the freeways, exited at Tramway and watched for the turnoff to the Juan Tabo picnic area and head of the La Luz trail. I hated to admit how many years it was since I'd been here, and I hoped I would recognize the turn.

My guest didn't seem to notice. She answered my conversation attempts with monosyllables and kept checking her phone. As bonding experiences go, this might not have been such a great idea. I found a parking spot and pulled in, ordering Freckles to stay in the back while I got organized, making sure the food cooler sat in a shady spot. I pulled out my cell phone.

"Let's leave our phones here," I said, putting my phone into the glovebox. "All week long I work in an office where the thing rings all the time, always someone wanting a piece of me. When I get out in nature, it's so great to ditch it and just listen to the birds and the wind."

She looked a little panicky.

"Once we get partway up the trail there's probably no signal anyway," I said.

"What if we need help?"

"Someone will come along. It's a popular trail." Mine was probably the last generation who would ever remember the freedom of being completely unconnected.

"I'll just zip mine into my pocket," she said.

If she'd been my kid I could have made it an order, but she wasn't, so I let it go. We started up the easy slope of the first section of trail. The full trail goes all the way to the top of Sandia Peak at ten-thousand-plus feet with some steep places which, this time of year, could still have snow on them, but my plan included no such heroics. Unless we felt especially inspired and hearty, I figured we would go the first half-mile or so, turn around and come back. A mile at this altitude feels farther than you think.

"I used to hike this trail quite a bit when I was your age," I told my companion. "Getting out like this was like the perfect antidote to school where I had all these classes on tax regulations. In fact, I think I was coming up on my accounting exams the day I hiked out here and ran into you guys with Elsa."

"That was funny," she said with a tiny smile. "Mrs. Higgins had her hands full with us, I guess. We'd run up the trail a ways and she would call out and tell us to stay in sight. We laughed and made a game of staying just beyond the limit. She got us when she turned around and walked away. We were watching from behind a big rock and saw her heading down the hill. Oh my god, we got so scared she would drive away and we'd have to walk all the way home."

"I know. Even in her eighties she could do so much. She's amazing."

"We sneaked back down, watching to see what she would do. I was ready to scream and run to catch up with her car, but Zayne was all brave, talking about how yeah, we'd hitchhike home if we had to."

"Elsa would have never, *ever* left you girls up here."

"Yeah, I know that now. But, you know, to a kid—" Her eyes misted over, her lower lip quivering.

"Her brownies used to get me to come running."

Clover blinked twice, coming back to the present. "Yes. That's exactly what she did. She got to her car and opened the trunk and we heard her say 'Now where did I put those brownies?' and we came racing down the hill."

I laughed over the memories and Freckles leaped around in circles, flushing a few quail from behind a bush. They ran across the trail, heads bobbing, tiny legs skittering a million miles an hour.

"Dang," I said. "I wish I'd had brownies to put in our lunch today. You're making me hungry."

We came to the bend in the trail where I'd planned to turn around. The view from here was spectacular, with the city spread out below yet looking close enough to toss a pebble and land it in one of the major streets.

"We need a selfie of the two of us," Clover said, unzipping her jacket pocket.

Had the girl actually begun to think of me as a friend? Wow.

She stepped close to me and stretched her arm with the camera facing us. Her pensive smile flashed bright for the photo.

"I'll Friend you on Facebook so you can see it. Bet we get a ton of Likes."

For one moment I wondered what it would be like to be nineteen again, so young and carefree. She posed another shot to get the panorama behind us, although most likely not a lot of it would show. We headed down toward the picnic area.

"I'll get the food," I said when we arrived back at the picnic tables. "You guys stake out a spot for us."

The dog wiggled with excitement. Clover took the leash and the two of them began examining the choices, looking for the best spot. I caught up with them at the site highest above the parking lot. I'd remembered to include a plastic tablecloth—you never know what condition public tables will be—and I spread it wide across the concrete surface.

When I brought out the goodies, Clover's eyes lit up.

"Cool—an actual adult picnic. Not that I wouldn't have been okay with peanut butter sandwiches," she amended quickly.

I found it oddly endearing that she cared enough to insert the little politeness.

"We aim to please," I joked, handing her the cheese knife while I unscrewed the tops on the water bottles. "Too bad Zayne wasn't around to come along with us."

A shadow passed over her face, something I couldn't interpret. A wariness, perhaps a dread that I would get into more of the same old questions.

"Oh, well, more food for us," I leaped in to say. "Her loss."

She sat stock-still for a full minute, her expression far away. Again, I couldn't read her thoughts but hated that we'd lost the lighthearted moment.

"Look, there's a roadrunner," I said, pointing about ten yards away.

The change of subject brightened Clover's face again. Luckily, the dog was still leashed and I distracted her with a tidbit of the cheese while the bird ran out of our sight.

"Let me see the pictures again," I said when Clover brought out her phone.

She turned it to face me and I reached out and swiped through them. She had a flair for this, good camera angle, great lighting. She'd captured a candid shot of me and Freckles at some point up the trail. I'd never realized she was aiming toward us. It was an appealing picture of the moment when I let the dog off the leash and she'd licked my face.

"You're pretty good at photography," I told her. "Ever thought about a career of it?"

"Oh, I don't know … I, um, haven't really thought much about the future. Zayne thought about getting into the film industry, doing something like my parents. They know a lot of people."

As she talked, I swiped back through the photos one more time. Before today's outing there were shots from the river party. I recognized Missy, the girl from the dorm, and the boy I'd seen at their house a few times. Before the party, there were shots taken inside the Delaney house— one twin about to bite down on a huge pizza slice, feet modeling a pair of new red shoes. One more swipe and I nearly dropped the phone.

Clover continued to drop famous names as she talked about her parents.

The photo on the screen showed Zayne sweeping her hair upward with one hand. She stood with her shoulder toward the camera, rear end jutted out, knees flexed in a model-like pose. The little tattoo was clearly visible. So was everything else, since she wore nothing but the red shoes.

I must have reacted because Clover looked back at me. I quickly swiped back to today's photos. *C'mon, Charlie, don't be a prude. They're not your kids. It's not your place to form judgments.*

I stared again at the photo of me and my dog. "Hey, can we email this one to me?" Drake's birthday was coming up and a framed photo like this one would make a great gift.

Clover looked at the picture. "Yeah, that's a good one. You and Freckles were so cute together."

I put my email address in and tapped a couple of buttons, sending the picture on its way. "Thanks. It was nice of you to take that shot."

She basked a little at the praise, and I wondered again how these girls, given such complete freedom at their young age, received their guidance and validation in life. I may have been on my own fairly young, but I had the stability of school and nearby family. I thought of the thousands of little compliments and smiles Elsa had given me over the years. I needed to show more gratitude for it.

Chapter 29

I checked my email the moment I got home. The photo was every bit as nice on a big screen as it had been on Clover's phone. I found some decent photo paper and printed it. The ink was barely dry when I heard a sound at the front door.

Quickly stashing the picture out of sight I joined Freckles in giving Drake a hearty welcome. With one arm around me and the other hand being kissed by the dog, he beamed.

"How was the job?" I asked.

"Uneventful. The best kind." As owner, operator and pilot of his own aircraft, the responsibilities sometimes weighed heavily on him. Days that didn't require a post-flight inspection to investigate a small noise or perform required maintenance were the easiest.

"Right now I just want a shower and then I'm thinking Pedro's for dinner," he said.

I'd had such a lazy afternoon, although technically I was on the job, having dinner out seemed in keeping with the tone of the day.

"I'm going to check in with Ron while you shower," I said, wondering whether my brother's larger-than-life houseguest was gone yet.

"Invite them along to dinner if you want to." He began peeling off his flight suit as he headed toward the bathroom.

I didn't get an answer on Ron's phone so I left a message stating our intentions and suggested they meet us if they didn't have other dinner plans. When I clicked off the call I noticed the Facebook app on my screen. I've so seldom used the thing I had to go look up my password and mess around with the various icons until I figured it out. The first thing I did was search for Clover and Zayne Delaney.

Clover had already posted several pictures from our hike, mostly selfies that included Freckles. She had tagged me in one where I was opening the picnic cooler. There was a shot of the twins together, posted yesterday, but the photo hadn't been taken then. In it, both girls were wearing sweaters. Our spring weather had been too warm recently. I stretched the picture and saw a fuzzy glimpse of what appeared to be Christmas lights in the background. Funny, she would choose that one now.

On Zayne's page, there were pictures from a party and the comment "OMG last night's frat party!" I didn't recognize any of the other kids, but the backgrounds suggested an outdoor setting. Each photo that included Zayne showed her miming a silly action—dancing with the beer keg, draping a flimsy scarf around her neck, pouring a cup of beer over a boy's head. The photographer's words came back to me, the man who'd talked about his teen daughter and the things her friends posted online. Maybe Zayne was called Zany for good reason.

Movement behind me caught my attention. Drake emerged from the bedroom, smelling of soap and fresh clothing.

"Hey, you're not going all teenager on me, are you?" he teased, looking at the phone in my hand.

"Only a little bit." I dropped it into my purse and told him the results of my call to Ron.

Freckles dashed willingly to her crate in exchange for a doggie cookie, and we walked out to Drake's pickup. A glance up the street showed both sports cars in the Delaney driveway. I suspected Zayne's Facebook post about a frat party was actually one of the river parties here in Albuquerque. Maybe she'd told so many people she was going to State now she had to keep up the pretense through social media. I shrugged off my doubts. It was anybody's guess what those girls were up to. I felt a tad guilty for befriending Clover when I only intended to spy, but I wasn't going to let it bother me tonight. I had chicken enchiladas on my mind.

Ron's car sat outside Pedro's, our favorite hole-in-the-wall restaurant just off the Old Town Plaza.

"You got my message," I said when we walked in.

He and Victoria exchanged a blank look. It's when I noticed they sat at a table for two.

"He's leaving his phone muted for awhile," she said. "Kind of hiding out."

"I'm not hiding out," Ron said with a testy grimace. "I just don't want to talk to Bobby Lorrento or his wacko wife right now."

I got the feeling something had happened in my absence this afternoon. Drake and I pulled up chairs and joined them without asking.

"Bobby and Marcie on the warpath with each other again?" I asked, accepting the margarita Pedro brought over.

"Lorrento's on the warpath with everyone at the moment, including you and me."

"Me? What did *I* do?" Wasn't my trip down to El Paso and the long drive back to deliver the ring last night going to count for anything?

"Someone switched the ring."

"Whoa, whoa—back up and fill in the gaps."

"Last night, Bobby was out when you delivered the ring. He came in late but I'd waited up, knowing he would be thrilled to have it back. He comes in, I hand it over, he takes one look and says 'this isn't mine'."

I felt the blood drain from my face. "It had to be. I looked at it before I handed over the money. It was never out of my possession until I gave it to you."

"How closely did you examine it?"

"Did I have a jewelers loupe and really check the diamonds? No. I just figured Livingston only owned it a couple days, he wouldn't have had time to commission a zirconia version."

My chicken enchiladas arrived but my stomach was in a knot and I couldn't take a bite.

"Ron, are you saying the ring is a fake?" Drake asked. He took my hand under the table.

"It's not a fake, it just isn't Bobby's. Remember how I said the whole team, the coaches, managers and everyone on the winning team gets those rings? This one belonged to an assistant coach. Its value is about a quarter of Bobby's.

The diamonds are smaller, the platinum is thinner, and that doesn't even count the value as a collectible."

I did the math in my head. "We just paid more than a hundred thousand for a ring worth twenty-five?"

"Well, Marcie did. With Bobby's money."

"My god, Ron, what are we going to do?"

"I told Bobby we'd stay on the case and find it. For tonight, I'm lying low and letting Lorrento get used to the idea. I got him a room at the Marriott and told him if he had to talk to someone, it better be his buddies. After he left our place, I called Marcie, explained the situation to her and suggested she not talk with Bobby. He's placing the blame squarely on her. Well, a little bit on us too. Once I feel like he won't come and bash my head in, I'll start working to find the real ring."

He had managed to polish off a huge burrito while he talked, obviously not as bothered by this whole mess as I was.

"I know you're still working on the Delaney twins deal, but I'm going to need you on this one too. You went to Livingston's house, met with him. We need to talk about that. See what possible leads you might give."

I stared at my untouched enchiladas. I couldn't think of a single clue, nothing I'd seen in El Paso that could lead us to the real Super Bowl ring. Drake prodded me to eat something, but my usually favorite dish held no appeal tonight.

Chapter 30

I lay awake long into the night, berating myself for not having examined the ring more closely before handing over the cash. Stupid, stupid, stupid. I'd checked the team name and year, both were correct. It simply hadn't occurred to me Livingston would have another team ring on hand to substitute. And that must be the case. He'd planned well in advance, and the scam was the big reason he'd been so willing to sell his new purchase. But still, if I'd only looked closely, handled the ring and read the inscription inside. I'd been such a fool.

On the other hand, Marcie Lorrento was the real fool, falling for Livingston's pickup lines when all he really wanted was money. It would be interesting to see her reaction to the betrayal.

After stewing for hours over my own culpability,

transferring the blame to Marcie and thoroughly chastising her in my mind, I gave up on sleep. I got out of bed to relieve Drake from my tossing and turning, pulled on a robe and went into his office. I closed the door, not wanting Freckles to think we were starting a new day already, and turned on the computer.

Where to start? At this point I had no idea whether Livingston was actually a collector or if he was in the business of turning a quick buck whenever he could. My guess was the latter, seeing as how he'd almost immediately agreed to sell his new purchase to me. I began my search by looking up football memorabilia for sale.

The search results were a bit overwhelming, with thousands of sites. I started with the largest and most popular. Several Super Bowl rings turned up, most with photographs from multiple angles and promises of squeaky-clean provenance.

I didn't find Lorrento's ring but I learned a bunch of the markers I should have checked. No wonder Livingston had been so cordial to me. He spotted me for the uneducated dope that I was. Again, I felt myself going down the blame path but steered the other direction. Whether my lack of knowledge or Marcie's hormones were to blame, it didn't matter. The job was now to retrieve the ring. Getting Livingston for fraud and grand theft would be the icing on the cake, and yeah, you betcha I planned to get this guy.

On to other sites listing football collectibles. Still no Lorrento ring. Okay, I decided, let's switch to finding the man if we can't find the ring.

Searches for Jay Livingston gave me a few leads. Unfortunately, there was an actor by the same name, a middle-aged guy who'd played minor roles in nearly every incarnation of *Star Trek* and had a list of film credits a mile long. His name came up with regularity in the searches, along with a John Livingston who made the circuit of motivational speakers claiming to offer the secret to make anyone's life perfect. None of these Livingstons appeared to be the one I wanted, unless the man I'd met had managed to lose fifty pounds and twenty years since the actor's publicity shots were taken. The speaker Livingston had the right physique, from what I could tell, but his sandy blonde coloring, vivid blue eyes and deep dimples didn't match.

Okay, so the internet didn't have *all* the answers. In the morning I would go back to square one, the pawnshop where Livingston had purchased the ring. Someone there would have a vivid memory of the man and maybe I could learn more.

I yawned and shut down the computer. Only when the room became dark did I realize I could see the faint light of dawn around the window shades. Cripes—I'd been awake all night. My eyeballs burned from the hours at the monitor. I blinked hard a few times to work up some moisture then tiptoed back to bed. Drake groaned and rolled toward me when I slipped under the covers. I nestled into his warmth and let the heaviness of sleep settle over me.

When I woke, bright sun cast a square of light through the glass block windows in the bathroom and beamed it via mirror to my shoulder. I squinted against it, but it pulled me toward wakefulness. Drake was nowhere in the room, but I could hear small sounds from the kitchen. A glance at the clock told me it was not quite seven-thirty. I'd had a full two hours' sleep. Ugh.

I rolled over and pulled the covers over my head but it was no use. Names and places and photos from my

hours online came rushing back at me. Even though I'd
found nothing useful, I couldn't seem to turn off the litany
running through my brain. I stumbled to the shower and
turned it as hot as I could stand, scrubbed shampoo into
my scalp and then turned the rinse water to a tepid chill.
Something in the routine would have to wake me up so I
could function today.

Drake stood at the front door, jacket on, ready to walk
out when I came out of the bedroom wearing my robe and
wet hair.

"Hey, sleepy," he said, walking toward me and planting
a kiss on my forehead. "I left you a note, didn't want to
wake you."

"You're headed out early."

"Yeah, today it's Fish and Game. We'll be up near
Bandelier. I'll call you when I'm ready to pull pitch. Well,
the note tells you all that." He stood back and looked into
my eyes. "You didn't get much sleep. You okay?"

I didn't go into the full extent of the ring disaster, nor
exactly admit my guilt over it, but I got the feeling he saw
more than I realized.

"It'll work out. It's just having two cases going at once
is leaving my mind a little scattered."

He gave me a real, long-lasting kiss this time and
promised to keep me updated about his flight. I watched
him drive away, toying with the idea of going back to bed
for awhile, knowing I'd never actually fall asleep. I poured
coffee into the biggest mug I could find and strolled the
back yard while I drank it. The flowering shrubs and trees
were starting to leaf out and the grass was getting a bit
long. If one of us didn't find the time to mow soon we
should call a yard man. I filed the task for later. There was

too much going on right now.

Back in the kitchen I couldn't think in terms of food yet, so I went into the bathroom to dry my hair and try to make myself presentable. I'm not big on primping. The whole routine took less than fifteen minutes, and I emerged with hair in a ponytail and a swish of blusher to show for my efforts.

Freckles danced around me, eager for another adventure today. She stuck by my side while I gathered my things and made certain she was at the car door the moment it unlocked. Up the street, I heard an engine and looked up to see the blue convertible coasting to a stop at the edge of my driveway.

"Hey, Charlie."

I tossed my purse on my seat and closed the dog inside.

"Clover, hey. How's everything?"

"Fine. Did you see the pics I posted after our picnic? The one with you and Freckles got a ton of likes. I put our selfies on Instagram and Snapchat too. Check 'em out."

I nodded a little absently, thinking what a pain it would be to check all these social sites.

She revved her engine as I was about to ask how Zayne was doing, and with a wave she was gone. Oh well. At this moment recovering our other client's diamond ring was far more urgent than wondering who liked me on Facebook.

Chapter 31

Ron and I arrived at the office at nearly the same moment. I found myself following his vehicle into the driveway and tracking his moves as we pulled into our respective parking spots. Sally's minivan was already there and I caught the whiff of coffee as we approached the back door.

"Did you hear anything more from either of the Lorrentos last night?" I asked my brother.

He shook his head. "Thank goodness—no."

"I spent the night on the internet," I said. "The ring hasn't shown up on any of the big auction sites."

He stepped back and let me precede him into the kitchen. "Damn. I hoped he would try to turn it quickly. Otherwise, he's likely to hold onto it for a long time. He'll have to assume Bobby would report this to the police."

"Why hasn't he?" I set my purse on the table long enough to rinse my favorite mug and fill it from the carafe.

Ron shrugged. "He still might. If we get a call from the major crimes division today it'll tell us what Bobby was doing last night."

"So ... maybe we should step back and let them take over?"

"Bobby left my house shouting 'This is on you. Find my ring.' I'm taking him seriously."

"Okay, then what's our next move?"

"I'll go talk to the pawnshop guy where Marcie originally sold the rings. Livingston seems to have a finger on the pulse of the business. I mean, he knew right away when this ring came on the market."

"Yeah, because he was sleeping with Marcie and she told him."

"True. But this local guy is probably familiar with his competitors, maybe knows of a place in El Paso where Livingston might try to move the ring. He's also heavily into the trade show circuit and watches auctions for certain items. I'm grasping for whatever leads we can get at this point."

I felt the weight of the task as I walked upstairs and settled at my desk. In the forty-plus hours since I'd seen Livingston he could have done any number of things. With a buyer standing by, all he needed to do was stick the ring into a box and send it by registered mail anywhere in the country.

On the other hand, maybe Livingston was an avid collector and wanted nothing more than to keep the ring for himself. I thought of his upscale home and his casual demeanor with large amounts of cash. If I met with him again, face to face, maybe I could convince him to undo yesterday's sale. If he cared a scrap for Marcie, he might do it if he thought she was in danger.

Across the hall, Ron was on the phone and the gist of the conversation was what he and I had just talked about. While he worked the local pawnshop angle, maybe I could follow my own instincts. I palmed the ring box and shut Freckles into her crate so she wouldn't panic at my leaving her behind. At the front desk I showed Sally the ring box and told her I was taking it with me.

My cell phone began to chirp while I sat in the drive-up lane at McDonald's. Drake. He went through his flight plan and said he would call again when he landed at the customer's job site. I made a note of his ETA and told myself it was better I didn't share my current plan. He needed to focus on his flight. I could handle this other business.

A frisson of worry coursed through me as I stopped to gas up. This was risky, heading on a probably foolish errand without telling anyone where I was going. But Drake had enough on his mind and Ron would stay happy doggedly tracking any leads the local pawn guy might give. This recent mess was my fault and I needed to be doing *something*.

The road felt very familiar as I hit I-25 southbound, holding my McMuffin one-handed and leaving Albuquerque traffic behind. Before I'd reached Socorro, Drake phoned again to close his flight plan and let me know he'd arrived safely at Bandelier.

"Your voice sounds shaky," he said. "Or there's a lot of noise in the background."

"I'm in the car." I told myself he didn't need to know more than that. Not yet anyway.

He told me he estimated his job to take six hours or so, and he would call again before he left the site. Standard protocol. Nothing to worry about. I was a little south of Socorro when my phone rang again. The readout said it was Ron and I could only imagine the chewing-out I was about to get. I increased my speed and let the call go to voicemail.

For the next two hours, I rehearsed my approach to Livingston. "Hi, Jay, remember me? Well, there was a slight mistake with the ring you sold me yesterday and I'm going to need the real one."

Geez, that sounded lame.

How about the emotional approach? "Jay, Marcie is devastated about this ring business."

Uh ... no.

Okay, I could always threaten. "Jay, this is big-time fraud and you know it. The money or the real ring, or else I take this to the authorities."

And exactly how did I think I would back up such a statement? He would laugh in my face and lock the door and, of course, I'd not planned very well or brought a weapon or any way to enforce my tough statement. By the time I reached the outskirts of El Paso my stomach was in a knot.

The directions to Livingston's house were still on my phone and I retraced my previous movements, pulling to a stop in front of the grand house. I took a deep breath and walked to the front door, pressing the doorbell button firmly, as if decisive action would grant me a measure of courage I certainly wasn't feeling. A minute went by and I pushed the button again, twice. No response, and I noticed there was no car in the driveway today. Well, rats.

I glanced at the houses across the street and took in the scene a little more fully. Funny, I hadn't noticed a For Sale sign in Livingston's front yard last time I was here. In fact, I was virtually certain it had not been there. Had he made a quick decision to sell?

I went back to the Jeep. I could sit out here awhile and see if he came home. Meanwhile, maybe there was a way to get his cell phone number without calling my brother. I dialed the number for the agent listed on the real estate sign.

"I'm at 4910 Desert Vista Drive," I said. "I was here two days ago and—"

"Oh, yes. You must have come for the open house."

"Uh, no … I'm just trying to reach the owner and hoped you would have a number for him."

"Normally, there's no contact between buyer and seller. It's why they have an agent, so we can handle all the negotiations."

"Oh, sorry. You've misunderstood. I'm not interested in buying the house. I just need to reach Mr. Livingston on another matter entirely."

"Livingston?"

"The homeowner." How dense could this lady be?

"You're at my listing on Desert Vista? I'm sorry but the owner's name is Cruikshank. I don't think there's anyone named Livingston associated …"

I looked again at my directions, then at the house, to be sure the address was right, took a breath. "I was here the day before yesterday. Jay Livingston answered the door and invited me inside. We sat in the living room, talked and conducted a little business. That's what I need to talk to him about today."

"Ma'am, I'm sorry I have no idea what you're talking about."

My thoughts swam. I began to think *I* had no idea what I was talking about. I forced myself to get on track while I had her on the phone.

"Sorry. Tell me more about the open house. Were you the agent on site?"

"Yes, from ten to four."

"And you never left?"

"Oh. I did take a short lunch break. One of my colleagues was supposed to take my place during the noon hour but she had a family emergency and couldn't make it. Her husband stopped by to tell me. He offered to watch the place and hand out cards while I ran out to pick up food. Really, I wasn't gone very long."

Just long enough. I thanked her and hung up, sitting in my vehicle with a zillion thoughts running through my head.

The only scenario that made any sense was that, somehow, Jay Livingston had staked out a house for sale and given that address. I had to wonder why, but there must be a reason and the reason surely had to do with keeping himself out of our reach. Unless he'd known in advance about the upcoming open house, he must have planned to break in somehow. The logistics of timing and coordination boggled my mind, but the fact was he'd done it. I marveled at how smooth he'd been, how perfectly at ease in convincing me this was his house. I was beginning to see more con man than collector in the man.

I'd passed a Denny's restaurant near one of the freeway exits and decided a decent meal would help my flagging energy and give me the time to plan my next steps. I took a table near the windows and ordered a chef's salad. My phone chimed with a little reminder I'd set a few days ago. Ignoring that, I remembered Ron's earlier call while I was on the road so I checked my voice mail instead. The chewing-out was fairly predictable. What was I doing, taking off on my own and where did I think I was taking the diamond ring? Yada, yada …

I laid the phone on the table when my salad arrived and resolved to forget about Ron, at least until I'd eaten. I'd been right about the food—eating did perk up my energy. It also became clear I wasn't going to have much luck stumbling around the city on my own looking for Livingston. The man could be anywhere in the world. I paid my bill and went out to the Jeep.

Might as well call Ron back now. He may have become more furious with the passing hours, but I figured facing the music with some miles between us was better than in the office tomorrow morning. I dialed his number and leaned back in my seat to await my fate.

Chapter 32

Ron's suggestion turned out to be the one thing I had not expected to hear from him: report the fraud to the local authorities. Since Livingston's residence was in Texas, and since the sale of the lesser-value ring had taken place there, we could sic their people on him. When he put it like that, I sort of relished the idea.

I looked up the address of the main police station and let the tiny map on my phone direct me to it. For a city of close to seven hundred thousand people, the police department seemed a bit skimpy in comparison to the nearby federal Border Patrol facility. I supposed that was the impact of budgeting law enforcement resources at the border. I parked and went inside, gave a synopsis of the reason for my visit to an information officer and was directed upstairs to the major crimes division.

Whether I'd caught the lunch hour or whether the division was hopelessly understaffed, I couldn't tell. The office I entered contained three desks, only one of which was manned at the moment. The guy's suit jacket hung over the back of his chair and his short-sleeved white shirt was unbuttoned at the neck, his tie loosened. He had cocoa skin and dark hair with a generous sprinkling of gray. His nameplate said he was M. Lujan. When Lujan asked how he could help me, his voice sounded bored.

I gave the basics: I'd been in contact with a local man with a collectible Super Bowl ring to sell. I'd brought the agreed-upon amount of cash and he'd sold me a ring worth far less. I received a knowing-but-tired look that said: you foolish people never learn to examine the merchandise, do you?

Lujan's expression closed further when I explained how I'd come back to find the house where we'd conducted this bit of business wasn't actually Livingston's house. A wry smile crossed his face when I told how Livingston had tricked the realtor into leaving it unattended long enough to pull his scam.

"I'll give him a B-plus for creativity," Lujan said, not looking up as he typed my statement on a form on his computer screen.

He printed the statement and had me sign it. He asked to see the ring—seemed mildly dazzled when the light hit the diamonds—and took several photos of it, including (naturally) the parts I should have looked at more closely before I forked over the cash.

I stepped out into the bright sunshine when it was all over, relieved to have shifted part of the burden to an authority figure, although Lujan had not exactly radiated hope that we would be seeing Bobby Lorrento's ring anytime soon. The police session had taken longer than I expected, my stomach was churning from the salad at lunch, and I would be late getting home. But nothing about staying away overnight appealed to me. I walked to my Jeep, got in and called Ron to report the last two hours' accomplishments.

By the time I went through Las Cruces, my gut was in definite rebellion and I pulled over at a gas station/convenience store to see what over-the-counter remedies might be available. With two packets of tummy treatment chewable tablets and a large bottle of water in hand, I continued my journey.

An hour later, a flashing dashboard light caught my attention and I noticed the Jeep's temperature gauge had gone into the red zone. I edged off the roadway as far as I could and shut down. I hadn't passed an exit in at least twenty miles and didn't remember signage promising another anytime soon. I powered all the windows down and hoped for enough breeze to keep me from becoming roasted Charlie out here in the desert.

Well, I'd been paying a little extra on my insurance every month for roadside assistance—this looked like the perfect time to use it. I grabbed my phone and the little card with the number from my wallet. The phone showed one bar of signal strength and the battery had ten percent left.

Crap. Would this fun day never end? Was it some misalignment of the planets or something? I couldn't seem to catch a break.

I connected—barely—with a perky young woman who wanted to go through a Q&A session, but I interrupted by giving my location.

"Look, I've got probably a minute or two to talk. My car's out of commission and I need to be towed to the nearest garage. I'd appreciate anything you can do to make that happen."

Her response sounded polite, although the scratchy quality of the signal didn't exactly assure me she'd heard everything I said. The phone went dead before she finished talking. Double crap.

I took another of my tummy soothers and blew out a breath of frustration.

Okay, Charlie, think.

Somewhere in here I had a phone charger cord. I hoped it was for the current device, as they all seem to have different connection plugs. I rummaged in the glovebox without luck, then tackled the little compartment in the console. Nothing there either. Sometimes stuff found its way under the seat. I leaned over and ran my hand beneath the passenger seat, coming up with a gum wrapper and a gas receipt before my fingers touched a cord. Aha!

I'd started to pull on it when all at once my Jeep rocked violently. I slammed against the dashboard. Something bit into my ribcage and my head whacked the glovebox door. I felt the car move, tires screaming in protest against pavement and gravel. Then it went still.

The whole thing happened instantaneously but it took me a long, stunned moment to figure out that I'd been hit by another vehicle. I groaned and pushed myself upward.

"Shit, man!" came a voice from outside.

"You hit a parked car, dude," said a second male voice.

They both giggled.

I managed to get myself upright, spun around to see out. My Jeep was no longer parked neatly parallel to the road, but sat nose-down where the verge dropped away, hind end still on pavement. A vivid-orange Trans Am's crumpled front end had taken out my left rear quarter-panel.

My karma for asking whether this day could get any worse.

A teenage boy stood at the collision point, while the driver was trying to put the car in gear and back away. The passenger spotted me and his eyes got saucer-like. He scrambled to get back in the car, which by now had steam spewing from under the hood.

"Oh, no you don't," I said, throwing my shoulder into my door to shove it open. "You're not going anywhere."

I said it with a lot more authority than my pounding head and screaming lower back really felt. I stomped over to his driver's door and yanked it open. Beer fumes rolled out, and I spotted a half-dozen empty cans in the back seat. Before he could stop me, I reached across the kid in the driver's seat and twisted his key from the ignition.

"Seriously?"

"Damn straight. You think you're gonna do this and just drive off?" The day's frustrations built to a head. "Give me your phone. Right now!"

He actually handed it over. Never in my life had I exerted such power over a teenager, and I have to say it felt pretty good.

I took a step back and pressed the button to activate the phone. It had stronger signal reception than mine had gotten earlier. I dialed 911 and waited for it to connect. The driver squirmed in his seat.

"You two. Stay right where you are," I ordered.

"I need to—"

"Shut it. You've capped off a shitty day for me and you'll just have to wait it out." I jammed his keys into my jeans pocket.

The emergency operator came on and I described the location and situation. "We'll need two tow trucks and the police should take a report."

My idea of being home drifted away with the steam from the Trans Am. The two boys didn't look happy. I envisioned lectures from parents, a court appearance on a drunk-driving charge, and whatever else their irresponsible act had brought down upon them. For me, I had a feeling my Jeep was toast. I looked at her and wanted to cry.

By this time, passing traffic had slowed to a crawl, although the accident wasn't blocking a lane. The impulse to stare couldn't be helped. I stomped up the road a ways and came back, having blown off only a little of my ire. In the distance, I saw a tow truck coming toward us.

The truck driver pulled to the median and made a U-turn, which really caused the traffic to bunch up. He steered to the front of my vehicle and got out.

"Road Care called and dispatched me," said the burly man with shaggy brown hair and a beard that seemed too much in the ninety-degree heat. "Didn't say nothin' about an accident."

"Yeah, well, that's because there wasn't one when I first called. My Jeep overheated and I was waiting for a tow when these two bashed me."

He gave a sympathetic nod.

"The police are on the way. At least I hope they are," I said. A glance toward the Trans Am showed both boys having a nervous conversation inside.

Sure enough, within a couple minutes a State Police

black-and-white appeared over the horizon, lights and siren going full tilt. The car made the same move the tow truck had, except it came to a halt behind the teens and a slightly built female officer got out. From the look she sent toward the boys, I guessed this wasn't the first time she'd responded to an accident involving beer-drinking college kids.

She bypassed the orange car and walked up to me. I went through the story of my breakdown and the crash, handing over the boy's keys and phone.

"This was good thinking," she said, indicating the keys.

"I doubt he would have gotten far, but he was sure willing to try," I said.

"Are you injured?" she asked.

"I don't think so."

The tow truck driver pointed toward my temple and I rubbed it with fingers that came away with a little blood. The officer took my statement and released me to ride along with the truck after he'd hooked onto my Jeep. It was a bit of a process, as he straightened the vehicle's position and lifted her onto the bed of his truck. Meanwhile, the officer did breath tests with the two kids and they both ended up in the back seat of her cruiser. A second truck arrived to haul their vehicle away as I was retrieving my purse, phone and charger cord from mine. Little black specks danced in my vision when I bent over, and my driver ushered me to his truck and gave me a bottle of water.

"We'll get you to T or C real soon and you can get some rest."

Any hope of making it home tonight quickly faded. My head throbbed, and muscles I didn't remember began to make themselves known. In the one thing I'd done right

all day, I remembered to run my hand down inside my
purse and make sure the twenty-five-thousand-dollar ring
was still there.

Chapter 33

Truth or Consequences, New Mexico, sits approximately in the middle of the state and as the nearest town to Elephant Butte Lake is a fairly major recreation attraction during the summer months. April being a bit pre-season for boating, I was able to get a room at one of the many lovely little strip motels after a long rigmarole of delivering my damaged Jeep to a fenced yard of other broken toys, clearing my possessions out of it and renting a plain-vanilla sedan to get myself home. I indulged in that most comfortable of comfort food, Kentucky Fried Chicken, and took my little boxed dinner to the room. The desk clerk was kind enough to provide me with a toothbrush, toothpaste and comb. I suppose my slightly battered face accounted for the sympathetic glances I received everywhere.

Fortified with food and pain meds, I took a deep breath and called home.

"I'm fine, hon, but there's not much way I want to drive back to Albuquerque tonight," I said, after glossing over the basics of my day.

"El Paso? When did that idea come up?"

I admitted the trip had been very spur-of-the-moment, but made something of a deal out of the new twist in the hunt for Jay Livingston.

"Okay, then. I've got Freckles here at the house," he said. "Ron brought her by when he left the office for the day, concerned that you weren't back yet. You might want to give him a call."

My head pounded some more at the thought, but I did it. Ron wasn't pleased to hear about the lukewarm response from the El Paso police, and I got the feeling he didn't hold much hope of catching up with Bobby Lorrento's diamond ring anytime soon. Finally, I told him I was achy and exhausted and would have to postpone any further lectures until tomorrow because, dammit, I wanted to go to sleep now.

Muscles were seriously cramping up now and, although I couldn't remember what time I'd last taken ibuprofen, I loaded up on more before peeling off my clothes and crawling between the sheets. Sleep lasted exactly as long as the pills. Four hours after taking them, I rolled over and felt every ache and pain again.

I indulged myself in a good bout of self pity, wanting my husband and my dog and my own bed. Seeing as how none of them materialized, no matter how much I whined about it, I took more pills and tried pacing the room a few times to walk off some of the soreness.

My body wanted rest but my mind was awhirl. This ill-conceived trip had certainly complicated my life. One of the first steps, I supposed, would be to call my insurance company and find out how long it would take to get my Jeep back in working order. According to the little wallet card, they had a 24-hour number to call for claims, and since I wasn't getting back to sleep on the hard-as-a-board mattress anytime soon, I called it.

A benefit, I discovered, of placing a business call at one o'clock in the morning is the call gets answered right away. No sitting on hold, no jingly music *ad nauseam*. The female voice at the other end wasn't exactly perky at this hour, but she did offer sympathy about the accident and asked if I was all right. She took all the information and said she would send a claims adjuster to the yard where the Jeep sat, cold and alone. The thought depressed me.

By the time I finished the call, I was tired again but couldn't shake the antsy feeling. I lay down again and actually dozed for a few hours. By daybreak I decided there was nothing holding me here. I gathered my skimpy possessions and got into my generic rental for the two-hour drive home.

Drake seemed surprised to see me when I walked into the kitchen in time for the coffee he was brewing. He set down the carafe and pulled me close. I moaned a little when his hug squeezed a sensitive muscle and he held me at arm's length.

"You okay?" he asked, running his finger gently near the cut on my forehead.

I nodded. "Yeah, I'm just going to clean up and change clothes before I head for the office."

He gave me a firm look, seeing past my brave façade.

The truth was, I felt bone tired. My plan to start the day early and continue full speed suddenly didn't seem so great. He steered me toward a chair at the kitchen table.

"Let me get us some breakfast," he said, "then you're going to take it easy all day."

"Is that an order?" I really hoped it was. Freckles sensed my vulnerability and laid her head on my lap.

I watched as Drake cracked eggs into a bowl and chopped some onions and tomatoes. In very short order he had made an omelet and toast and set a plate in front of me.

"Eat. I'm calling Ron to let him know you won't be in. After breakfast, you can have a nice, hot shower and then I want you to sleep as long as you possibly can."

It sounded heavenly. He hovered over me and even wrapped my favorite big fluffy robe around me when I came out of the shower. I barely heard him say something about keeping Freckles out of my way for the day, as he closed the bedroom door behind them. I sank into my luxurious mattress and pulled the bedding over me, cocooned in another dose of muscle relaxers. A brief thought intruded, of talking to Ron about Jay Livingston and the diamond ring, but I shut it firmly out.

The room was dark when I woke, momentarily confused about the time of day when I saw the clock said 8:19. Had I slept nearly twelve hours?

I could hear the soft sounds of the television in the other room, and there was a strip of light under the bedroom door. A shadow crossed it and the door gave a slight rattle. Freckles somehow knew I was awake.

I stretched and discovered I was less sore than I'd been earlier. Slipping into soft sweats and a t-shirt, I brushed my teeth and ran a brush through my hair. The view in the mirror brought me back to reality. The cut on my forehead wasn't bad, but a huge, purple bruise had bloomed on my right cheek. The red scuff on my chin meant I must have scraped it on the carpeted floor mat. No point in trying to hide it from Drake—he'd already seen it all—but I would have to scrounge up some foundation makeup before I went out in public.

"Hey, sleeping beauty," he teased when I emerged from the bedroom.

"I feel more like Rip Van Winkle. It is still Wednesday, isn't it?"

"It is. But I would have let you sleep several more hours if you needed them. You've been pushing pretty hard recently."

True. The two trips to El Paso in three days had exhausted me. Not to mention I was tired of all the games between Bobby and Marcie Lorrento and Jay Livingston. For all I knew Marcie and Jay had cooked up the idea of substituting another ring and the two of them might be about to head south for a lengthy vacation together. It wouldn't hurt my feelings at all if they did so, as long as Bobby didn't try to break down our door again.

"You have a few messages," Drake said. He'd paused his TV show and left the couch. He pointed at a note lying on the coffee table. "Want something to eat?"

I picked up the slip of paper. "No, thanks. I'm fine for now."

"Oh, besides that one, Ron called to see if you were coming in today. That was around noon and I told him not to count on it. I guess he wanted to tell you about some pawnshop guy. And Victoria offered to bring soup, but I assured her we already had a pot of stew from Elsa. It's in the fridge, whenever you're ready for it."

"Wow. Lot of fuss over my tiredness."

"And the accident. Everyone's concerned." He nodded toward the paper in my hand. "That's the insurance adjuster who went out to look at your Jeep."

The note only contained a name and phone number.

"He didn't give you any information?"

"Well, yeah, he did. It's not good. He said the body damage to the rear hatch, door and quarter-panel would cost more to repair than the vehicle's current value. So, they're going to total it and give you the book value."

I sighed. "I was afraid of that. All the way home I was thinking about it. Sally had a repair job done on her van awhile back and I was astounded at how much body work costs. Hers was minor and it was over a thousand dollars."

"The man suggested you can keep the car if you'd rather, spend just enough to get it running again and not repair the body damage."

"Yeah, and drive around in a bashed vehicle with doors that barely open and close." I remembered having to give a hard shove just to get my driver door open. "I don't see that working out too well."

"We could go car shopping tomorrow."

Next to dental procedures, I hate car shopping the most. The whole scene where you walk onto a car lot and immediately become targeted by every sales person around. *No ... no ... don't make me do it.*

"I'll think about it. Maybe I'll have some of that stew after all." I wandered toward the kitchen, halfway wishing I'd just stayed in bed.

Chapter 34

Drake postponed a client's job in the morning and we spent a few hours at the car mall, where the experience was every bit as delightful as I'd imagined. When, at the Ford place, the third sales guy bee-lined his way toward us, I took Drake's arm and we ducked between pickup trucks. Our dash for freedom felt so good I couldn't force myself to go back.

"Why don't you shop around online and see what you find?" he suggested as we pulled into the parking lot at Souper Salad for lunch.

Why hadn't I thought of that? Most likely because my head recently had been filled with all the natter of teen girls, rich people's marital drama, and the blunder I'd made with the hundred-thousand-dollar diamond ring. The auto crash was the thing that topped it all off.

We loaded plates with salad and bread and found a table. I stared out at my rental car in the parking lot. With the daily meter ticking, the decision about new wheels wasn't something I should delay. I pulled out my phone and browsed the subject of cars. The problem was I didn't even know what make or model interested me, and trying to make decisions based on the tiny images on a phone screen wasn't making the task easier.

"A few more days with the rental isn't going to matter," Drake said, reading my mind. "Take your time. Um, as long as you deliver me back home to get my truck. I do need to get back to my business at some point today."

Ron had texted me twice, and I knew I needed to get back to RJP business as well. We finished our meal and headed home. Drake gave me a kiss and got into his truck. I headed for the front door, planning to retrieve Freckles from her crate and take her to the office with me. We were headed back to the white sedan when the blue Corvette coasted to a stop at our curb.

"Hey, where's your Jeep?" Clover asked.

I explained the situation. She eyed the plain little car with sympathy.

"Bummer."

"Yeah, and the worst part is deciding what to replace my Jeep with."

She bit at her lower lip, thinking. "You could drive Zayne's car," she said.

I looked up the street at the red convertible in their driveway. A flutter resembling excitement went through me.

"Aw, I really can't take it …"

"I'll let you. Um, I mean, her being back at school now, you know."

I *didn't* know. I had to give her credit for sticking with her story though.

"It's just ... I'm not sure about the fallout. You know, what if she comes back and is furious? Or what if your parents blow a gasket over your giving permission for something they didn't agree to?" And yet, the lure of that gorgeous car tugged at me.

"Call 'em. Except they're off somewhere crazy right now." She said it so simply, confident it would be no problem at all to loan an expensive car to a neighbor who'd just wrecked her own.

Still ... no one on earth could say the 'Vette wasn't at least a hundred points higher on the coolness scale than the boring little sedan in my driveway.

"I'll call your Aunt Donna. If she says it's okay, I'll consider it."

Drake would say I was stretching toward a midlife crisis. Ron would be so envious he would turn purple. My own practical streak told me there was no way to follow or surveil anyone on any of our cases. But the latent kid in me said *yes! Go for it!*

Clover sat there at the curb, looking at me. She meant now. I pulled out my phone where I'd stored Donna Delaney's phone number. I'd no sooner said hello than Clover held out her hand, wiggling her fingers. I handed the phone over.

"Aunt Donna—hey. Charlie needs to borrow Zayne's car for awhile but she's embarrassed to ask, so is it okay? It is, right?"

I grabbed the phone away.

"Donna, hi. Look, this wasn't my idea but it would be a big help. I'm paying for a rental but I still need a few days to get something new lined up for myself."

"Charlie, you didn't really even need to ask. I know both girls think highly of you, and those are their cars, not mine. Take it if you need it."

"Wow. I—well, this is so generous of you."

"Not me. The girls. Really, it's fine." She paused a second. "I know you can't really talk with Clover right there, but do let me know sometime how you're coming along with locating Zayne. Okay?"

I wished I had better news for her, but promised another call in a day or two. Now the pressure was *really* on.

Clover had picked up the gist of the call, put her car in reverse and hit the gas. It whined its way back home, and I trotted up the street to catch up.

"So, I'll grab the key," Clover called out, halfway to their front door when I walked up the drive.

She popped back outside a few seconds later and we spent a few minutes together while she gave me some tips and tricks to know about the car. I slipped into the driver's seat and breathed deeply. I wouldn't say it had the new-car smell—after all, a teenager had driven it for a year or two already—but it was *way* new compared to mine. Once again, it hit me how unlikely it was that Zayne had gone away to school without taking this baby along.

Clover seemed distracted. She hopped back in her car and waved goodbye while I sat in the purring sports car.

Wow. Okay. Things had taken a turn and I needed to think of practical considerations, such as turning in the rental and getting to the office, but the lure of simply putting my foot to the gas pedal tugged at me. I carefully backed it out of the Delaney driveway, getting used to the different configuration of blind spots, put her in gear and cruised to my own house.

Ten minutes later, with Freckles perched on the

passenger seat, I roared into my parking slot at the Victorian in fine style.

The whole point of driving a car like this is for people to see you in it, and that urge was met with gratification for me when Ron opened the kitchen door and openly gawked. I clambered out of the low-slung car a little awkwardly. It was a whole different set of moves from merely sliding off the seat of my higher-riding Jeep.

"What's this?" he asked.

"It's on loan." Drake had already given him the highlights about the crash, my night in the hotel and my subsequent day of rest.

Ron gave the car a skeptical sizing-up.

"I know, I know. How many times have you told me a red sports car wasn't your best choice either," I said with a pointed glance at his Mustang. "I'm not keeping this car."

"It is very cool though."

"It's *very* cool."

We both stared at the car while Freckles made her rounds of the back yard. I supposed I *could* consider a sports car of some kind. Maybe not quite this flashy, maybe a more subdued color ... Well, it was a decision I didn't have to make this minute.

We walked through the kitchen, where Ron picked up the mug he'd been filling when I drove up. I went up to my office and he joined me a few seconds later.

"So, the week has been eventful," he said, settling onto my sofa while I turned on my computer.

"I don't hold much hope that the police in El Paso will put a lot of effort into catching Jay Livingston and getting Bobby's ring back."

I described the cramped office and lone detective who'd taken the report, ending with the fact I had no intention of traipsing back and forth on that long stretch of highway again.

"Couldn't Bobby just file an insurance claim for the ring being stolen, show them the cheap substitute he got in return?"

"If he carried a rider on his policy for jewelry of that value, sure, I suppose he could."

"If he's not too embarrassed for the story to spread that much further …"

"Yeah, that too."

"You think he'd do that?"

"Who knows? Right now he wants me to keep working on it. While you were away, he and Marcie started to make up. He went back home last night."

I felt a groan rise in my throat. Those two were a pair, all right.

"So, can we drop the case? That's my question."

"I'm meeting with Bobby later today and I'll tell him. I need to fill him in on my visit to that pawnshop guy, which is to say I basically didn't learn anything, but I did convince him to get his attorney to settle out of court for the punching incident."

"Yeah, well, have fun with that. I am *so* done with both the Lorrentos. I think they deserve each other *and* whatever happens to their fame and possessions."

Ron grinned and headed toward his own office. I could only hope he agreed with me.

Chapter 35

Hopeful I'd seen the last of the battling Lorrentos, I turned my attention back to our other case, figuring out how I was going to verify both Delaney twins were all right and get a picture for their aunt. Even this morning, Clover was sticking with the story that Zayne was living in Las Cruces, although I smelled deceit all over the tale.

Somehow, I needed enough proof to confront her and get the real skinny on it. I leaned back in my chair and thought about the reasons an otherwise gregarious young woman would choose to disappear.

A man.

I don't know why it hadn't occurred to me before. The most likely reason Zayne wasn't around was because she'd run off with some guy. In another era, if she'd become pregnant she might have been sent off to a home for unwed mothers and returned a few months later. But times had changed and I couldn't see such a scenario now.

Still, there were other reasons people moved away. The guy promised exotic travel, or he lived in another city, or there was some reason she needed to keep the relationship secret. I could see the desire for secrecy if this was someone her family didn't approve of, but Rick and Jane were hardly around and they certainly didn't appear to have set any limits on their two daughters.

The other puzzle I kept asking myself: how much does Clover know? Surely she was in on the secret. It didn't seem logical her twin would have gone away without a word, not to mention Clover's lack of worry and the cover story about Zayne being away at school. No, she was in on it.

My challenge was to get close enough and find the opportunity to get her to talk about it.

How would I do that? I drummed my fingers on the desk. Maybe Clover had inadvertently handed me the answer: social media.

I opened my browser and went to Facebook. Over the past few years, several friends had suggested I set up accounts, including Twitter and Instagram. I'd done it, friended a few people, and discovered I either needed to monitor it constantly to keep up with the crowd, or I had to forget about it. Life being busy enough already, I did the latter. Now, my social media skills were severely lacking.

I found the little cheat-sheet where I'd written all my passwords and logged into my Facebook account. A few dozen comments awaited my viewing, but I discovered most were hopelessly outdated tidbits from friends who had, no doubt, given up on hearing from me. A few friend requests waited to be accepted or denied. Deleting the obvious scams from handsome soldiers in military uniform, men I'd never seen in my life, I noticed two of the requests came from Clover and Zayne. I accepted both.

Clover's page contained the photos from our hike and picnic. She was right—the one of me and Freckles touching noses had received a lot of likes, along with comments like "Awwwwww, how cute!!!!!" Apparently, drawn-out words and loads of punctuation were the way to bring extra emotion to short and simple messages. At any rate, I found myself a little flattered by the attention.

On her timeline, a day after the picnic with me, Clover had posted a charming heads-together shot of herself and Zayne dressed up and maxed out on their makeup. The caption read: Checking out RADZ! Best time ever!!!!

I recognized the name of the club that had opened a year or so ago to lots of media attention. Apparently, it had caught on with the younger crowd. It might be worth a trip if I could spot the two girls together, and if not, perhaps I could get a conversation going with their friends and learn more. I could mention it to Drake and see if my dear hubby was up for a night out on the town.

Then I quickly discarded the idea. Not only was nightclub life not at all his thing, the two of us would stand out just as badly as someone Clover's age walking into a retirement home. With the touches of gray in his hair, Drake would most likely be taken for law enforcement. If the kids smelled a narc they'd scatter like roaches in the light.

It would be better if I walked into the club with a girlfriend. Who did I know with the playfulness, not to mention the clothes to dress us up properly? I needed a pal who would inspire me beyond my preferred stay-home-with-a-book demeanor. The Facebook page was still open and I scanned the photos of my friends. Geez, we were becoming a dull crowd. Linda was a doctor with such a busy practice she rarely stayed up past ten o'clock. Sally was younger but had a husband and two kids. With the toddler, she was barely awake most days, much less into the evening hours.

Victoria. My sister-in-law has sparkle and energy. She's a classy dresser, but she knows fashion well enough to young-it-down a bit. She'd be the one to come up with something we could wear. I called her.

"I'm tied up with something tonight," she said. "Could we make it tomorrow night?"

"Sure." An extra twenty-four hours to work up my courage would be a good thing, right?

I put the phone down and went back to the computer. Zayne Delaney's Facebook page showed a half-dozen selfies. Prominent in the recent ones were posts about how she was loving college life. Interesting.

I scrolled to one that read "In dorm room with BFF Missy." It was the girl I'd spoken to briefly outside her dorm at UNM, the one who'd gone to the river party, supposedly with Zayne, although I hadn't known how to positively identify her at the time. Okay, if Missy attended school here in Albuquerque, how was it going to fool anyone to imply she was now down in Las Cruces at New Mexico State? The background behind the two girls certainly did look like a dorm room. I could see scattered clothing and the general clutter that defines living quarters of kids all over the world.

Another post, dated two weeks ago, showed Zayne wearing a studious-looking pair of glasses which reflected the glare of a computer screen. "Late night studies," said the post. The girl's surroundings showed muted colors in a dim room. I clicked the photo and it came up larger on my screen. The blue and tan color scheme seemed familiar but I couldn't immediately think where I'd seen it.

I read the comments her friends had made, commiseration over the tough schedule and encouraging little prods like "Don't work TOO hard. Hahaha!!!"

I zoomed the picture, trying to spot Zayne's tattoo, but in each photo she wore her hair in front of her ears, concealing her neck. I scrolled back over her timeline, looking for some indication when she'd left for college or wherever it was she'd gone. Prior to last October, nearly all the photos on both of the twins' pages showed the two together. Since then there were a lot more of each girl individually. Something felt different about the things they talked about. Something just a touch *off*. But what? I couldn't, for the life of me, figure it out.

I spent another hour zipping around Twitter and Instagram, looking for activity by either Zayne or Clover Delaney. There was plenty, and pretty soon the whole scene began to blur in my brain. The frequency of posts, both with the girls I knew and with their many friends, was mind boggling. A lot of importance was placed on receiving approval—Likes, and little smiley faces, hearts, flowers, the occasional sad-face or frown.

Observing them closely, there were undercurrents of the sort I remembered from the horrible, hormonal middle-school years. I thought of the importance these kids placed on social media 'likes.' From an adult perspective, it seemed so needy and desperate but I was young enough to remember the pressures.

It really seemed doubly needy when I considered these were no longer thirteen- and fourteen-year-olds but grown young women. Sad to know so much importance rested on popularity.

My shoulder ached from steering the mouse and my neck was screaming in protest. I needed to move. I wandered across the hall to Ron's office but his chair sat empty. He may have told me he was going out—I didn't remember. Scary to think how absorbed I'd become in the social media world, and how quickly.

I glanced at his desk and saw his computer monitor still lit. Okay, so he couldn't have gone too far or for too long. The image on the screen caught my attention. Apparently, it was the home page of Innocent Times, the alibi company Bobby Lorrento had been using to help cover his tracks during his little cheating escapades.

An idea leapt into my head. I sat in Ron's chair and put my hand on the computer mouse. Clicking the About Us tab on the page, I found a phone number and an email address. At the bottom of the page was the required tagline with the site owner's company name and address. I found a pad of sticky notes and a pen and wrote it all down.

Chapter 36

I frightened Ron into sloshing his coffee when I left his office as he was coming up the stairs.

"You need me for something?" he asked, checking the front of his shirt.

"Nah. Just stretching my legs."

I hurried back to my desk where I placed a call to Innocent Times and requested an appointment with Rex Stoddard. I may have given the impression I was interested in their services. I may have also given the impression I was important enough only to deal directly with the company owner. It could have been because I threw the name Bobby Lorrento into the conversation in a way that was not entirely truthful.

Ten minutes later, I was out the door and heading toward the uptown area that tends to house brokerage firms and insurance offices. Innocent Times was located in an unprestigious suite of offices on a third floor where I imagined—if they'd had windows—the view would consist of some treetops and the windows of the building next door. I supposed it was the sort of business that didn't need to impress its clients with a lot of frills. The inner-sanctum look was more in keeping with their mission, anyway.

Rex Stoddard greeted me in his office with the word Private on the door. I supposed it was to differentiate it from the other two doors beyond the tiny reception area, one of which I suspected might be a restroom. Somehow, I had pictured the operation being a whole lot bigger. It could be my name-dropping had nothing to do with getting an appointment with the owner.

Stoddard was about forty, with a round body, round face and receding sandy brown hair. Somehow, I'd pictured a guy who would start a company to cover up infidelities would be the sort who had needed those services himself. Sitting across from the geeky guy here, I wasn't getting a match to that image.

"I know what you're thinking," he said. "This guy couldn't possibly juggle multiple women because he'd never have more than one date at a time. Right?"

I felt a blush coming on. He'd pretty well nailed it.

"But don't you see? I was *the guy* in high school and college—the one all the other guys used as their alibi. 'Honey, don't worry about it. I was studying with Rex. Honey, Rex and I only went out for a couple beers.' They'd buy me a six-pack if I would come up with a receipt showing two beers purchased at some innocent enough spot like Applebee's. I got where I could finesse those receipts to show the exact day and time the friend wanted. I mean, those little slips of paper looked so real the restaurant employees couldn't tell they were fake. "

Okay, call me impressed.

"Pretty soon my buddies were sending their other buddies … I quit swapping the favor for beer, and it was amazing how much cash these men were willing to come up with, especially once we all reached the age where they were starting to have wives. I branched out to include receipts from airlines and hotels, little backup materials a guy could leave lying around when he said he'd been away on a business trip. There I was, going for a degree in accounting and making four times more with my alibis than I would ever bring in as a CPA. I dropped out and turned my little venture into a business."

"You didn't feel guilty about all this?"

"Hey, I wasn't the one doing the cheating or telling the lies. All that's on them."

I supposed he had a point about that. I also wondered how much money he was really making. He certainly wasn't working out of glamourous digs here.

"Yeah, I know," Stoddard said. "You'd think I would be in the penthouse suite of offices, right?"

I really needed to work on my poker face. This guy was *too* good at reading my mind.

"I don't waste money on non-essentials. My clients don't pay for me to have an office with a fabulous view. These days, most of 'em never even come here or meet me face-to-face. Low-key is the thing. I've got a staff of four, a stock portfolio in the millions, and three homes on two continents. It's all I need."

Sounded like plenty, to me.

"So, what can I do for you? You don't really look like the typical cheating wife." A glance at my wedding band. "If you want an admission from me that your husband is one of our clients, sorry. No way you'll get that info from me."

I actually laughed. Drake and I worked together so much and shared all our financial information. Neither of us could possibly fit a sneaky affair into our days, much less cover it up. I handed him my RJP business card and explained I was here about the *how*, not the *who*.

"I'm looking into a case of twins, thinking one of them is covering up for the other, but I haven't exactly figured out how she's doing it."

"Twins—nice. Identical?"

I nodded.

"Oh, man, they've got it easy."

I told him about the social media pages and the selfies. "I'm thinking one girl could be posting for both of them. With the log-on information for both accounts, I suppose even I could manage that much."

"Yeah, easy peasy."

"The one girl claims to be away at college but the photos on her page look to me as if they could be locations here in Albuquerque. Is there any way I can find out where she was when she put the pictures up on Facebook?"

He nodded slowly, contemplating. He picked up the handset of his desk telephone and punched a button. "Buddy—in my office for a minute?"

He replaced the phone and looked at me again. "I started old-school and my specialty still is printed documents. Buddy handles all that tech stuff."

I heard one of the other doors open and close and a

moment later a young man appeared. He didn't look more than fifteen but I supposed he could be in his mid-twenties. Guessing ages is getting increasingly difficult these days. He had longish, curly brown hair and wore jeans and a vintage rock band shirt with Tour 2006 above the group's photo.

"Yeah, boss?"

"Buddy, this is Charlie. Charlie, Buddy Blue." Buddy leaned against the doorframe, not offering to shake hands, acknowledging me with only a nod.

I asked whether it was possible to find out where a particular text message or social media post came from.

"I could do it," Buddy said.

"Is it possible for someone to fake their location? Say, a person here in Albuquerque make it look as if they were in Las Cruces when they posted."

"Is either of these girls super tech savvy?"

I thought of Zayne in her platform shoes, fitted jeans and designer bags. Clover was somewhat outdoorsy but still dressed and acted like the fashion diva rich kid she was.

"I doubt it," I told him.

"She'd have to know a bit about advanced forward link trilateration timing, if she can get into the network. Or there's always a way of interpolating antenna signals …"

He pretty much lost me after the word *advanced*. I got another idea.

"If I could bring you one of their phones—could you get the information?" I hated to use the word *hack*, but that's what it amounted to.

"Sure." He backtracked a little. "Depends on how far they went to cover up, you know. But, talking about your average college kid, yeah I can probably do it."

He went back to his lair and I talked price with Stoddard. The figure was a little shocking but I knew we were going to pass it along to the Delaneys, and any parents who didn't keep better tabs on their kids deserved what they got when it came to the cost of tracking them down.

Back in the parking lot, I climbed into the red Corvette and listened to the soft roar of its engine as I put her in gear and zoomed out of the parking lot. I wondered if I wasn't getting a little *too* accustomed to driving the fun machine.

Chapter 37

Back at the office, I'd started upstairs when I heard voices from the conference room. One was definitely Ron's. The other was female. I peered around the corner and saw the back of Marcie Lorrento. What on earth did *she* want?

I shamelessly edged over to the wall beside the doorway and eavesdropped. With Sally gone for the afternoon, Ron hadn't thought to close the door. How convenient.

"... just that I'm concerned about him," Marcie was saying.

"I know." Ron has developed this soft-and-gentle method with the clients. "You do realize that Jay Livingston cheated you and Bobby out of a lot of money?"

I'm standing there thinking, *and wasn't actually ever interested in a relationship with you.*

"Some police detective from El Paso called me," Marcie said. She sniffed a little and her voice broke. "I didn't quite understand why they're after Jay."

"Let me spell it out. Jay bought Bobby's Super Bowl ring at the pawnshop. He put the word out the ring was for sale—he's not a collector. He had a cheaper substitute ring ready, which he sold back to us, using your money, pretending the ring was Bobby's. Now he's in possession of the cash *and* the real ring. It's enough money to classify as grand theft, and that's what the police are interested in."

"But—"

"Picture it like this: You go to a shop and see a pair of Manolo Blahniks that you know are real. You love them. You buy them at full price. You get home and open the box to find the clerk substituted a different pair. They look similar but you and all your friends will immediately know they're fake. It's kind of like that."

I stepped into view. "Let's not forget the elaborate scam he set up to make me believe he lived in an upscale neighborhood, and the pains I took to try to recover your money." For emphasis I touched the big bruise on my cheek, although Livingston couldn't directly be blamed for my vehicle accident.

Marcie blanched a little when she saw my injuries. "Oh, gosh."

Ron intervened again. "Marcie, we'll continue to cooperate with the police and attempt to recover the ring, but I'm not going to track down Jay Livingston for you. You need to sort out your own marital woes. If I can offer a little advice? Get yourself straight about what you want with Bobby—stay with him or leave him, I don't care—but don't bring another man into the picture unless you are completely out of your marriage. There are way too many pitfalls, and you've only discovered one of them, being swindled by a crook."

I gave a little amen to that. By the expression on her face, I had little hope she would take Ron's advice to heart. This whole messed-up relationship could still go any which way.

Ron pulled Marcie's chair out for her. I held up her purse. Yes, it was a not-too-subtle effort to simply get her out of our offices. We watched from the front window as she got into her car and drove away.

"Is it true?" I asked. "You plan to work with the El Paso police on this thing?"

"They haven't asked for my input," he told me. "If they do, I'll give whatever info I can."

"It might be worth a call, just a follow-up to see if they've found Livingston yet."

He gave me a long-suffering stare. "You can if you want to. I only told Marcie what I did to get her out of here."

It wasn't like my brother to get rid of a client. As long as they were willing to pay us to do something, anything at all, he would normally stick with them. Looked as if even Ron was tiring of the power couple and their antics.

"How's your search for a car coming along?" he asked as we climbed the stairs to our offices.

"I'm liking the borrowed Corvette, for now."

"Don't get too used to it."

"I know. I know."

I got to my desk to find Sally had left me a note saying Donna Delaney had called. She might have changed her mind about my use of Zayne's car, and maybe Ron's suggestion was a little prophetic. I called Donna's number, got voicemail and left a quick message, then I went online for a little research on what vehicle I should consider buying.

Sports cars were appealing, especially given my newfound infatuation with zipping around town in the borrowed one. But, in reality, a two-seater wasn't at all practical for two of us and the dog to pack up for a weekend in the mountains. I gazed fondly at a few models on my computer screen then switched my search toward vehicles with a bit of roomy cargo space. Before I could get to the research data on safety and reliability (and, yes, I'm a little obsessive on that stuff), my phone rang. I saw Donna Delaney's name on the readout.

"Hi, Charlie, glad you called. Just thought I'd check in."

"Afraid I have nothing new. I'm working on an angle that might tell us more about the social media posts the girls are doing. So far, Clover seems to be in her normal routine around home and I haven't had a call from Zayne ordering me to give her car back."

"Keep it as long as you need it. If she can't touch base any more frequently than this, well, she can just wait for the car."

"I'll get together with Clover again soon. With my own car out of commission, I've been scrambling a bit to wind up another case and spend more time on yours. I will—I promise."

She was nice about it, but I couldn't help feeling I should be doing more. The twins weren't children, but their youth, money and good looks certainly put them in a vulnerable position. Again, I told myself to let Ron handle the Lorrento mess so I could devote more time to this.

Sidetracked by Marcie, my online search for a car and now this phone call, I did a quick refocus. I was missing some important clue in the Delaney case. I felt sure of it. But what? I had to figure that out.

Chapter 38

I called Clover's cell phone but it went immediately to voicemail. Knowing how readily she usually dropped everything for a new phone call, I wondered if she was dodging me. I decided not to get paranoid about it and shut down my computer in readiness to leave for the day.

A truck from A-1 Landscape Service was the only vehicle in evidence at the Delaney house. I recognized Tommy, the guy who cares for several neighborhood lawns, and waved up the street at him. He waved back but didn't miss a beat with his noisy edger machine.

Freckles was a little miffed at being left home all day. I let her out of the crate and she followed me to the kitchen for a cookie. Eyeing the gazebo out back, I was tempted to make myself a lemonade and do nothing for the rest of the afternoon but kick back until Drake came home. However, seeing as there'd been no shortage of fast food in my life recently, it would be smarter to get some exercise. I clipped the dog's leash to her collar and we headed toward the park.

As I tossed a tennis ball about a hundred times and watched my little sweetie race to bring it back, I thought of my earlier conversation with Buddy Blue at Innocent Times. He'd said he might be able to answer my question about the location of the calls and social media posts if I could bring him the phone they'd been posted from. Once again, I chastised myself for not grabbing Zayne's phone that night I'd had the chance. It was beginning to look as if I would have to come right out and ask to borrow it, and I could come up with no logical reason for that.

As before, I wished this whole thing could be as simple as walking up to their house, finding both girls home at the same time, and snapping the photo I needed. It wasn't going to happen. I knew it. This was a silly fantasy.

I informed Freckles she'd done enough fetching. You'd think a dog would figure this out when her tongue hung out and her feet began to drag. We leashed up and headed back toward home.

The landscaper's truck was gone when I sighted the Delaney house. For one brief moment I toyed with the idea of sneaking around back to see if my former route into their house was still available, but it was broad daylight now. I figured I'd better not push my luck.

I realized, belatedly, that I really ought to tell Clover about the easy access. She was there alone a lot of the time, and the unlocked doors invited danger. On the other hand, I couldn't very well admit I knew about the two unlocked doors; I'd had no business in their backyard in the first place. Next time I was legitimately in the house I would saunter through the kitchen and simply lock the connecting door myself. Sheesh—what a tangled web I'd woven.

All those thoughts flashed through my head in an instant, and by the time we were adjacent with the house Clover came roaring up the street in her blue 'Vette. With a squeak of tires on concrete, she stopped inches from their garage door. She got out of the car and slammed the door. Her eyes looked red, her face blotchy.

"Clover? Everything okay?" I called out.

She halted in surprise, as if anyone wouldn't have noticed her dramatic return.

Freckles spotted the girl and tugged urgently at her leash. I let go of it and watched her race toward Clover while I crossed the lawn at a more leisurely pace. The energetic dog wiggled her whole body, hoping for a smile.

"Sorry. I didn't mean to let her rush you like that," I said. "You seemed upset just now."

Clover gripped her car keys so hard I thought she would draw blood. She ignored the eager pup and turned toward her front door. We'd not been invited but Freckles and I followed anyway.

"Is it about Zayne?" I asked.

The wings of her long hair concealed her face as she took her time going through the four keys on her key ring. From the depths of her oversized purse, I heard her phone ding with an incoming text message. She ignored it and settled on a key for the front door. When she looked up, her eyes were moist.

"Damn Ryan," she said through gritted teeth. She seemed to realize I was waiting for an answer to my question. "It's fine. Everything's fine."

"You don't look fine," I said. "Hey, how about coming over to our house for awhile? I've got lemonade and it's a nice afternoon to sit out back." I realized how *Elsa* the invitation sounded.

Her phone chimed again and she sniffed. "That's okay. I've got ..."

The words trailed off and she waved vaguely.

Not to be ignored, Freckles danced around both of us. When Clover unlocked her front door, the dog nosed it open and dashed inside.

"Freckles!" I stomped madly at the trailing leash, trying to halt the dog, but she was way ahead of me.

Clover stood aside, a little dazed, and I rushed to catch up with my dog, who had already discovered a bag of chips on the living room coffee table. She managed to tip it off the table and had crunched down a bunch of them before I could get my hands on her collar.

"Oh my gosh, I'm so sorry," I said.

When I looked up, I saw Clover was smiling.

"Sorry." I picked up the bag and held it high above my head. Freckles stared wistfully, completely oblivious as to why I was upset with her.

At least the incident had diffused Clover's anger. She reached out to the dog and began ruffling her fur while I carried the near-empty bag to the kitchen.

"It's not like I was going to eat the rest of it anyway," she said with a sad note to her voice.

When I came back, she had dropped her large purse on the sofa and a few items spilled out, including two cell phones. One of them chimed again and the screen lit up. Little banners showed the two messages from the past few minutes.

"Sorry," she said, "I need to get that."

She let go of Freckles and scooped up the phone,

turning toward her bedroom. There I stood, looking at the phone in the bright pink case, the one I'd been wishing I had *borrowed* the last time I spotted it. Clover was out of sight. The phone sat right there, in easy reach.

Yeah, I'll admit it. I went for the easy grab. In a half-second, the phone was in my back pocket. For good measure, I tipped her purse a little farther, scattering a few more items onto the sofa so the missing item wouldn't be so obvious.

"I'll catch you another time, Clover," I called out from the front door. "Maybe we can do something later in the week."

She appeared at the bedroom door down the hall. "Yeah, sure."

I kept facing her so she wouldn't see my pocket, but her attention was riveted on her text messages. Freckles didn't quite understand why I was so eager to leave all the enticing scents she had discovered in the kitchen trash, but I was insistent with her.

A couple minutes later, in the privacy of my own home, I pulled out the card from Innocent Times and dialed their tech guy, Buddy Blue.

Chapter 39

Buddy suggested we meet at five-thirty at Rubio's, which I gathered was his favorite after-work watering hole. It was convenient for him, not so much for me, as I would be driving across town in rush-hour traffic. I budgeted some extra time and was ready to head out the door when Drake pulled into the driveway.

"Hey you," he said, pulling me close for a kiss when I opened the front door for him. "I've got some exciting news."

"Is it quick news? I'm suppose to be meeting a tech guy in forty minutes." I glanced at my watch. "Unless you want to come along and talk while I drive?"

He pointed to his flight suit, which was a little grungy at the knees. He'd obviously been assisting with maintenance.

"I'll make it quick, then fill in the rest when you get

back. I've got more details about that little cabin. It's been tied up in an old woman's estate and no one has been up there in more than twenty years. I think we can get it."

I hadn't said anything, but I'd found myself thinking more and more about the little mountain place in recent days. My auto accident hadn't been serious, but it got me thinking about the risks of everyday life and the missed opportunities Drake and I had when I was out chasing down bad guys. Finding a place to truly get away from reality for awhile seemed like heaven. I told him where I was going and he said he would have dinner ready when I returned.

Rubio's is one of those places that had a huge heyday about twenty years ago. Big hit when it opened, always crowded, it boasted great steak dinners and a bar where Albuquerque's business crowd hung out. The allure lasted a good five years—almost a record for this town—until the next new dazzler opened and the crowd drifted six blocks up the street.

For the past ten years or so, Rubio's has held on by its teeth, supported by guys like Buddy Blue who come by for a beer after work and rarely stay through the dinner hour. The menu has scaled way back, with the big sellers these days being nachos and chicken wings.

Buddy sat at a roomy booth with a mini laptop open on the table. I sat across from him and handed over the phone I'd swiped from Clover's bag. I'd already asked him what he would charge to hack the account and he said it depended on how long it took. He made a couple of little um-hm noises, which didn't tell me a whole lot, then pulled out a cord and plugged the phone into his computer. Quicker than it takes to tell about it, he unplugged it and handed the phone back to me.

"That's it?"

"Just the beginning. I have the phone's data—it's registered to a Zayne Delaney. Now I have to search through it. What was it you wanted to know, exactly?"

"Text messages, social media posts and phone calls from the past couple months—were they made from here in town or somewhere else? If elsewhere, I'd love to know where."

He tapped keys and scowled at his screen. Maybe I should tell him if he keeps that up he'll have permanently deep eyebrow wrinkles by the time he's thirty.

"Okay … let's see …" His finger zipped around over the touchpad. "Phone calls were definitely made locally. Did you look at this before you brought it? More than half these were made to a number registered to Clover Delaney. There's a few international. I think the country code is for Egypt? Not positive about that."

The parents. Donna had said Rick and Jane were on location in the desert somewhere.

"Are there incoming calls from Egypt, too?"

"Yep. Sure are."

I noticed his beer was empty, asked if he'd like another, and flagged down the server to bring it, along with a glass of water for myself and some chips and salsa for the table. My tummy told me lunch had been a long time ago and dinner was still a way off.

Buddy reached for his new beer without taking his eyes from the computer screen.

"Text messages … looks like the same thing, although there's a ton more numbers exchanging those. We've got Missy, Ryan, Mom, Delfina, Clover, Jen, Ashley, Connor … You want a list of all the names?"

It seemed that would be a lot of work, but while

I pondered the usefulness of the information to me he continued to tap away.

"Never mind," he said. "It's simpler to copy them all and let you sort it out. What's your email?"

I gave it to him and a moment later heard my phone's familiar alert tone. I tapped the icon and spotted the message from Buddy. Scrolling through, I saw it was a long list. I would check it carefully later. Glancing around the room I noticed couples at other tables, each person in his or her own little world on an electronic device. I wondered if anyone seeing us at a glance would think Buddy and I were a similar couple. I stifled a chuckle and picked up a tortilla chip.

"So, that's it for the simple part," Buddy said, dipping into the salsa for the first time. "How much deeper do you want me to go?"

"What's the cost and what would we learn?"

"I could get into the account and watch it live, in real time. Give you the person's movements and let you know who they're contacting. We can even go with text alerts to you if we see anything unusual. Rex bills my time at two hundred an hour."

I gulped—it was quite a bit more than we were charging Donna for our time; I'd already sat here more than a hundred dollars' worth.

"Tonight's not on Rex's clock. Buy me a burger and the beers, and we're good for the little bit I've done here."

"Thanks. I appreciate that. In this case, I pretty much know who's using the phone and I don't think knowing her movements step-by-step will make much difference."

He didn't seem especially disappointed. I got the feeling Innocent Times kept him plenty busy.

"I'd be happy to get you something fancier than a burger," I said. "Name it. Anything on the menu."

"Burger's good. Maybe some extra fries."

I flagged the server again and placed the order, letting Buddy know I needed to head home. I had a good idea what Clover was up to, using Zayne's phone. I still had no idea why the elaborate cover-up.

I puzzled over it as I drove home, and then it hit me. Most likely, Zayne was up to something she wanted to conceal from her parents so she'd left her phone with Clover so the calls to mom and dad would show up coming from her number. She'd probably run off with a guy and got herself a new phone, one they knew nothing about.

Now that I had a logical answer, I wondered how I could go about proving it. Again, the only idea that came to me was to get closer to Clover and hope she would talk to me. Obviously, she was in on the game.

Chapter 40

We sat out under the gazebo, Drake and I, late into the evening, bundled into a warm comforter with mugs of hot chocolate at hand.

"I talked with a young woman named Maria Greenwood," he told me. "Her great-grandparents built the cabin in the 1930s and started a goat farm. Their name was Locke. As Maria recalled, the story was the goat venture didn't succeed and the couple moved to Albuquerque to raise their children. When her husband died in an accident on the highway road crew where he worked, Sarah Locke became a writer. She moved to the cabin full time once her two daughters were grown, and she lived there into her nineties. When she died, the estate was sort of a mess. The next generation was aging and no one wanted the place. Maria said she'd only been there a few times as a child and couldn't even remember how they got there except it involved an extremely long walk."

"I wonder how such an elderly woman could manage."

"I asked the same question. Maria said Sarah kept a horse and would load her groceries and such into saddle bags."

"Wow—I can't imagine." Here I'd been buzzing all over the city in a speedy sports car. We take so many things for granted in modern life. "Earlier, you said you thought they would sell the place?"

"Maria is checking with the remaining heirs. Apparently, not thinking of the repercussions, Sarah left this, her only remaining property, to all her heirs, to be divided equally. It gave each of them such a pittance no one took charge. In the meantime, Sarah's daughters have passed on and the next generation consists of Maria's mother and an uncle who lives in Texas. Maria said she couldn't see any reason they wouldn't sell. We're apparently the only people who've expressed an interest in the place in decades."

I snuggled beside him, my thoughts vivid with images of an old woman living in the tiny cabin, writing her books and rarely going to town. I wondered how I would be in my senior years and found there was something immensely appealing about the pictures of Sarah Locke living independently, away from civilization. Next thing I knew, Drake was lifting my empty mug from my hands and suggesting we go to bed.

I dreamed of the little cabin in the mountains but, in the weird way of dreamland, it now had three bedrooms, a hot tub and a backyard pool. I woke with a start and wondered at the strangeness of the human psyche.

The sun was well above the top of Sandia Crest when

I walked out to the driveway and got into my borrowed Corvette. I really did need to get serious about vehicle shopping so I wouldn't be responsible for this expensive toy much longer. I'd started the engine when I looked up to see Elsa coming across my lawn. I shut down again and stood beside the car.

"Hey, I've been meaning to ask you how things are going?" she said in greeting.

My brain zipped backward through recent thoughts—new car, mountain cabin ... but I knew she meant the Delaney twins.

"I still don't know anything for certain, but we're getting closer." I didn't think it was a great idea to admit I'd taken Zayne's phone and had a professional hacking job done on it. "The girls seem to be in touch with each other and with their parents, so I'm sure everything's okay."

There was no point in going into the details of everything I'd learned. I thought I could trust Elsa's discretion, but what if she blurted out something when she got together with her card ladies? Better to be vague at this point.

I gave her a hug and got back into the car. Traffic was picking up by the time I reached the office. I was the first to arrive so I started the coffee maker and switched on lights as I walked through the rooms. I checked voicemail where a call from an insurance adjuster waited for me.

She told me the dollar amount they were paying for my totaled Jeep and asked me to come by their office to sign a release and collect my check. I blew out a breath. It wasn't nearly enough to buy a new one.

Ron came in the kitchen door just then, interrupting my moody reflections. I joined him at the coffee machine.

"How's things?" he asked in such a chipper voice I

knew it probably meant he and Victoria had great early-morning sex.

I filled him in on what I'd learned from Buddy Blue. "Clover Delaney is obviously a part of whatever her sister is hiding. Maybe if I spend a little more time with her I can get her to open up and tell me about it."

He dumped two heaping spoonsful of sugar into his coffee and gave it a stir.

"What about your case? Any word on Bobby Lorrento's ring?"

"I called the detective in El Paso late yesterday. He didn't have much for me. Said he would call if there was progress."

I suppressed a wave of impatience. Two cases. Vague clues but no answers. Last night's conversation with Drake about the cabin had turned my thoughts toward our plans and future, and that's where I wanted to go right now, not traipsing about in circles that involved the problems of spoiled rich people. I carried my coffee and the message sheet where I'd written the insurance lady's name to my office.

Ron's head appeared at my doorway. "Meant to tell you—Vic says she has to cancel tonight. We've unexpectedly got the boys for a couple days."

I'd nearly forgotten our impromptu plan to go to Radz nightclub. Oh well. I most likely wouldn't have learned anything new about the Delaney girls, anyway.

"That's fine," I said. "I wasn't much up for it any more."

Back to the insurance lady. I phoned her and we made an appointment in an hour's time. She said I would need to bring the title to my Jeep, which meant a dash back home to get the document from the safe.

I turned into the neighborhood right behind the blue

Corvette and followed Clover to our street. As I began to pull into my driveway, I noticed her movements became erratic so I parked the red 'Vette and walked over. Her car sat at a skewed angle in their driveway and Clover was leaning out the open door as if she couldn't work up the energy to stand up.

I rushed up to her side. "Clover, what's wrong?"

She looked up at me with bleary eyes.

"Sweetie, it's nine in the morning. Are you drunk?"

"Prob'ly."

I extended a hand to help her out of the low car seat.

"Come on, let's get you inside so you can sleep it off."

"I slept already," she insisted. "Think I passed out at the party. Missy went off with some guy from a frat house."

It was so hard not to deliver a lecture, but she wasn't my kid. I took her hand and she got to her feet. She fumbled for her keys, which she'd forgotten to take out of the ignition. When she stood up and faced me, I was shocked at how ravaged her face was. She looked ten years older than the last time I'd seen her.

"Clover …"

"I know. I—I hate my life." Her eyes welled up and tears spilled down her cheeks.

"I know, hon. Life is hard at this age." I hated my patronizing tone.

We stumbled toward the front door. I thought of my appointment across town, but I couldn't leave her alone in this state of mind. Who knew what she would do? I took her key and unlocked the door. She tripped over a shoe that had been left in the middle of the living room and flopped onto the big sectional sofa. In thirty seconds she was snoring softly.

Great. Now what?

I took my phone from my purse and called the insurance lady, explaining I'd run into a little snag, and moved our appointment ahead another hour. I eased a small pillow under Clover's head and draped a knitted throw over her. She didn't move a muscle in the thirty minutes I watched her, and I found myself getting antsy to complete my meeting at the insurance company.

Wondering whether Clover would even remember I'd been here, I wrote a note suggesting we have lunch if she was up to it. I propped the note on the coffee table so it would be the first thing she saw when she opened her eyes, locked her front door securely and headed back on my mission.

Chapter 41

The insurance woman had probably never finalized a claim so quickly. I signed what she told me to and collected my check. She started to say she hoped I would insure my next car with her agency, but I was halfway to the door before she got her sales pitch off the ground.

Outside, I got out my phone and checked my bank balance. There was enough in savings to cover the difference, and having the insurance check in hand meant I had no further excuse not to get myself another car. I cruised past the dealerships all crowded together on Lomas but couldn't make myself stop. Clover's state of mind hadn't been good; already I was worried I shouldn't have left her alone.

The late-morning traffic in this part of town wasn't bad, and this time I edged the red 'Vette into the Delaney driveway beside the awkwardly parked blue one. With hands cupped around my face, I peered through the front window. It gave me a limited view across the dining table and into the living room, but I couldn't see the girl on the couch from this angle. I was debating whether to ring the doorbell when I saw movement.

Clover emerged from the hall that led to the bedrooms. The afghan was wrapped around her shoulders and her long hair fell across her face. At least she was upright. I stepped to the door and it opened before I could press the button.

"Hey, Charlie." Her face had a foggy look.

"Hey. You doing okay?"

She nodded but couldn't quite come up with a smile.

"Can I come in?"

"Sure." She pushed the screen door open.

"Sounds like you had a rough night," I said, looking around the room. Nothing had changed.

"So … you *were* here."

"Yeah. You don't remember? You drove yourself home." Scary, scary thought.

"I … yeah, I woke up in my car out in front of one of the fraternity houses on campus. I drove home okay, then it seemed like …" She tucked a strand of hair behind one ear. "Like I just didn't want to think anymore. Thanks for bringing me in."

I wanted to fire questions at her: what potentially lethal combination had she drunk, snorted, swallowed or shot up last night; where was Zayne; what kind of game were the girls playing; why did she tell me she hated her life? But the vulnerability was still there. It would be like firing a gunshot next to a baby deer. She would probably tuck herself into a ball and cower in fright. I took a different tactic.

"Look, I was hoping for some company today," I said. "Drake and I found this little cabin on the east side of the mountain and I wanted to walk up for a closer look. You feel like getting outside a bit?"

It was probably a dumb idea. She looked like she needed about twenty hours sleep followed by a salon makeover.

"Can we get some breakfast on the way?" she asked.

"Absolutely. I know a great place."

She stared down at the short-shorts and tank top she'd been wearing when she came home. "Let me shower and change out of these clothes."

I made two travel mugs using their machine with the plastic cups of specialty coffees, helping myself to supplies in the messy kitchen. Clover emerged twenty minutes later, looking like a new person. She'd pulled her wet hair up with a clip, and her face looked fresh and younger without the heavy eye makeup. Her manner was still subdued, but for someone who'd dragged herself home after an all-night party she was moving amazingly well. I supposed I could have done the same at nineteen. I pulled out the keys to the loaner red sports car. Despite Clover's improved appearance, there was no way I would trust her to drive.

Rush hours were over and the lunch crowd not quite out yet, so traffic was almost sane as we headed east on I-40.

"Where are we going?" she asked, shifting in her seat as we entered Tijeras Canyon.

"There's a little café up here. You can't see it from the freeway but we discovered it a few years ago. The guy makes the best breakfast burrito." I glanced her direction with a smile. "The biscuits and gravy are absolute heaven, too."

She leaned back in her seat and closed her eyes for a moment. "Umm. I bet the last time I had biscuits and gravy was when Mrs. Higgins babysat us as kids."

I had to laugh. The dish was one of Elsa's breakfast specialties. She'd filled my young tummy with it many times. I found the café, which looked smaller and more rustic than I'd remembered. Clover gave it a skeptical eye. The Corvette stood out among the pickup trucks in the small parking lot.

"I really do need to get serious about shopping for a vehicle," I said, once we'd taken seats at a corner table and made our menu choices. "Any ideas?"

"I always liked your Jeep. Get another one." Now, on her second cup of coffee, she'd revived. "If it were me, I'd get the sportier one. Some of the models look like any old sedan. You're a sporty person, Charlie."

"Thanks. Coming from someone your age, that's a high compliment—I think."

She gave me a wan smile, the first since dragging herself out of her car and informing me she hated her life. I wanted to get into the subject, ask the difficult questions, but our food arrived and the moment was lost.

As we dug in, our limited conversation turned to the meal and the fact that Mr. Randel's biscuits really were just a little better than Elsa's. Our neighbor had him beat on the gravy, though. There was something about the way she seasoned hers. By the time we finished eating, Clover's mood lifted and she'd nearly convinced me to run back to town and visit the Jeep dealership.

"My dad is really good friends with the guy. He could get you a good deal on a new one," she offered.

"Except he's in ... some other country right now."

"Well, yeah. I'd talk to him for you, if you want."

"Thanks. I'll think about it. I'm not above doing a little name-dropping if I go there. I'll tell him your dad is my neighbor."

By her smile, I realized she had very few opportunities to help people and she'd enjoyed offering me this one little thing.

"So, ready for a walk up to this spectacular cabin I told you about?"

"I thought you said it was a tiny place."

"Spectacularly tiny? Yeah, it's not much. I want to see if it's as good on a second view as I thought it was the first time."

Clover grabbed the breakfast check, pulling a debit card from her purse to pay. I let her cover the meals and I laid a little cash on the table for the tip. Taking the role of an adult was new to her and she seemed to enjoy it.

Back in the car, we put the top down and let the warm spring air tousle our hair. I felt reassured at Clover's improved disposition. Maybe her comment this morning had been made in the aftermath of a hangover.

We cruised along the eastern side of the Sandia mountains, through the little village of Cedar Crest. I'd printed an aerial view of the cabin and hoped I would spot the turn. We would be driving past the small towns of Golden and Madrid, where I'd spotted Bobby Lorrento that day at the wine festival. At some point after that—about seven miles farther on—there should be a narrow dirt road with a turnout. Maria Greenwood had described her family parking alongside it when they went to visit Grandma Sarah. After that, we would be on foot.

The four-lane road narrowed to two when we passed

the turn to Sandia Peak. A big portion of the traffic always went that way, up to the ski runs in winter, to the picnic areas in summer. It was a winding scenic drive nearly all Albuquerque natives had taken at some point in their lives. I slowed my speed to adapt to the road's width. Clover had become quiet.

"Everything okay?" I asked, hoping she wasn't about to lose her breakfast or something.

She nodded but her face was pale.

"I can stop if you're feeling ill."

She took a deep breath. "No, no. I'm fine." She attempted a smile but it didn't reassure me.

I watched from the corner of my eye as I came up with inane conversation to take her mind off her stomach, taking the curves in the road more slowly. By the time we'd passed through both of the east mountain towns, where she'd declined offers to stop, I supposed she would be all right. I concentrated on finding the landmarks for the turnout I was seeking.

Maria had said there used to be a mailbox on a post, but I was skeptical it would be there all these years later. She'd also remembered a tall pine tree, the only one in an area where most of the vegetation was piñon, sage and cedar. The tree could also be long gone. I intended to rely on Drake's sectional map, together with the aerial photo. We had done some measurements and calculated the path to the cabin began six-point-nine miles from the ballpark at Madrid. I had my eye on the odometer.

We rounded a curve in the road and there it was, the pine tree and the turnout. I passed it a little too fast and had to turn around. When I steered the low sports car onto the dirt edge, I saw a battered old mailbox lying on the ground. Its post was missing, but this had to be the place.

Clover still seemed preoccupied, although she followed willingly enough as I scouted the area until I discovered the old, well-worn path.

"This has to be it," I said.

She nodded and followed as I started out. A dozen yards up the trail, obscured by a thicket of dense chamisa and a big cottonwood tree, stood a small fenced paddock. This must have been where Sarah Locke would leave her horse tied when she went to town for supplies. With a rugged enough vehicle and a little clearing of the current-day brush, it could serve as a parking spot out of sight of the road.

The faint trail led upward, the ground rising steadily a couple hundred feet in elevation, until it disappeared. Clover and I reached the spot and saw it dropped down to a dry arroyo where a narrow stream probably ran only after a decent rain. The path followed the streambed, where vegetation grew thicker. A couple of times I had to push through and look around to see where the worn trail began again.

Maria's estimate of a half mile seemed fairly accurate. We rounded a few turns and soon I could see the cabin's roof beyond the next rise.

"Good thing we wore our hiking boots," I said to Clover when we reached the clearing where Drake had landed the helicopter that first day.

I unzipped my small daypack and pulled out two water bottles, handing one to my companion. "Ready for some of this?"

Clover nodded, but she hadn't said more than a dozen words in the last thirty minutes.

"Let's sit on the steps," I suggested. "You still look kind of pale."

She complied without a word.

"Clover, what's happened? You say you feel all right, but you don't look it."

She stared at her water bottle.

"Did something happen at the party last night?" Another thought occurred to me. "Is it something to do with Zayne?"

She chewed her lower lip a minute. I remained quiet while she put her thoughts together.

"It's Ryan Subro, the jerk. Just because he was popular in school, he acts all entitled. He's started doing the same thing to me."

"What's that?"

"Asking for, um, photos. Last fall, he was doing it with Zayne. She ignored him awhile, him and his friends. They all do it. One night she got really drunk and she sent him one."

I'd been through the photos on Zayne's phone, and I had a feeling I knew which pictures she meant. Several showed parts of her anatomy in ways that would certainly be provocative.

"Once she'd sent the photo, he said she owed him sex. He wanted ..."

I cleared my throat, hoping she wouldn't describe the acts.

"He wanted everything. Problem was, the minute she gave in he started saying she was a slut. All his friends started harassing her—put out or we'll trash you."

I put an arm around her shoulders. "Oh, god, that's awful." No wonder Zayne had decided to get out of town.

"Where did she go?"

Tears dripped from her chin and she shook her head.

"It's okay, sweetie. It's okay."

Chapter 42

I left Clover on the porch to compose herself while I roamed the property and took a few measurements of the cabin. There was still no way to get inside without breaking something, but I got a rough idea of the interior layout by peeking, as well as I could, around the edges of the curtains. There were no surveyor stakes, so it was a wild guess where the property lines were.

By the time I finished my notes and drank the rest of my bottled water, the girl's expression had calmed. She almost smiled when she saw me, but from her earlier breakdown it was clear she wasn't ready discuss her sister's whereabouts.

Conversation on the way home revolved around my decision on a vehicle. I got the name of her father's friend at the Jeep dealership. It couldn't hurt to have a contact. Drake was on a job near Santa Fe today, but he'd be home tonight. If all went well, I might actually have my new Jeep without having to pull his attention away from his business.

I dropped Clover off at her house and headed for the RJP offices. Ron was—no surprise—on the phone. I assumed the conversation was another employment background check.

I logged onto my computer and started to take a serious look at the new Jeeps. The local dealership claimed the best prices in the state and a whole lot of other razzmatazz designed to get a person to click buttons and sign up for news. I just wanted the basics. Clover was right—the Wrangler was definitely a sporty-looking vehicle. The Renegade bridged the gap between sporty and sedate, and it got better mileage. Plus, it came in some very cool colors. This was starting to get complicated.

Normal office noises went on in the background as I read specs and reviews, and my head began to swim. When Ron appeared in my doorway, I was happy to take a break from my research.

"Guess who that was," he said.

"No clue."

"I called Detective Lujan with the major crimes unit in El Paso."

My brain had to switch multiple gears to remember this was about the missing Super Bowl ring. I made an impatient little hurry-up gesture.

"So, it seems Bobby Lorrento's ring isn't the only item this Jay Livingston has scammed someone on. Lujan found several other complaints in the El Paso and southern New Mexico area where a man of his description has sold memorabilia that turned out to be fake or of lesser value. In at least two other cases, he used the 'borrowed house' ploy to make it look as if he lives in an upscale neighborhood."

"Have they caught up with him?"

"Not yet. But here's where it gets interesting. They traced his real residence to an apartment building—nothing special, just an average furnished place in an average neighborhood. No sign of Livingston so they talked with the manager. It seems our guy moved out last week without a word, even though his rent was paid through the end of the month. Just packed his few possessions into a bunch of suitcases and loaded it all into his vehicle. The van had New Mexico plates."

Which means very little. El Paso is not more than a few minutes down the road from the state line.

"Information from New Mexico DMV showed the car registered to Jay Livingston with an address in Albuquerque."

"He lives here in town, after all?"

"Don't know that, yet. He could have provided a false address on his car registration, so I'm going to check it out before I mention it to anyone else."

Much of what we knew about Livingston, so far, had been fake. For all we knew, he could be on his way to anywhere in the world.

"Want to ride along? You've actually met him. I only have a driver's license photo, and we all know how lifelike those are."

"I ... um ..." I glanced at the vehicles on my computer screen, decided I was tired of reading specifications. "Sure. I'll go."

While Ron drove, I told him about my vehicle search.

We hashed that over until the subject was dead, well before we reached the southeast heights address.

We pulled up and parked across the street from a plain-Jane apartment building, the kind usually occupied by young marrieds or college kids. Tan stucco, dark brown trim, painted iron railing along the skinny second-story walkway. It had twelve units—six on the ground floor, six on the upper. Ron said Livingston's was supposed to be apartment twelve, the last one on the west end, second floor. It did not look like the residence of a man with hundreds of thousands in cash, that's for sure.

"Maybe he's just frugal with his money," Ron said, when I mentioned it to him.

"Or he's here temporarily. I get the feeling he's a guy who moves around a lot."

"That, too." He'd trained a pair of binoculars on the one window of the apartment, but I doubted he was getting much through the closed blinds.

I took in the bigger picture. There was only one car in the building's parking lot, a ten-year-old black Celica in front of unit one. If I had to guess, I'd say it most likely belonged to the manager.

"Do you think he's actually here?" I asked.

"Doesn't look like it," he mumbled from behind the binoculars, "but it's getting close to the time people come home from work and school. It's worth watching to see who shows up."

He'd no sooner spoken than a pickup truck pulled up in front of apartment three. A young guy in jeans and t-shirt got out, slinging a heavy-looking backpack over his shoulder as he locked the truck. He loped to the stairs at the east end of the building, took them quickly and went into number nine. Before his door was hardly closed, another car parked and discharged a college-aged girl, who apparently lived in unit two, next to the manager. Two more residents came home in the next twenty minutes. I felt myself itching to do something. The diamond ring was probably sitting inside just waiting to be retrieved by me.

"I could go check out Livingston's place," I offered. "There's enough activity, no one's going to notice."

"Right. And have Livingston come waltzing up the minute you've cornered yourself inside? Forget it."

"But the ring. It's in there, calling my name."

"Yeah … no. We need to catch Livingston *with* the ring."

I didn't see why we couldn't just nab the ring, take it back to the Lorrentos and be done with this whole case. What would Livingston do, report me to the police for stealing his ill-gotten property?

"He won't be happy to see you, Charlie, and he'd probably come after you."

Damn. How *does* he read my mind like that?

"He'll be along. If the ring is in the apartment he's not going to leave it for long. Most likely, a small item like that, he's carrying it with him."

I hate it when my brother makes sense. I pulled out my phone and called Drake to let him know where we were. He had finished his flight and was back at Double Eagle airport, and he still had maintenance to do before heading home.

An hour passed. I'd used up all the fun activities, such as poking through Ron's glove compartment. Nothing interesting there— just the usual assortment of outdated insurance slips, a wad of napkins from fast food places, a plastic straw, three twist-ties, a near-empty tube of sunscreen and two small screws that didn't appear to belong to the vehicle. Oh, and the Colt pistol he's licensed to carry anywhere. I took a moment to ponder the question of whether people actually ever used their gloveboxes for gloves. I, personally, had never seen it. Moving along, under the front seat, my hand encountered a dust-covered gummy worm and I quickly gave up that search.

"Will you stop fidgeting," he demanded after about ten minutes of my restlessness.

"Surveillance is boring."

"Yes, it is."

I should have known, when he suggested the outing, we wouldn't simply walk up to Livingston's door and get what we wanted. Experience should have told me this would become the sum of my afternoon hours.

"I'm hungry." My biscuits and gravy and the bottle of water had long since worn off.

"There's a gummy worm under the seat." He actually managed to say it without a smile. "If we get desperate, my survival kit is in the back."

I'd seen his survival kit. It consisted of a warm coat, a space blanket and a collection of vending machine goodies. Cheese and crackers, packs of Oreos and fried pork skins comprised the menu, and I would bet a dollar everything in there was way past its sell-by date. It would do in a pinch, but I wasn't *that* hungry yet. Two blocks north, we'd passed a Carl's Jr. on Central. I could walk over there and back a lot quicker than it was taking Jay Livingston to get home.

I'd no sooner voiced the thought than I sensed Ron's body tensing. A white van had pulled into the apartment parking lot, taking the slot at the far west end.

"Take a look," he said, handing me the binoculars. "Is that him?"

I aimed toward the vehicle and the man who was climbing out. Same slim build, same dark hair with a bit of curl. He wore similar jeans and jacket as the first time I'd met him. He stood beside his car a moment, door open, glancing all directions. I lowered the binoculars.

"It's him."

Livingston's gaze switched toward us. Oh, crap. Had the setting sun flashed off the binocular lenses? I started to slide down in my seat but he'd spotted me. Our eyes met for a long moment and I knew he recognized me. Smoothly as a snake moves, he slipped back into his van. It whipped out of the parking lot and headed east with a squeal of tires.

Chapter 43

Ron peeled through the apartment parking lot, making a wide turn that put us in the same direction as our quarry, but the white van was out of sight.

"He turned left at the corner," I said.

Ron followed, and I could see his vehicle ahead at the intersection with Central. Traffic on the major street was backed up solid.

Bad move, Jay.

We caught up. With only two cars between us, surely Livingston already knew we were behind him. Livingston edged forward until a kindly soul held back and let him turn right into the traffic stream. With two more vehicles waiting their turns, we knew Jay could be miles away before we ever moved.

"There's a light at Girard," Ron said, making a tight U-turn back to the last intersection we'd passed.

He zipped, way above the speed limit for these residential streets, three blocks east before turning left. We came to the traffic signal and saw it was green in our favor.

"He's back there," I said, staring to the left, my heart racing a little. "He's about four cars back, waiting in the left-turn lane."

Livingston would turn exactly into our path if he didn't pull some quick maneuver to do otherwise. I couldn't tell whether he'd seen us. My guess was he would be watching his rearview mirror.

Ron crossed the intersection. "Okay, this is a different wrinkle. We're tailing someone that's about to end up behind us."

"He's sure to spot this car. Red doesn't exactly blend into the background." I thought fast and hard.

"Grab my Stetson from the back seat," Ron said.

I handed him the wide-brimmed hat and he swapped his ball cap for it.

"Duck down. With any luck, he won't realize it's the same Mustang."

I slid my seat back and did my best to tuck into the scanty legroom below. "You watch the road," I said. A collision in this position would definitely maim or kill me.

Ron slowed his speed and hung to the right-hand lane. "I'm letting cars pass me while we still have two lanes here. If he continues past Lomas it'll narrow down to one and I'm stuck with whatever the traffic pattern is at that point."

I concentrated on breathing in my bunched-up position.

"Okay, he made the turn and he's tailgating the guy in front of him. I think he has his eye on me." He draped his arm over the steering wheel, a casual gesture Livingston wouldn't expect from a driver chasing him.

I heard a car pass on our left. As the next one approached, Ron yawned and brought his left hand up to cover it.

"He passed me. Kind of gave me a look but didn't react. I'm going to let one car get between us, then I'll edge over into his lane."

"Let me know when I can sit up again. Feeling a little vulnerable here with no seatbelt."

Ron was probably thinking of the pricey ticket he'd get if a cop stopped him and found me in this position.

"Approaching Lomas .... Looks like he's going to turn left."

"Maybe he's making a big loop, planning to head back home now that he thinks he's lost us."

"Let's hope so. It would simplify things." I felt the car ease into the left lane and make the turn. The motion, along with stopping and coasting, gave my stomach a rolling sensation.

"What's happening, Ron?"

"Traffic's moving better here than on Central," he said.

"Can I get up?"

"Uh ... yeah, you'd better. Looks like he's gonna get on the freeway."

Great. I unfolded myself from my tiny compartment and planted my butt on the seat, reaching for my seatbelt. My eyes refocused just in time to see Livingston's van get into the lane for southbound I-25.

"This is looking like quite the loop," I said. If he stuck with it long enough, Livingston could make the trip all the way back to El Paso by going this way.

Ron glanced at his instruments and back at the road. He'd allowed three vehicles between ours and the white one. Jay ignored the Gibson exit, the last one which would have conveniently taken him back to the apartment.

"What do you think he's up to?"

"No idea, Charlie. All I can do is follow."

A lot of the traffic dropped away at the Broadway exit; now, no one blocked our view of Livingston's vehicle. Or his view of us. I had a feeling he knew we were there—may have known all along—and was set on creating a long chase.

Ron sighed. Aside from a casino coming up soon, it would be fifteen miles or so before another chance to get off the interstate.

Livingston passed the casino, even though the billboards said Ringo Starr and his group were appearing tonight. Who could *not* want to see that show? Ron actually let out a chuckle when I questioned it aloud.

"You don't even remember him, kid."

I was searching for a response when we suddenly noticed we were catching up with Livingston—rapidly. Ron slowed, but the white van was definitely coming to a stop. Our man had edged to the side and was pulling off the highway. Ron tapped his brakes to alert the drivers behind, then he followed Livingston's moves as he came to a complete stop. We halted less than ten feet behind his vehicle.

"Surely, he doesn't think speeding up now will gain him any advantage," I said.

"I think his engine shut down." Ron left the Mustang running and waggled his fingers toward me. "Hand me the Colt."

I did as instructed, holding my breath in hopes this whole scenario wasn't about to go horribly wrong.

"Stay in the car," he said. "If he takes off again, I don't want to have to wait for you."

He reached into his shirt pocket and handed me his cell phone. "Scroll through my phone contacts and get the number for Tom McPeel. He's with Major Crimes at APD, the contact the El Paso police gave me. Call and tell him what's going on. Ask him to dispatch some state troopers to our location."

Ron waited until two cars whizzed by before opening his door. With the Colt tucked into his waistband, he edged toward Livingston. I couldn't help it. I had to find out what was going on. I opened my door and stood behind it, listening as Ron approached.

"Hey, man. Why'd you stop?" Ron asked.

I couldn't catch the words, only the fact of a short, mumbled response.

"Wait right here." Ron turned to me and called out with a huge grin on his face, "He's out of gas."

"Tell him I'm calling roadside assistance," I shouted back. I hit the button for Detective McPeel.

Chapter 44

Word got out quickly. Two state police cars showed up within ten minutes, dispatched from the nearby town of Belen. The sun had set, making me wish I'd remembered to bring a jacket. Why is it I can never seem to understand that surveillance drags on forever and I should be prepared for all temperatures and all hunger conditions?

The officers had quickly transferred Jay Livingston to one of their vehicles, and a call was put out for a tow truck to take his. The flashing lights brought traffic to a crawl, gawkers unable to resist trying to catch a glimpse of blood. Ron and I were in the process of telling how we happened to be there when Drake called.

"Hey, what's up?" he asked.

I caught the fringe of worry in his voice.

"We caught our suspect. Just talking to the police now."

"Does this happen to be at the side of the highway?"

"Why? What have you heard?"

"It's on the news. Traffic reports say I-25 is backed up for miles, and the overhead shots make it look serious. I thought I recognized Ron's car."

Oh boy. With the traffic and cacophony of voices, I hadn't even heard the news helicopter. I assured him there'd been no injuries and all was well. I'd be home as soon as I could possibly manage. The long day was suddenly closing in on me.

When the detective arrived, I begged off any more roadside questions, asking whether we could take this up again in the morning. He gave me a look that said police work isn't only nine-to-five, but then he took pity and told us we could come by his office anytime within twenty-four hours and give our statements for the record.

Even so, it was nearly eight o'clock before I dragged my weary body into the house after Ron took me back by our office to shut everything down and retrieve my loaner Corvette. Drake greeted me with a long hug and the offer of a sandwich, but by that time the hunger had passed and bed was all I wanted. I showered, fell between the sheets and didn't wake up for many hours.

By the time I roused a little, Drake was already gone. He'd left a note on the bathroom mirror, letting me know he had to be out early for a spring elk count with the Fish and Game Department. The tone of the message was that he *really* hoped we would have a nice evening together. Poor guy. I'd hardly been around in the past few days.

I breakfasted on two leftover blueberry muffins, played with Freckles in the back yard awhile and, when she was finally tired out, I made ready to leave for the office. Ron and I had agreed to go together to speak with the detectives. I wasn't looking forward to the questions, but did have to admit I was curious about Livingston's motives and whether the expensive ring had been recovered.

I met Ron at the office and rode downtown with him. Detective McPeel met us with a gruff expression that hinted he'd been up late into the night on this case. Hey, not my fault. He could have locked his suspect into a cell and gotten a good eight hours' sleep like the rest of us.

We each gave our version of events, mine including the two trips to El Paso and discovery that Jay Livingston's living arrangement was a sham, which had led us back to Albuquerque in pursuit of our client's missing ring.

"We got a lead on the apartment on Rucker Street and were surveilling the place. We had hoped to talk to him there. There was always the *chance* he'd mistakenly given me the wrong ring during our transaction and would trade it back for the correct one." *Yeah, and pigs can fly.*

McPeel's skepticism was every bit as evident as my own.

"You searched his apartment last night, I'm sure. May I ask if you found Bobby Lorrento's Super Bowl ring?"

A long moment went by as he decided whether to share information.

"Let's just say the ring you're looking for … it's only a fraction of what we found."

"Livingston had *more*? What—more sports memorabilia?"

"I'm not at liberty to say. A full investigation is ongoing."

"But—okay. You are saying the ring I bought back for

Bobby Lorrento is among all this?"

"We believe so."

Ugh. Why do cops speak in such roundabout ways?

He printed my statement, had me sign it and told me I could go. I wasn't sure which room Ron had gone into. I hesitated in the hallway, wondering where to look for him, when I heard a slight commotion. From around a corner, two officers appeared with an orange-jumpsuited prisoner. It was Jay Livingston. This time he didn't look quite so debonair.

"Where's my stuff?" he demanded. "I need to get home and check on my stuff."

"We're not headed home right now, sir. You're on your way to your arraignment."

"For what? I purchased everything in that apartment."

Neither officer responded. I pressed myself against the wall as they passed. Livingston gave me a long, hard stare. One of the officers took his arm and kept him moving forward. The other peeled off and ducked into a side room where I caught the pungent scent of strong coffee.

I eased toward the open doorway and stood to the side, intent on the phone in my hand, as if I was busy with an urgent message. From the break room I could hear two cops talking.

"That was the jewelry guy?" one said. "I heard the search was pretty unbelievable."

"Yeah, no kidding. Closets jammed full—I mean *full*—of the stuff. Lots of cash, too. We were up until four, logging it all into evidence." A noisy yawn. "A cup of this stuff for the road and then I'm outta here. Gotta get some sleep."

The other man chuckled. Footsteps approached the

door and I moved a little farther away.

Before either of the men left the coffee room, I heard another door open at the far end of the hall. Ron appeared, relaxed and smiling. I caught up with him and we left the building.

"Guess what," I said as we walked through the parking lot. "Bobby's ring wasn't the only thing Livingston took."

"I know."

"I just heard two cops talking, saying there were closets full. And cash."

"I know. McPeel told me some of it."

"How is it you always manage to get cops to talk to you? He wouldn't tell me anything."

He shrugged and unlocked his car. When he asked if I was up to some lunch at Pedro's, of course I was.

"Livingston was squawking about how it was all his stuff, how he'd paid for everything in the apartment."

"Well, technically, he did. He just paid a whole lot less than it was worth."

"But ... he'll probably get off. Can they make the charges stick?"

"It'll be complicated."

We arrived at Pedro's where I ordered my usual— chicken enchiladas with green chile and sour cream. Ron got the beef burrito. We're *so* predictable.

"So. Does this mean we're done with the Lorrentos? Police have the guy. Case closed?"

He took his time over the chips and salsa. "I'll have to write up a final report for Marcie. Technically, she's the client. I could do it this afternoon and then, yeah, I guess we're pretty much done with them."

"I'm sensing a *but* ..."

"But, nothing really. I'm just curious about a few things. I might do a little follow-up. See if I can piece together a whole picture."

"A little lecture to Marcie on choosing the wrong guy to fool around with?"

"Well, she wasn't too smart about it, was she?"

I didn't think cheating was ever a good idea, but our food arrived at that moment and I got a little too busy to talk about it.

My phone rang as I was about to pour honey into the middle of my sopapilla. When I saw it was Drake, I wiped the oil off my fingers and took the call.

"Hey there," he said. "I'm on my way back from the job and was thinking about an early dinner at Pedro's."

"Ooh, a little late for that decision. But I'll bring home whatever you want." I felt badly that our timing hadn't worked out a little better, but I soon had a takeout box of enchiladas for him and was on my way home.

It felt good to have wrapped up the Lorrento case, but I felt an unease about the Delaney twins. Clover's admission yesterday bothered me. I just couldn't put my finger on what to do about it.

Chapter 45

The next morning, Drake offered to help me finalize my new car purchase. I'd accessed the inventory online for the local dealership, chosen the Jeep I wanted and was now ready to talk deals. Well, okay, I wasn't really ready to dicker with them, but with Drake at my side I figured we could get through it. We fortified ourselves with a decent breakfast at CeeCee's and strode onto the car lot, full of confidence.

Two hours and a chunk of money later, I drove away in my new black Renegade. It wasn't nearly as flashy as the red Corvette, but I liked the sort of ninja feel. Plus, it would be a whole lot more practical as we got closer to owning mountain property. Weekend gear and Freckles would fit right in, a fact that was a big plus.

Life settled down for a couple of days. Drake was handling details on our purchase of the tiny mountain cabin. While I was at the office this morning, he planned to meet a surveyor up there to establish the property lines. I'd hoped to run into Clover and take her to lunch as a thanks for the loan of her sister's car, but I hadn't seen her around. I should call—her cell number was right there in Zayne's phone. I'd missed an easy opportunity to return it the night Clover passed out, so putting it back in their house in some sneaky manner was another item on my to-do list.

I called Donna Delaney and updated her with what I'd learned from Buddy, the tech guy from Innocent Times. She agreed that her nieces were probably pulling some scam on the parents.

"I've been thinking a lot about this. My guess is Zayne has gone away with a guy, and it's probably someone she doesn't want Rick and Jane to know about," I said. "Clover is covering for her and has become very upset each time I've brought it up. I'll get in touch with Clover and try again."

I didn't want to lose the girl's trust, but the only way to get straight answers might be to present her with what I knew about the phone calls and texts.

"Whatever you think, Charlie. I'm sure it's all right." Donna hesitated a moment. "It's just … I don't have unlimited money to spend investigating."

I assured her I wasn't going to send a whopping invoice for my time. I'd just hung up the phone when I heard Ron's booted feet clomping up the stairs. He peered in at my doorway.

"I just had lunch with a most interesting man," he said.

"And here I thought you were completely devoted to Victoria."

He rolled his eyes. "Why else would I have such a dweeb little sister, if not to make fun of me and twist my words." He started to turn away but I called him back.

"Tell me about the lunch. I'm guessing this is a client?"

"A lead. I'm tying up loose ends on the Lorrento case and I happened across an old buddy of Jay Livingston's from his high school days. I followed the friend-of-a-friend thread on Facebook and came up with Larry Vaso."

He came into my office, sat on the sofa and took the end of a tug-toy Freckles brought to him.

"Larry told me Jay has been a con man since his earliest days. His dad used to fascinate the boys with stories of ways to make a quick buck by tricking people. They would laugh over his antics but, when Larry would go home and relate some hilarious episode to his own family over the dinner table, he'd get a stern lecture about right and wrong. He says he tried talking to Jay about it, but Jay just laughed it off."

Freckles gave up tugging with Ron and went to chew quietly on a rubber bone.

"The Livingstons acted as if they were rich, Larry told me. They lived in the biggest house in the neighborhood, and Jay's dad had a new car every year. Larry said it was hard for him to understand—if his friend's dad was a crook, how did he become so successful. His own father kept telling him it would all come crashing down someday."

"Well, Jay certainly wasn't living the high life when we found him," I said.

"No, and I guess that's where the rest of the story comes in. The senior Livingston did eventually crash and burn. The boys were off to college by then. Jay had a flashy car and a high-limit credit card, and he didn't take his studies seriously at all. He spent his time making money by selling fake term papers. Apparently, once, he sold a master's thesis for thousands of dollars and it turned out he'd blatantly stolen it from the archives at another college.

"Back at home, the old man pulled a jewelry job—I'm guessing something like what Jay's in trouble for now—and got caught. The whole house of cards came tumbling down when it turned out everything he owned was either mortgaged, rented or stolen. He showed up at his son's dorm room, begging a place to hide out from the police."

I felt my eyes go wide. Holy cow.

"This is where it gets interesting."

It wasn't interesting enough already?

"Larry and Jay watched his dad get hauled off to prison. For Larry, it validated everything his father had told him for years. He knew he would stick to the honest way of doing things, and never again would he believe in someone else's appearances."

"Jay obviously didn't mend his ways, though."

"Larry said Jay just got weirder and weirder. He didn't stop scamming people. The liar's mindset was deeply ingrained. But instead of spending his gains on a showy lifestyle, he started to hoard all of it. The cash, the jewelry—by the time the police caught him this week, he had trunks and boxes full of it."

I remembered Detective McPeel's comment about the tip of the iceberg.

"Yeah," Ron said, "that crappy apartment where he lived held several million dollars worth of stuff."

"Wasn't he afraid of being robbed?"

"He wasn't foolish. He'd rigged up the most sophisticated alarm system I've ever heard of, and not the kind that calls the police. The kind that traps the intruder.

Without his codes, walking into that place could get you hit with a Taser or shot."

"Seriously? Rigging something like that is illegal, isn't it?"

He gave me a patient stare. "Pretty much everything Livingston did was illegal."

Well, true. From stealing jewelry and *borrowing* other people's houses, to sleeping with married women, his life consisted of unethical and illegal activities. I pondered the impact parents have on their children, and it was fairly mind-boggling. I felt a sense of relief I'd never had kids of my own.

I must have remained lost in that pensive mood quite awhile; when I looked up again, Ron had left the room. Maybe he was thinking of the extra time and attention he needed to give his own boys, especially as they approached their teens.

Chapter 46

Bringing my mind back to the other young people in my life at the moment, I promised myself I'd try to have a heart-to-heart with Clover when I got home. Ron had gone back into his own office, Sally had left for the day, so I couldn't see much reason I shouldn't head home and try to catch up with my young neighbor. I called out to my canine companion and the two of us headed for the back door.

My new Jeep would provide the excuse for a knock at Clover's door. She, after all, had been the one to send me looking at a similar vehicle to my old one. I started it and began the drive home.

What I *should* be doing was to return Zayne's phone. My data expert had extracted what we needed from it and there was really no excuse to keep it. A guilty pang shot through me. Here I'd been making judgments about Jay Livingston's dishonesty, and look what I'd done. Yes, I could justify my little thievery all sorts of ways, but it was time I came clean and gave it back.

I turned onto my street, automatically glancing toward the Delaney's house. Sure enough, both Corvettes sat in their driveway. From the front yard next to mine, Elsa looked up. No one can convince me all old people have failing eyesight. She spotted me behind the wheel of the Renegade and began waving madly. I pulled to the curb in front of her house.

"Wow, Charlie," she said. "Drake told me you got your new wheels today. I like it!"

She eyed the vehicle from all angles.

"We'll have to plan a demo ride pretty soon," I told her. "I was on my way to the Delaney's to return a, uh, borrowed item."

She gave me the grandmother look, the one I used to get when I fudged the truth as a teen.

"I talked to Donna earlier. She still wants me working on the case."

"Well, I should hope so. We still don't know where Zayne is."

I filled her in on my theory that Zayne got a new boyfriend and went away somewhere. "Donna thinks that's probably the case, but I'd still like to verify a few things with Clover. So, can we do a rain check on the car ride?"

"Sure thing. Oh, did I tell you my lettuce out in the garden is already producing bunches? I need to pick and bring you some." She wiped her hands on her apron. "I could do it now, if—"

A car took the corner a bit too fast and veered toward

my rear end as it sped up the street, grabbing our attention. Elsa actually took a few steps away. I gripped my steering wheel, but the car narrowly missed mine.

He swerved to the right side of the street and came to an abrupt halt in front of the Delaney place, sending out a long blare of his horn. I recognized the car as Ryan Subro's white BMW.

"Rude," Elsa said. "In my day—"

I'd heard it a million times. In her day a young man would never sit at the curb and honk for his date.

Date?

A warning shiver went through me. Surely Clover wasn't dating Ryan now. Not after what she'd told me at the cabin about his behavior toward her sister. I kept my eyes on the house and, sure enough, Clover came out. She leaned toward the open passenger window and the two exchanged some words. I tried but I couldn't tell what they were saying, even with my side windows down.

Clover didn't seem happy to see him, but whatever he said convinced her to get into the car with him. I didn't like the looks of this.

"Gram, I gotta go."

I followed the BMW to the end of the block, mimicking his turns, tracking him out of the neighborhood. Ryan and Clover seemed to be having an intense discussion inside the car. He rarely looked at his rearview mirrors and, despite the fact I wasn't being terribly subtle at tailing him, he didn't seem to realize I was behind.

At Rio Grande Boulevard, he took the ramp onto eastbound I-40. I stayed within a half mile all the way, letting traffic and the Albuquerque drivers' penchant for filling the smallest available space keep me from becoming too obvious to Ryan. From Clover's admission that this guy had been bullying her sister, I worried that he was now trying the same thing with her. Of the two girls, I would have picked Zayne as the more assertive. If Ryan Subro intimidated her into doing things she didn't want to, I worried about Clover's ability to fend him off.

In a series of moves eerily similar to the drive I'd taken the other day with Clover, Subro drove through the city, entered Tijeras Canyon, and exited at Cedar Crest, following the same route north on Highway 14. A number of cars came the same direction—it was, after all, a fairly populated area—but eventually they had all turned off the highway to smaller roads and driveways, until I was the only one behind the Beemer. When he made the turn onto Sandia Crest Road, I followed. That's when he must have spotted me.

He sped up and began taking the turns faster and faster. The low-slung sports car could handle it. In my new SUV I wasn't so daring. Within a couple minutes I was only catching occasional glimpses of him ahead. I spoke up for the hands-free phone to activate.

"Call Drake," I commanded. A reassuring ring tone sounded over the speakers.

"Are you still near the cabin?" I asked.

"Just pulling pitch to head home."

"I need you to detour. I'm following a white BMW convertible up the road toward Sandia Peak and he's getting ahead of me. He might be headed for one of the picnic areas or for the top—I don't know."

"I'll stay overhead and let you know." Bless my dear husband for being able to read the situation and react.

I dropped my speed slightly. It wasn't worth taking

chances in a vehicle I was still getting familiar with. If I didn't see the BMW at one of the few turnoffs, I'd stay the course and let Drake tell me where it stopped. We kept the phone connection open, although noise from the rotor blades and turbine engine made casual conversation impossible.

Within minutes, I heard the helicopter overhead. I wondered if Ryan would notice, but since it was not a law enforcement aircraft I doubted he would think anything of it, even if he spotted it above. I kept my eyes on the winding road where switchbacks occasionally gave glimpses of the white car, although I couldn't see well enough to know if either person inside was looking back toward me.

The ride seemed interminable. I would swear it never used to take this long, but the perception was surely my own impatience, along with nerves over what would happen when I caught up. We passed the turnoff to the lower ski area terminus. The winter season was well over now, and there was no sign of activity. Large patches of dirty snow and black mud provided the only evidence there'd been a ski season at all in recent months.

Drake's voice came over the phone line again. I couldn't make out the words and asked him to repeat.

"The car is—"

The line went dead, the connection lost.

Chapter 47

I tapped the redial button, slowing to concentrate on the tight curves in the road. For a moment, I thought we'd reconnected but the crackle cut off immediately. I backed off my accelerator and began watching every possible wide spot where the car might have turned.

It appeared suddenly when I rounded a bend. The BMW was parked in a designated space where one of the many trailheads began. Hiking?

Could I have misread Clover's body language when she approached Ryan's car? I pictured the exchange between them. Clover was wearing shorts, a t-shirt and sandals. She knew this side of the mountain, at this altitude, would have patches of snow for a few weeks yet. There was no way she'd planned on hiking.

Surely she was up here against her will.

I parked, blocking his car from leaving, and tried to think what to do. I saw no sign of them and wondered if Ryan was armed. I didn't have my pistol with me, not that I would use it other than for self defense anyway. But it could have made a good intimidation tool to get him to let her go. I rummaged in my purse for another idea.

Zayne's cell phone. I'd intended to return it, but what if I could use it as a distraction? I tapped into the contacts list and found Clover's name. When it began to ring, I heard a very faint riff of rock music from the woods ahead. The two were much closer than I'd imagined. The music continued to sound in the distance. Then it quit.

I whispered to Freckles to stay in the car and be a good girl. Grabbing my jacket from the back seat and closing the door with the softest possible click, I tapped the number again. Surely, Clover would see Zayne's name on the screen and know this was her chance to speak to someone who would summon help.

The music chimed again, this time a bit farther away.

Pick up, pick up, I pleaded silently.

"Hello?" came a tentative voice.

"Clover, it's Charlie." I kept my voice to a whisper. "Pretend it really is Zayne calling. Carry on conversation and let me ask you some questions."

"I *can't* ..." she wailed.

"Yes, you can. Just pretend." Dammit, girl. You're good at pretending.

"I—"

There was a scuffle. "Who's this?" demanded a male voice.

Oh shit. I didn't have a story ready for this.

"Oh, hey. I'm a friend of Clover's. I need to ask her something real quick."

"No you're not. It says the call is from Zayne. Who are you?"

I had to let Clover see me, but I needed to be armed in case Ryan was.

"Uh, my name's Charlie. I think we met once. You're Ryan, right?" I bent down and picked up a fallen tree branch, a chunk about four feet long. It was hefty enough to do some damage.

"Clover's gonna have to call you back later," he said. The call went dead.

I dropped the phone into my pocket and lifted the branch with both hands, wielding it like a sword. The bark was rough, and I had no idea if the thing had been deadfall for a long time. It might shatter into splinters at the first whack. With luck, I wouldn't need any more than one shot.

I caught a glimpse of pink through the trees. Clover's tank top. My heart rate picked up as I approached with as much stealth as possible. Still, Ryan heard me a moment before I walked into the small clearing where they stood.

He had a grip on Clover's upper arm. When he saw me he spun her around and drew a knife from his belt. With a sharp click it switched open and he held it to her throat.

"Get out of here," he said. His handsome face was contorted with rage.

"Ryan, calm down." I scanned the area, looking for an easy escape path for the girl.

"I *said*—get *away*!"

That's when I noticed they were standing at the edge of a precipice.

Chapter 48

I dropped my two-handed grip on the tree branch, holding it down at my right side.

"Take it easy, Ryan. This isn't what you want to do."

"How the hell do you know what I want?" He tightened his grip on the knife handle and Clover let out a small whimper.

"Ryan, that helicopter overhead? The one that's been keeping an eye on us. It's the police. More officers are on the way." I prayed that part was true.

"Oh yeah?" He taunted me, but I saw him give a quick glance at the sky.

"The police know everything that's already happened, Ryan. The bullying, the nude photos, the name-calling online."

His sneer told me he didn't care. What was the penalty for bullying someone into leaving town? Probably nothing at all. I took a different tactic.

"Okay, it doesn't matter to you. Tell me then, what *do* you want? What do you hope to gain from this?"

I could tell he hadn't thought that far ahead. His gaze went skyward for another split-second as he thought about it. I tightened my grip on the branch, down at my side.

"Ryan, it will go easier if you let Clover go now. Harming her will only make the situation worse."

Drake … I sent all the telepathic signals I could toward the machine hovering four hundred feet above our heads. *Send me some backup now.*

"Ryan, c'mon. Let her walk over here by me. We'll leave you alone."

He gave a sharp laugh and pointed at me with the knife. "You're crazy, lady."

It was exactly the chance I needed. I brought the branch up like a baseball bat, stepped in, took aim and swung. It hit his wrist with a sickening *crack!* The knife flew through the air.

Clover screamed, frozen at the edge of the sheer drop.

I followed up with a whack to Ryan's kneecap and he went to the ground, doubled over in pain, shrieking.

"Clover! Take this." I yanked the cord from the hem of my windbreaker and handed her the end. "Pull 'til it rips, if you have to."

She acted quickly once she had instructions.

"Tie his wrists. Tight."

His right wrist and hand were already swelling but, sorry, I had no pity. We couldn't take a chance he would try to take control again. The moment he'd been secured, I let one hand off my weapon and picked up Ryan's knife. A narrow line of blood rimmed the blade's sharpened edge. I looked at Clover.

Her neck showed a two-inch red mark that oozed a trickle of blood. An inch over, slightly deeper, he would have cut her carotid and there would have been no way to save her life this far from help. I felt a rage well up in me and it was all I could do not to kick the man while he was down.

He'd begun screaming threats at me. His father was an important man in this town. He'd sue me. If anything happened to the use of his hand, I'd be paying, for life. I ignored him and turned to Clover.

"You okay, sweetie?"

She nodded mutely, but her body began to shake violently as she walked toward me.

I pulled Zayne's phone from my pocket and punched in Drake's number. Thankfully, this time we had a connection.

"Help's on the way," he said. "You all okay down there?"

"Sort of. Get them here as fast as you can, if you have to lead them in."

"I can see lights just down the mountain, hon. They'll be along soon. I won't leave until I see they've reached you."

My own legs didn't feel any too steady as I dropped my bat and embraced Clover, never taking my eyes off Ryan Subro. He continued to rant, upping the intensity of the words when she broke away from me and walked toward the drop off, pointing toward its depths.

"Clover, get away from the edge. You'll be okay, I promise."

She shook her head. I sprinted to her side and pulled her back.

Ryan screamed her name and called her several choice words.

"You—shut up!" I shouted at him. "Leave her alone."

My words seemed to ring through the air, but when I paused to listen it was actually the sound of sirens. Within a minute, they wound to a halt nearby. I heard voices as the officers got out of their cars.

"We're over here," I called, still not trustful enough to turn my back on Ryan. He'd begun to writhe on the ground, trying to get to his feet, but his injured knee didn't give him much success. Lucky for us.

It seemed like a long time, but in reality only moments passed before four officers in Bernalillo County uniforms— three men and a woman—emerged from the forest with guns drawn. Clover and I held our hands up in plain sight.

"What's happened here?" the female officer asked.

I quickly explained how I'd followed the pair after observing what seemed to be a kidnapping at knifepoint. Okay, that last bit might be a twist on the truth. I hadn't actually seen the knife until I stood here.

"My husband is the one who called from the helicopter."

"Got it. He didn't give much detail. I'm afraid we'll have a bunch of questions for you." Her name badge said she was B. Ramirez.

At that instant, Clover swooned against me. I reached out to steady her.

Ryan, who'd remained quiet all of three minutes, began another rant. "Don't listen to anything she says. I had nothing to do with it."

I had a hunch. "Clover? He's talking about something

other than today—this particular incident—isn't he?"

Two of the men dragged Ryan to his feet and forced him to limp away with them.

"They'll take him downtown," Ramirez said. "He can't get at you anymore."

"Clover, can you tell me what he was talking about?" I asked gently.

She sobbed and fell to her knees, pointing toward the cliff where Ryan had a grip on her such a short time ago.

Officer Ramirez and her partner stepped toward the edge. "Oh, shit," the male officer said.

Ramirez turned back toward us, wiping a hand across her face.

Before anyone could stop me, I walked over to see what they were looking at. It took a minute to spot what they were focused on, but when I did, it took my breath away.

Forty feet below, on a rock ledge lay a body. Leaves and boughs partially covered the badly decomposed remains, but one thing gave it away immediately. It was a young woman and she had long blonde hair identical to Clover's. This is where Zayne Delaney had been for the past six months.

Chapter 49

Officer Ramirez treated Clover gently but, nevertheless, she was being considered a 'person of interest' until the full story of her sister's death could be unraveled. A crime-scene unit arrived and the rest of us were quickly shooed out of the area. When Ramirez ushered Clover into the backseat of her cruiser, I got into my Jeep and followed.

On the way to the downtown detention center, I phoned Donna Delaney.

"I'm sure Rick and Jane will want her to have an attorney on hand," she said. "I'll find out who that is and make a call."

"She kept hanging onto me," I said. "Do you want me to see if they'll let me stick around until the attorney comes?"

"If you could, Charlie. That would be wonderful. The family owes you extra for all this."

"It's not about money, Donna. She's so shaken up, my heart just goes out to her."

By the time I negotiated downtown traffic, parked and got into the county lockup, the miracle of overseas phone calls in the modern age had gone into effect. Ramirez came out from somewhere in the innards of the building and told me an attorney was on his way to meet with Clover Delaney.

"She really wants you present," Ramirez said. "Says she doesn't know her parents' attorney."

"Would I be allowed to?"

"She's not under arrest yet. As long as the attorney is present and doesn't mind, I can't stop you."

When the lawyer arrived, it turned out to be someone I knew. Ben Ortiz had represented my brother once, not that long ago.

"What's your relationship with the Delaney girl?" Ben asked as we stood near the elevators.

I explained how I'd known the girls their entire lives, the scenario of babysitting at a young age, and how we'd recently been asked by the aunt to look into the whereabouts of the absent twin.

"Seriously, I thought she'd either gone away to college as Clover stated, or she'd taken some other whim and left of her own accord."

"You think Clover will open up more readily with you around?"

I shrugged. "Maybe. We've been getting closer in recent weeks."

"Come along, then." He held the elevator door for me

and we went up to a room where he said the conversation would be private.

When Clover came in she looked marginally better than out in the woods. At least she'd washed her face and hands. Someone had given her some sweats and a jacket, and she was no longer shivering like a flower petal in the wind.

Ortiz advised Clover to tell him the full story, not to leave out details that could later come back to haunt them both if she were arrested and the case went to trial.

Clover took a deep breath. "It started with Ryan and his friends hitting on us through our social media accounts." She shifted in her chair. "Well, it goes back even further. We both started posting selfies when we were in ninth grade. You know, the glamour shots. All the girls do it. You want to look good. There's a lot of pressure about that. Lots of girls get depressed over their looks and popularity."

Ortiz looked as if he wasn't buying the seriousness of it, but I remembered enough of it to believe her. Girls, especially in middle school, could be so cruel. Remarks about weight, bad hair days, the wrong clothes and pimples really stung.

"If a girl doesn't photograph well, she'll do exotic makeup and use Photoshop to make her picture look better. We'd spend hours on it, doing each other's makeup. Everyone wanted to look like Kim Kardashian. Zayne even dyed her hair dark for awhile, but it just didn't look right with her pale skin. She got called Zombie Zayne so she switched it back."

"So, girls were posting pictures that didn't really look like themselves? To, what? Impress boys?" Ortiz quit making notes.

"Yeah. You know, to look our best."

"Obviously, at some point it got a lot more serious than mere photo enhancement."

"So, yeah. Through high school we stuck with pictures that made us look our best. Dad gave us credit cards and never asked questions, so we could buy all the cool clothes we wanted. But still ... you know, you fantasize about boys. What's the first kiss going to be like? And other things ... you know ... well, sex. What will that be like?"

I remembered those concerns, as well.

"So, like, junior and senior year the pressure's really getting intense. Nearly all our friends had hooked up, like, lots of times. Zayne was more, um, open about it. Flirted a lot. She said she hadn't actually had sex yet, but I wasn't sure. Some of the kids she'd go off with when I decided to hike or read a book ... well, they were the wilder crowd. Kids had called her Zany Delaney, like, forever, and she got a kick out of it. She wanted to live up to the nickname."

The lawyer, clearly, was beginning to wonder where all this was leading.

"So, it was prom of our senior year and Ryan Subro had transferred to our school from public school. In private school, it's mostly kids of successful people like our parents. Big-name businessmen around town send their kids there, too, so it's kind of clubby. You know. Anyway, Ryan started trailing around after Zayne like she was the prettiest girl ever. He asked for nudes and she sent a couple earlier in the year, but she was basically stringing him along, finding out if he was really into her or was just being a horn-dog.

"I guess Ryan didn't realize we were twins for awhile. He'd say things to me sometimes when he obviously thought he was talking to Zayne. I talked to her about it, about how she shouldn't be so open with him unless she was serious. Anyway, it's close to prom and he figures it out, and he's, like, all wow, 'I could have two prom dates' and stuff. Then he starts hinting around about having us both in, uh, you know ... in the bedroom."

She wiped her palms on her sweatpants leg and tucked her hair behind her ears.

"Zayne actually suggested it to me, that we go along with him. I said hell no, no way. I always thought Ryan was way too full of himself. You know, thinking he's all hot. And he isn't."

"What happened then?" I asked.

"So, we get through prom and graduation and all, and I haven't let anyone take a nude picture of me, but Zayne had sent Ryan a couple and then she's shocked to find them popping up on Instagram and Whisper. And I say 'why are you surprised?' I mean, did she honestly think Ryan respected her privacy, and those photos were for his eyes only?"

"Maybe she did think that."

"Yeah, that's what she said, but she's all depressed because he's posting these pictures and saying she's a slut. In the same breath, he's calling me a prude because I wouldn't go along with his little fantasy. And then his friends join in and they're saying it too." She took a shaky breath. "My folks always offered us a big trip each summer, so last summer we took it, went to Greece with them. Just got outta here for a few months, and it was good. It was all good. I figured by September Ryan would have been sent off to some east coast school and we'd never hear from him again. I mean, seriously, he had to grow up sometime, right?"

I was guessing not.

Ortiz spoke up. "Let's talk about the day Zayne died. That's what the police are going to question you about."

Clover reached over and took my hand.

"We didn't know what to do—Zayne and me. Every time we went out, Ryan was all over her, really putting the pressure on. So, last October, I told Zayne, we need to get him away from the crowd where his friends are, like, egging him on. Maybe, away from those other guys he would be more ... more *real*, I guess. You know, where we could talk to him and let him know how we felt. I suggested the hike in the mountains. I knew the trails and all."

I squeezed her hand for encouragement.

"So you three went up to the place where it happened?" Ortiz asked.

"Yeah." Clover's voice grew quiet. "It was a mistake from the start. Ryan misread everything. He thought we three, up there in nature, it would be fun and kinky. Right away, he pulled out his camera and wanted us to open our shirts and let him take pictures. Zayne tried to laugh it off, like she always did, but I yelled at him and told him to grow up."

Her pressure on my hand increased.

"He got really ugly then, like, all in a rage. He started screaming all these filthy names at us both. It made me furious. I just felt this awful anger inside me and I wanted to push him off the edge of the cliff. He charged at me, and I swear I would have let him fall." A deep breath. "He was pretty agile, though, and when he got right to the edge of the drop-off he, like, swerved to the side. He grabbed for Zayne—or maybe she grabbed for him. I don't know for sure. It happened really fast. She went over the edge. We looked down and there she was—"

A sob escaped.

"I swear, it just happened so fast. I was stunned." Her voice was ragged.

"What did Ryan say?" Ortiz asked.

"He was panting and looking scared for a minute, but then he stood up straight and looked right at me. 'You pushed your sister,' he said. And I said, 'No. No way. *You* pushed her.' But I didn't know. It happened so fast. I had some scratches on my arm and he pointed to them and said, 'See? The cops see those scratches and they'll know it was you.'

"He started to come toward me, and I could tell he was thinking about pushing me, too. I ran toward the car and he caught me and threw me on the ground. 'You aren't telling anyone,' he said to me. 'Not the police, not your parents. No one.' He said if I told anyone at all, he would come back and kill me, and it wouldn't be a quick death like Zayne got."

She'd nearly crushed the bones in my fingers by now, but I couldn't ask her to let go. The poor girl was reliving the trauma she'd held inside for months.

"Go through it with me now," the lawyer said. "Tell me exactly what you did next."

"Ryan had his hand at my throat and he made me promise to go along with what he suggested. I was so close to blacking out, I just agreed with him. The first thing he did was ... oh, god ... he raped me. He was brutal and excited all at the same time. Afterward, I cried and the more I cried, the more he smiled. I felt dirty and cheap, and I was such a fool."

"He's a sick, sick person," I said. "You didn't deserve that."

Ortiz's pen had paused over his notepad.

"Okay." Clover took a ragged breath. "I know you just need the facts. Ryan got up and started finding boughs from the trees, leaves, pine needles and stuff, and he started tossing them over the cliff onto Zayne's body. After a couple minutes, he grabbed me by the arm and dragged me back to his car. All the way home he made up the story and told me what we would say."

The lawyer was making notes now.

"He said it would be up to me to convince everyone that we all three came back from our hike that day. I was to say my sister was alive and perfectly well. I was to go out with her friends and pretend to be her. Once we were sure no one was questioning anything, we'd come up with another story—tell people Zayne had gone away to school or that she'd met a man. He stayed at our house for three days, drilling me on the story, making sure I wouldn't change my mind. We even went to a party the next day, with me posing as Zayne, to establish she was fine."

"You used Zayne's phone to make calls, even to your parents, and you imitated her. You posted to her social media accounts and everything."

"Yeah ... how did you know?"

I turned to Ortiz. "Several people became concerned— neighbors, the girls' aunt—so I started trying to spot the two girls together."

"You were spying on me?" Clover seemed shocked.

"They just wanted verification you both were okay, sweetie. You didn't really think you could keep Zayne hidden forever, did you?"

"We thought the story of Zayne going away to school would work. Then we'd say she'd met an older man and moved away with him. Ryan said if her body was ever found, the other man would be the natural suspect. We—" Her face crumpled and tears flowed. "We just couldn't think past the next few days at a time."

"How did Ryan treat you after that day?" Ortiz was clearly looking for something he could build into a defense for her.

Clover dissolved into hysterical sobs and buried her head in my shoulder.

Chapter 50

Clearly, the girl was exhausted. The harrowing events on the mountainside and reliving the tragedy had taken a huge toll. I convinced the attorney to let the rest of the story come after giving her a break, although I knew Clover would have to repeat the events many times—to the police, the court and her own family, before it was done.

It all came out in grueling detail over the next few weeks. The media leaped on the "Twin-Killer" story as if it were the trial of the century. I'm sure a bad terrorist attack could have redirected attention from the local story, but for now it was Albuquerque's moment in the national spotlight.

The Subro family hired a famous attorney, who proceeded to paint Zayne and Clover as vixens who'd led their wholesome son into a life of sin and crime. So, naturally, the Delaney family rallied. Rick and Jane flew home and started volleying cannons of their own toward the Subros, making it known all along that they'd left the set of a major Hollywood motion picture to be at their daughter's side.

Both young people were out on hefty bonds. I didn't know about Ryan, but Clover had become basically a prisoner in her own home because of the media vans out front. Endless shots of the two Corvettes in the driveway were about the only thing of interest they could broadcast, but lack of compelling video didn't stop them.

I had to hand it to our local legal system and the hardworking people who ignored the media and the chest-thumping of the families and took the time to ferret out the clues and evidence. The charges were manslaughter and obstruction of justice against Clover. Ryan's DNA on Zayne's clothing still had the authorities deciding whether his actions were to be considered manslaughter or premeditated.

I visited Clover a couple of times before the trial, times when we mainly reminisced about playing Candy Land at Elsa's house and about the year I'd helped hide the Easter eggs. I'd thought she and Zayne were so adorable in their fluffy pastel dresses as they hunted them. One talk turned serious when she asked what I thought would happen to her.

"I don't know. No one does, at this point. I do think if you'd reported Zayne's fall as an accident right away, the police most likely would have believed it. The elaborate hoax is what makes it look so bad."

"I know. I should have never gone along with Ryan. Even now, my folks say he's trying to make it look like I caused everything, right from the beginning."

I nodded.

"He's really twisted, you know." She stared down at her hands. I knew she was wondering whether she would be going to prison.

"Yeah, he is."

I didn't talk about the stuff that was being said in the media. None of it made either family look good.

Back at the office, I found Ron in the conference room with Bobby and Marcie Lorrento. I tried to make myself invisible so I could sneak up the stairs unnoticed, but that didn't work. Ron called out to me and I stepped to the open doorway to say hello. Two men I didn't recognize sat with them. Ron introduced them as court-appointed officers.

"Jay Livingston negotiated a plea today," Ron said. "He gives up the valuables and cash found in his apartment in order to make restitution to his victims."

I nodded, seeing part of the picture. Bobby and Marcie were victims. It was almost hard for me to see them that way, but in the eyes of the law I supposed they were.

"Mr. Lorrento's Super Bowl ring was among the items retrieved," said one of the court officials.

Two jewelry boxes sat open on the table. The spectacular ring, which nested inside one of them, clearly outshone the other. If I'd been able to see the two rings side by side when I met with Livingston, the choice would have been obvious.

The man who hadn't spoken yet was counting cash onto the table. When a significant stack had accrued, he called everyone to attention and counted it again so all could see. Although I had work to do upstairs, I had to admit the scene with all the loot held my attention. I watched as the money and the larger of the two rings were passed to the Lorrento's side of the table before excusing myself.

A half-hour later, Ron came up to my office.

"What a mess," he said.

"Looked as if they all got what they needed."

"Yeah, Livingston is doing a short prison term—three to five years. I don't envy the cops, trying to figure it all out. Bobby and Marcie were only a tiny piece of the puzzle. Now they have to meet with the person the other Super Bowl ring belonged to and return that item. And then there are a couple hundred more things."

"Wow."

"Yeah. Livingston had been at this for years—buying, selling, collecting. There were two old-fashioned trunks full of jewelry and other goodies. And the cash—suitcases of it. While he does his time, the authorities have to sort out the mess. Even Jay himself can't seem to remember where each and every item came from. He's lived all over the country, so his victims are all over the place. It's an unbelievably complicated mess."

Some of the targets had most likely filed insurance claims for their losses, and those companies would have to be reimbursed. When I thought of the complex web of connections, it boggled my mind.

"At least we're done with them," I said. "We *are* finished, once and for all, with the Lorrentos, aren't we?"

"Yeah." He leaned against the door frame. "I have no idea how things will eventually go for them. Aside from the fiasco with the ring, there's still the infidelity and their general crappy attitude toward each other. The court recommended they get counseling, which I think is a fine plan—if they'll stick to it."

Basic respect for each other would have gone a long way toward saving the relationship. I wondered if they would ever get it back.

I finished my computer work, called out to my dog and left. All the way home, I thought about the twins and the still-unsettled mess the Delaney family had become embroiled in. It was such a sad story, all around.

Drake met me at the kitchen door with a glass of wine in hand. "I've got steaks ready for the grill," he said.

I set the wine aside and gave him a long, appreciative hug. "And I have a birthday gift for you."

"I thought we weren't making any birthday fuss this year," he said.

I went to the dining room china cabinet where I'd stashed a blue gift bag. "It's not exactly a fussy thing."

He pulled out the tissue-wrapped photo frame. A soft look came into his eyes as he studied the picture of Freckles and me. "I love it."

"The rest of the gift comes later," I said. "There's another bag in the bedroom, one with something red and lacy inside."

He gave an eyebrow-wiggle and set the framed photo on the kitchen table.

"I can't stop thinking about these two recent cases," I said, picking up my wine glass again. "Basic respect between people, especially for the opposite sex, would have kept either situation from getting out of control."

He nodded as he tossed the salad.

"This boy, Ryan, who basically blackmailed two girls for sex—is this a new thing, or was it always that way? I remember guys pressuring girls, back when I was in school.

I just don't remember it going so far. The pictures, the text messages …"

"Hon, as long as kids have hormones, there's going to be desire between them. What you said about respect— that's the key. If someone says 'no' you leave them alone."

I thought back to the day of the backyard barbeque at Ron's and my conversation with his son, Justin. He'd denied sexting with girls, but said he knew boys who did it. Maybe I should make time to get together and discuss it with the nephews. I suspected many of the kids who found themselves caught up in it didn't feel they could talk with their parents, and they didn't have the confidence to walk away from so-called *friends* who put pressure on them.

A knock came at the back door.

"I invited Elsa for steaks, too," Drake said. "She seemed a little lonely out in her garden when I got home."

I kissed him as I went to open the door. "You're the best."

Later—after we'd polished off a filet each, plus baked potatoes, fresh asparagus, salad and a portion of birthday cake—we three sat around the table, trying not to groan from overfill.

"Gram, thank you for putting up with me as a teenager. Watching the kids nowadays, I can't imagine how you did it."

"Kids today. I blame it on those smart telephones," Elsa said. "I saw a whole TV show about those app things they use. They say programmers design those things to get kids addicted to their phones because there's huge advertising money aimed at keeping them on those pages. The kids can't live now without having people *like* them. It's a reward system for being beautiful or popular or whatever, and they get real upset when they don't receive good feedback."

I had to wonder. Clover had definitely made a point of telling me how many positive comments her photos were getting. I'd seen the way she followed the apps with complete, rapt attention. Perhaps *addicted* wasn't too strong a word for it.

"Another thing—the kids now will say anything to anybody. In my day, you had to stand in front of the other person and say what was on your mind, face to face. It kept us all a lot more civil. If these kids had to do the same, a lot of problems would never happen."

I smiled at her wisdom. She definitely had a point.

Chapter 51

We rolled into one of the hottest summers on record, but Drake and I had our little cabin project to keep our spirits up. By August, we'd signed our closing papers and received the key. The route by air across the city was becoming familiar. Most often, though, we drove around the east side of the mountain; the cost of jet fuel was simply too much to be practical for everyday trips up there.

In the cooler mountain air we took stock of the little house's needs. The big ones were reinforcing the flooring, applying fresh paint, adding indoor plumbing and buying modern kitchen appliances. We discovered it would cost a small fortune to have the electric company run a line up to the place, so we investigated and opted for a solar system. Sunshine is one thing we have lots of in our part of the world.

Back in the city, I kept track of what was happening to Clover Delaney. The attorneys insisted Clover and Ryan stand separate trials, which I thought was a good thing. Clover was required to spend the duration of the trial in a jail cell, and it seemed the telling of the story dragged out far too long. In the end, the jury found her guilty of obstruction of justice.

Her parents' behavior was off-putting because of their arrogance and frequent mentions of their Hollywood connections. At least, that was my perception from the media coverage. I never was able to get one of the few seats in the crowded courtroom.

Luckily for their daughter, the judge had a kind heart and ignored the media's "trial by television" and stayed with the actual facts. She sentenced Clover to the jail time she'd already served and probation of two years, stipulating that Clover couldn't leave New Mexico and she needed to find gainful employment during that time.

Rick Delaney sputtered a little at the idea of his daughter actually working for a living, but the judge's lecture on the subject was clear. An affluent lifestyle the girls hadn't earned, in the judge's opinion, was part of the cause of their getting so far off track. Ben Ortiz, the Delaney's attorney agreed, at least in private, and told the family they'd better be grateful they hadn't lost both daughters. I learned all this from Clover when she rode up to the cabin with me the day after she was released.

As for Ryan Subro, his father's high-power attorney pulled out all the stops and managed to get his son completely off the hook for his actions. However, in a karmic way, the negative publicity surrounding the case sank the Subro auto dealerships way into the red financially. With little fanfare, Mr. Subro gave them up and the family moved out of state. Speculation in the neighborhood was that they went to Texas because it was big enough to get lost in. Personally, I didn't think Ryan had learned a lesson at all and, knowing the law-and-order mentality of Texas courts, I was betting the destination was somewhere else, somewhere the Subros could count on leniency for their wayward son.

In truth, none of us cared enough to check. We were thrilled to see Clover get out from under Ryan's control.

Clover received a few job offers, but all of them scared her—hostess in a popular bar, television traffic reporter, publicist for one of her dad's upcoming films. She wisely realized all of them only wanted her for the notoriety her face would bring to their businesses. She wanted out of the limelight, so Drake and I offered to pay her to help us with remodeling the cabin. She jumped at the chance, although I warned her she would have rough hands and broken nails within a week. I found it heartening to see the flighty girl disappear and the genuine one show up each day to work.

As the weather cooled toward autumn, carpentry for the porch seemed in order—we decided to enlarge it into an actual deck where we could cook and dine outside. Clover quickly learned how to use the power tools and worked alongside both of us as we built the flooring and added lattice around the bottom of the deck to keep larger critters out. The wood siding needed new paint and I decided to stick with the colors that had appealed the first time we saw the place. Drake teased me about being a sucker for rustic charm. It was true.

Although I loved the look of the old woodstove Sarah Locke had used for cooking, the hassle and extra heat generated by it soon convinced me to bring in a microwave for summer meals. We could keep the old one for winters, and I pictured myself making big pots of stew on snowy weekends.

The biggest indoor project involved partitioning the one room to create a separate bathroom and a cozy bedroom alcove. Drake drew up plans, we all helped dig a trench from the well house, and we installed pipes and a pump. Clover built two-by-four framing for the new rooms and delighted in the praise when we saw what a great job she'd done.

"You do realize this whole project would be way different within the city limits," Drake told us. "Codes exist for absolutely everything, building inspectors, the whole works. We're getting by with this because it's out in the sticks and it's not a full-time dwelling."

"Sarah Locke lived here just fine," I reminded him.

"In a whole other era."

It made me sad to realize a lot more than fancy phones had changed in the space of a couple of generations.

"How about taking a break?" I suggested. "We've subsisted on sandwiches and chips for weeks now. Let's drive down the road and see if there's decent Mexican food to be had."

Truth be told, I missed Pedro's more than I wanted to admit.

We hiked down the hill to where I had parked the Jeep then headed toward Madrid. I'd driven through the little art colony more times this summer than in all my previous years, but aside from the day we discovered our cabin, when the photographer had been with us in the helicopter, I hadn't stopped to meet the locals who would soon be our nearest neighbors.

Next to the general store stood a little café whose sign announced: Burgers, BBQ, Mexican, Vegetarian.

Something for everyone. We patted the sawdust off our clothes and walked in. The woman behind the counter looked familiar—long blonde hair, tortoiseshell glasses and a ready smile.

"Oh, hi," she said. "Haven't seen you folks around in awhile."

"The food and wine festival." It clicked. She was the one who, back in the spring, had been offering samples at the wine tasting booth. Seeing her nametag—Susie Scott— reminded me.

"Did you catch up with the guy you were looking for that day?" Susie asked, bringing three sets of flatware to a table near the windows.

"Wow—what a memory. I barely remembered it myself." It was at the beginning of the Lorrento case, when I'd spotted the football player with the other woman. "Yeah, we did catch up with him."

"I'm good with faces and details," she said.

We sat down and she stood by the table with hands on hips. "So, since it's after Labor Day, I'm afraid we're on a modified menu. We're totally out of the vegetarian specialties and the last of the barbeque went yesterday. Cook can make you a burger, nearly any style, and all the Mexican dishes are available."

She kept talking as she bustled to the counter and brought a pitcher of water to fill our glasses.

"Sorry about the limited menu. It's just, once summer's over, the crowds are gone and it's not worth our while to keep much in the freezer. We use it all up then we close for the winter. Cook makes up some pretty creative things, though. Today's special is the pulled pork burrito with green chile sauce and *papitas*. They're real good."

My mouth began to water as she described it. We each

ordered one. Susie busied herself behind the register and I gathered, from conversation with the cook, she was the owner. She tended to a dozen little duties but kept our glasses filled and asked whether we needed anything more. When she came by with our check, she focused on Clover.

"You're the girl from the news, right?"

Clover was used to the question but didn't like to respond, so I spoke up and steered the conversation another way.

"She is. We're neighbors. In fact, we'll be almost-neighbors of yours. Drake and I just bought a little cabin up in the hills."

Susie blushed a little and faced Clover again. "Oh, I didn't mean to pry. I felt so sorry for you, honey. I'm sure you were hounded to death by the press. I just wanted to ask a favor and see if we could help each other. Part of the reason we close here in the winter is there's a ton of stuff to do for the store and the café—the place gets bombarded by tourists all summer, so, yeah, the maintenance is fierce. Thought I'd see—you know, if you need a job—if you'd be interested. You could live in one of the little bungalows out back, help me with the work …"

I watched Clover's face.

"I'm an artist," Susie said, "and I like to use the winter months to paint a lot so I have some new things to sell the next summer. But I end up spending too much time building and fixing stuff. It's hard for me to get around to everything myself. There's a place for you to stay out here where it's quiet, and I can pay you a bit."

Clover gave the most genuine smile I'd seen in months. "Ms. Scott, that's so nice. Can I think about it for a little while?"

"Sure, hon. Just let me know."

We split the check. I was pleased to see Clover chip in her share but not make a grandiose gesture to pay for everything with a credit card the way she used to do.

Back at the cabin, we picked up where we'd stopped— bracing the framing for the new room partition. I held the partition in place while Clover hammered the supporting pieces.

"So, that was kind of a surprise," I said. "Susie Scott offering you a job."

"It was nice of her, and I think I'd be interested. I wanted to talk to you first, though. See, I had another idea." She got shy all of a sudden. "Since we've been working on the cabin, I ... well, I *really* love doing this."

I waited to hear the rest. Did she hope we could keep her employed on our job forever?

"So, I've been thinking a lot about it, and I want to go to trade school. I want to become a carpenter."

"Clover, that's great!" For the kid who'd thought of nothing more serious than shopping at designer stores, spending on an unlimited credit card, and keeping up with Instagram, this was a huge breakthrough.

"I mentioned it to my dad on the phone a couple days ago and he flipped. Said if I was so damn sure of myself then I must not need his money anymore."

"Oh, gosh. I hadn't thought of that." I let go of the partition. She'd braced it well.

"I don't care," she said, setting her hammer down. "I got an offer for Zayne's car the other day and I'm selling it. That'll cover my first year in school. I'll sell mine and get a more practical vehicle, like a little pickup truck. And now ... well, I think running into Susie today was fate. I can do what she said. Live out there in Madrid, go to school during the week and help her on weekends."

"You're sure? It doesn't sound as if your parents will be very happy about this."

She nodded. "I did things their way for a long time. The social friends, the contacts *in the business* ... Ugh, it's all just so phony. Someday, I want what you and Drake have. I want a partner who loves the same things I do, a genuine guy who's my best friend, the guy I'll want to spend time with and do projects together."

Her expression turned sad. "I can't believe Zayne or I ever thought Ryan Subro and his friends were interested in us. Not the honest kind of interest I really want."

"Do those kids ever contact you, try to get you back in their circle?"

"While I was in jail, and even before the horrible days of the trial—not *one* of them called or texted me. They don't care about me. They care about appearances. Things got back to me, things they were saying about me. You wanna know what I did?" The quirky grin was back on her face.

"What?"

"Threw them away."

"Your old friends?"

"In a way. I threw away my phone. All the contacts— gone. All the social media accounts—I'm done with 'em."

"You won't miss them or wish for the contact?"

"It's not like any of them miss me, is it? No, I don't need those kinds of friends. I got myself a plain old phone that does nothing but make calls. If I ever need to talk to Missy or any of the others, I'll call them, but so far my parents, Elsa and you are the only people's numbers I've programmed into the new phone."

The afternoon sun had gone behind the mountain and there was a distinct chill in the air. Drake came in and announced he had the pump ready to hook up to the new line, first thing tomorrow.

"You ladies look kind of serious," he said, giving me his questioning *everything okay?* look.

Clover laughed first. "Everything is perfect."

We grabbed our jackets and locked the cabin before starting down the hillside.

"Charlie? Could we make a stop on the way home?"

"Certainly."

"I want to tell Susie Scott my decision."

"We absolutely can stop for that. And Clover? I'm so proud of you."

She gave me one of the most heartfelt hugs of my life, and all at once the months of worry and the agony I'd felt on behalf of my young friend—it all melted away as I watched her embark on her new and steady path.

Author Note

The idea that this story would become *about* teens and their relationship with social media came to me after reading the book *American Girls: Social Media and the Secret Lives of Teenagers* by Nancy Jo Sales, and after watching a *60 Minutes* episode on the subject, which aired in spring 2017. If you have a child or grandchild who spends hours a day with cellphone in hand, you might want to read it, too. The fictional scenario in *Alibis Can Be Murder* is, sadly, all too real for many teens today.

Thank you for taking the time to read *Alibis Can Be Murder*. If you enjoyed it, please consider telling your friends or posting a short review. Word of mouth is an author's best friend and much appreciated.

Thank you,
Connie Shelton

Sign up for Connie Shelton's free mystery newsletter
at connieshelton.com
and receive advance information on new books,
along with a chance at prizes, discounts and other
mystery news!

Contact by email: connie@connieshelton.com
Follow Connie Shelton on Twitter, Pinterest,
Facebook, Amazon and BookBub

Get another Connie Shelton book—FREE!
Go to connishelton.com to find out how.

Connie Shelton is the *USA Today* bestselling author of more than 30 books, including her two mystery series, three nonfiction titles and two children's books. She has taught writing courses and was a contributor to *Chicken Soup For the Writer's Soul*. She and her husband live in northern New Mexico with their two dogs.

94811087R00191

Made in the USA
Middletown, DE
22 October 2018